Never Been to Me

Never Been to Me

GiGi Gunn

URBAN
Renaissance

www.urbanbooks.net

Urban Books, LLC
78 East Industry Court
Deer Park, NY 11729

ISBN 13: 978-1-60162-236-5
ISBN 10: 1-60162-236-8

First Printing September 2010
Printed in the United States of America

10 9 8 7 6 5 4 3 2 1

This is a work of fiction. Any references or similarities to actual events, real people, living, or dead, or to real locales are intended to give the novel a sense of reality. Any similarity in other names, characters, places, and incidents is entirely coincidental.

Distributed by Kensington Publishing Corp.
Submit Wholesale Orders to:
Kensington Publishing Corp.
C/O Penguin Group (USA) Inc.
Attention: Order Processing
405 Murray Hill Parkway
East Rutherford, NJ07073-2316
Phone: 1-800-526-0275
Fax: 1-800-227-9604

Never Been to Me

By
GiGi Gunn

Other Novels by GiGi Gunn:

Cajun Moon
Rainbow's End
Living Inside Your Love

Acknowledgments

Besides my usual inner circle—you know who you are—I'd also like to thank, for their continued support, encouragement, time, interest, inspiration, and expertise:

Vocalist Sandra Y. Johnson, saxophonist Lyle Link, Kevin Dwyer, Brenda Owen, Diane Taber-Markiewicz, Janice Sims, Sabrina S. Scott, Faye Putty, Elaine Gordon, Effi Barry, Arlene Jones, Alexis Baham, Martha Bridgeforth, Lareeta Robinson, Zina McNeil, La Tanya Samuel, Dana Lyons, Laurien Lynn Dunlap, Camille Lucas, Joan Conway, Vanessa Moore, and Sarah Lipscomb; Cover To Cover, M'tinis, Get Your Read On, and Turning Pages Book Clubs', the Ladies of Miss Conway's Literary Event, the Ladies of Miss Juanita Jones Reading Guild, Ladies of the Diamond Red Hat Society, and everyone who read and enjoyed *Never Been to Me*.

GiGi Gunn invites readers to visit her Web site at: www.gigigunn.net and e-mail her at gigi@gigigunn.net.

Dedication

To D.C.
Washington, D.C.
The capital of the free world,
my hometown.

If you dance to the music, sooner or later, you're gonna have to pay the piper.

— Mama Sinclair

CHAPTER 1

Paradise Cove
Bora-Bora, South Pacific

Drenched in the tropical sun's rays, she stood perched at the end of the wooden pier and scanned her tranquil surroundings. The solar heat warmed her body with delicious abandon so unlike the cold, gray winter days she'd left behind in D.C. The ocean, laid out in an aquamarine fantasy as far as the eye could see, lazily tumbled toward her, before slowing to lap, like bathwater, against the weathered post. Gentle trade winds swirled around her bikini-clad curves and carried a constant scent of hibiscus, plumeria, antriums and other exotic, undistinguishable fragrances. No sounds but those emanated and sustained by nature; the unspoiled earth at God's best; at His purest. The universe as He had intended.

Persi let her eyes meander over her environment and thought how Paradise Cove personified its name. A string of plush grass huts punctuated a pier that jutted out into the Pacific Ocean, insuring privacy while hiding an interior elegance. On the horizon, four men fished in an open canoe, as their ancestors had done for thousands of years, catching their dinner for the night. As with all vacations, the ten days were going too fast and, no matter how hard she tried, she couldn't convince time to slow down.

She dove into the welcoming wet, letting her copper-brown body part the water like the Red Sea, knowing she'd miss these early-morning dips once back in frigid, dreary D.C. She touched the pristine white sand of the Pacific's bottom and looked up though the crystal-clear water where prisms of solar rays rippled on the surface, and beyond that, the cloudless blue sky. *Paradise*, she thought. Neon fish, brightly painted electric blue with yellow stripes or bright orange dotted with black spots, playfully engulfed, then darted around her. She smiled as she swam in the gigantic aquarium. She floated under the transparent bubble of their hut, which formed the dining room floor where they'd spent many of their nights eating and watching the psychedelic aquatic life frolic below for their amusement; the same view shared from the living room, bathroom, and bedroom. This hedonistic paradise, designed solely for pleasure and decadently catering to every whim, had no kitchen. Native men clad in white dinner jackets balanced trays of sumptuous treats supplying sustenance, day or night, to the mostly newlywed patrons. Paradise Cove lived up to its honeymooner's haven reputation: no children, no scheduled activities, no pets, no tours or happy hours to destroy the lush peace and serenity.

Persi came up for air, flipped onto her back and invited the sun's full blast to kiss her face. She lay there, buoyed by the water, absorbing all the perfection of the past few days.

She smiled and thought of how she and her man began and ended their twenty-four hours whenever they wanted or not. Staff cast no aspersions on the privacy sign hanging on a hut door for days in a row: *KAPU*, which translated to *Forbidden–please do not disturb*. Reclusiveness was encouraged by management who remained unobtrusively around and ready with a solicitous "Anything you wish, Mr. or Mrs. Shelton?"

Persi began treading water and in the distance saw Brad still on his cell phone; she hated that intrusive contraption. She'd left a capable staff to manage her assignments during her absence, but Brad couldn't do that with his "girls." Three daughters he talked with each morning here, before they went to bed there. If the true test of future behavior is past behavior, she expected the same paternal devotion when they had their children, hoping to give him a son. Each morning, she went for a swim to give them their privacy, soothing herself with the thought that she had "Daddy" all to herself the rest of the day, week and total ten day stay.

She looked at his tanned-brown form whittled against the backdrop of the powdery white sand; as magnificent and beautiful to her now as he'd been when she first laid eyes on him. As a ninth grader, she'd been transferred to Roosevelt High School's science program where Brad Shelton was a senior. As she tried to find her chemistry class, her vision was stolen by six feet, two inches of all man, wrapped in an ROTC uniform as he strutted toward her. The sight of him stopped her heart. More than the dress blues and the scabbard diagonally projecting from his muscular body, he was a visual symphony in copper, his coloring so stunningly odd: light copper skin and blondish-brown hair peeking from under his hat. She fumbled and dropped her books and then glanced up into the most gorgeous, symmetrical face she'd ever seen, with light, piercing honey-sage eyes set below an explosion of thick lashes, balanced on high cheekbones. And his lips—full, wavery, and seductive; at fourteen years of age, she didn't even know what that meant, but she knew she wanted to kiss them. Touch them to hers. She'd just stared up at him, gap-mouthed and awed, and watched him walk around her without a backward glance. Not only was their age difference and the fact that he was way out of her league problematic, but he was probably bored with girls reacting to him this way.

Persi chuckled thinking of it now. It was love at first sight for her—as he walked on by, she scrambled to collect her fallen books. He walked on by her his entire senior year. But she noticed him every chance she got.

She now looked over and saw that he was off the telephone. She began swimming toward him. Always pensive after getting off the phone from home, her job was to cajole him around to the vacation mentality—an assignment she savored.

"Everything all right?" she asked, emerging from the water like Botticelli's *Venus*.

"Fine," he said tersely and then smiled. "The little one lost her tooth."

"Cute," Persi answered in kind. "So what do you want to do today?" she asked, her body dripping wet as she climbed between his legs.

"Whatever you like."

"You know what I like." She licked, then nibbled on his lips, tugging them into a half smile, then a full kiss.

His dry hands slid over her drenched flesh and he found her skin moist and hot to the touch. His body reacted and any thoughts of home evaporated in the seductive, steamy heat. He gathered Persi in his arms and they disappeared into their hut.

After they made love, Mr. and Mrs. Shelton hired a jeep and toured the botanical garden, where she studied the native, indigenous plants, then bought souvenirs before they dined in town for the first time since they'd arrived. They preferred each other's company until their ten days was up. As they packed, it was now Persi's turn to be pensive. She detested that their vacations, which had begun as twice or more times a year, had been scaled down to once a year and always ended too soon. Although they'd been to exotic locales like the Maldives in the Indian Ocean, Barbados, and Curacao, she hated being restricted as to where they could go; no quick weekend getaways to closer and more accessible Bahamas, Jamaica or St. Thomas.

Brad noticed her usual expected, quiet, sullen behavior the night before they went home. He always thought that they should make the most of their last night together, but she'd always turned morose.

"How's my girl?" he asked, stroking the side of her cheek, wanting to feel her nude body, exquisitely tanned to a deeper copper brown, beneath him on their last night.

"Hmm."

"You're still my girl? My number-one lady?" He offered his boyish smile and looked playfully into her eyes. His eyebrows arched and a smile split his striking face.

She ignored his charms and handsomeness and fanned away his searching hands. She unapologetically leveled her eyes at him and said, "Until we touchdown in D.C. and you go home to your wife and kiddies."

CHAPTER 2

The drone of the plane hummed in Persi's ears despite the expensive headsets Brad gave her as a gift one year. Firmly ensconced in the front cabin, as far away from each other as possible and still in first class, this was the arrangement agreed upon early in the relationship. They'd landed after their vacation from the Maldives and, once lighting from the plane and heading down the ramp, he'd glimpsed his little girls with signs and balloons emblazoned with *Welcome Home Daddy!* Instinctively, Persi'd hung back as he proceeded out into the open arms of his wife and girls. There she was. . . the wife. The wife who didn't understand him. The wife he no longer slept with. The wife he was staying with for the sake of the kids or at least "until the girls reach high school age."

"Tsk," Persi now scoffed. She'd believed him. On that particular day, she'd walked off the plane ignoring the happy family—all strangers to her. Later, Brad appeased her with a piece of jewelry—either the necklace or the earrings. The price of her pride should be higher.

Still awake and restless, Persi glanced over at his reclined, sleeping form. She rotated the small, personalized movie screen back into its place and saw him stir. He had it all: an excellent position, a sterling reputation in the community, a loving wife, three children, and a mistress of five years who was crazy about him. She hated him. She hated herself. Persi fooled herself during their rendezvous at her place or in posh hotels or quickies after hours in his office; it felt good during the tryst. . . damn good—but she always despised herself afterward. She was disappointed in the situation—in herself, but was hard-pressed to change it.

Like any relationship, it'd begun with an innocent hello. She'd officially met him at a Black Caucus event while still full-time at the National Institute of Health. After more than ten years, on that night, she'd seen him at a distance and couldn't believe how unbelievably handsome he still was. When her friend Doxie came over with a "guess who I saw?" Persi already knew. "Brad Shelton," Persi'd answered. Doxie looked disgusted and asked, "Don't tell me you still have the hots for him?"

"Is he still fine?"

"I'm sure his *wife* thinks so."

From a respectful distance, like in high school, Persi kept tabs on his movements all evening until suddenly they were face-to-face. Their eyes locked and he offered that old "you look familiar" line.

"And with that old, tired line, you must be so married," she'd quipped.

"Married ain't dead," he'd said as his honey-sage eyes swept her body. "Does that mean I can't speak to a pretty girl when I see one?" He'd flashed that famous Brad Shelton smile and she was back at Roosevelt High School, an awkward ninth grader standing in front of homeroom, and he a senior ROTC officer who, instead of walking by her, had stopped. History rewritten.

She'd been so restless and giddy that night that she couldn't sleep. The usually aloof but brilliant chemist Jean-Luc Etienne noticed her the next day at work and asked about her distraction.

"I saw an old, ah, classmate over the weekend and he's still beautiful."

"Classmate? I think you wanted it to be more, eh?" Jean-

Luc asked in his thick French accent. "Some feelings never change. They hibernate until chemically stimulated again. Then you are right back to where you were then. Eh?"

The *fasten your seat belt* light dinged and the pilot announced turbulence ahead. Persi glanced over at Brad as he'd turned over and pulled the blanket up and over his shoulders.

He's lived a charmed life, she thought with a touch of resentment. As the first son and second child of Dr. Clayton Shelton, Brad never had to work too hard or do too much, but be the oldest son of the renowned Dr. Shelton. His older sister followed their father into medicine and the father's established practice and Brad felt no compunction to do or be anything exceptional when mediocrity was all that was required. He'd squeaked by on DNA and privilege and his current success in the business world was directly attributed to his father's and mother's connections and standing in Washington, D.C. society. He'd taken his time earning his degrees, first at Howard University, majoring in charm and minoring in schmooze, until forced to grow up while earning his MBA at Columbia University. He'd married Patricia "Trish" Davenport, heir to the Davenport Insurance Company of South Carolina; deemed the wedding of the century—a prince marrying a princess. They lived an idyllic life. Persi had only formally met Trish Davenport Shelton a few times, though they shared mutual friends and connections. Persi had been privy to and obligated by the perfunctory, social Washington introduction done about three times and never taking; when unsuccessful at avoiding Mrs. Shelton, someone would say to Trish, "You know Persi Sinclair?" To which Trish would answer, "Why yes. Lovely to see you again," when she really meant "Who? And how would I know her?" Persi was intimately familiar with these social niceties as she'd been guilty of the same pleasant, anonymous intros.

That was how Persi and Brad were reintroduced at a Multiple Sclerosis Society fund-raiser at his Potomac, Maryland home. Persi purchased tickets as a favor to Doxie, taking Rucker Jackman, the celebrity football wide receiver who left a sizable donation and a significant impression on the crowd.

As Brad served hot dogs from the backyard's built-in grill, he said, "I remember you, from the Black Caucus event. You're Bruce."

"What?" Persi laughed as he laid the hot dog into her bun.

"Yeah. That real smart girl who got the full scholarship to MIT back in the day. Chemistry, right? You got a Master's and Ph.D too."

Persi's face erupted into the widest, blushing, little-girl smile that even Doxie had seen from the tennis courts.

"I read my *Alumni News*. You're more than a pretty face."

Persi was speechless. Brad Shelton knew her. Not back then, but he knew her now.

"You got some big-time position at NIH," he'd continued.

"Not really—it pays the bills."

"Hey, got someone I want you to meet over here," Doxie had interrupted as she rounded the pool. "Hey, Brad," she said as she attempted to drag her friend away.

"See ya, Bruce," he'd said with a flirtatious smile.

"Persi. Persephone. Persephone Sinclair."

"Right. Percy. I knew it was a guy's name. But you're certainly no guy," he'd said with a wink. "Anyone else call you Bruce?"

"No."

"Then that's what I'll call you."

And call he did. The following Tuesday he'd tracked her down at NIH.

She yanked up the phone and identified herself. "Dr. Sinclair."

"Bruce?"

She almost wet herself as Jean-Luc looked at her suspiciously.

Persi now remembered it like yesterday. If she'd hung up on Brad, or had a polite conversation and then declined his invitation to lunch the following Saturday, things would be different. But he headed up a science group of Roosevelt students and wanted to meet about her speaking to them on careers in chemistry; especially for the girls to hear from a woman chemist. *That was the hook*, Persi now thought in retrospect. She should have known when she wouldn't mention the conversation to Doxie she was careening toward trouble. She rationalized this was a respectable reason for her to accept a lunch invitation from a married man on a Saturday. She'd never dated a married man before; the best part of him already taken, and Persi wasn't inclined to share or be part of a harem. Yet she heard herself accepting Brad's invitation as they decided on a quaint café in old town Alexandria. *What am I doing?* she'd asked. She wasn't raised to be the "other woman" and her parents would die if they knew. She and Brad met for lunch and, subsequently, she spoke with the students. In three months, Brad got Persi out of her designer clothes and into his bed. That was five years ago.

"Prepare for landing," the pilot said as the flight attendant swapped the lukewarm towel from Persi's tray and left a buttermint with the airline insignia.

As the plane taxied to a stop at a Dulles International Airport gate, Brad helped Persi get her carry-on bag full of bikinis and cover-ups from the overhead compartment.

"It's late, '*they*' won't be meeting me. I can take you home," he said into her ear.

They, she thought wryly. "We can never be too careful, can we?" she said with an edge to her voice.

"Let me see you home."

"I have my car and you're practically home."

"Then tomorrow."

Just as the flight attendant threw open the plane's front door, Persi looked up into his mournful, honey-sage eyes and said, "Bye."

She sauntered down the enclosed corridor into the open space. Then she saw them, the wife's view obstructed by the head of the sleepy little girl she held, as the other two waited anxiously, looking past everyone not their father. Persi passed by them like she was on a Paris runway, making no eye contact. She couldn't acknowledge them because then she'd have to acknowledge to herself what she was doing. She wasn't ready for that.

Almost to the shuttle, she heard a loud chorus of "Daddy!"

Tears of regret and torment accompanied her as she walked to her car. Why was she doing this? It wasn't worth it. . . not the toll it took on her and her sense of self.

She sat in the car, wiped away angry, cold tears and breathed a few times to relax before she fished for the ticket and money to get out of the lot. "Home," she directed her sporty Audi as she cruised the beltway before venturing onto the streets of D.C. Quiet, somber, sober streets coated with a thin veil of either sleet or drizzle. "No matter where you roam, there is no place like home," she thought of her mother's words every time they pulled into the driveway when they were children. That stuck better than "home again, home again, jiggy jig."

Persi chuckled. She hadn't followed the predicable path to home ownership that four generations of native Washingtonians dictated. Her great-grandparents had begun on U Street N.W. Not the famed U Street of the Booker T. or Republic Theaters; not "historical U Street" of black celebrity where its regal members appeared on the silver screen for their segregated enjoyment. Not the U Street that halted at the Negro nexus of Northwest where four corners of 1940s black D.C., give or take a block, converged; north to south, Seventh Street became Georgia Avenue and, east to west, the infamous U Street turned into Florida Avenue. But the quiet, residential section of U Street reached by taking a sweet left off of Florida Avenue onto Second across Rhode Island Avenue then a right at St. George's Episcopal Church and stretched up to North Capitol Street. Her great-grands had a row house on the left side and Persi recalled how she loved the high ceilings, fireplaces in every room, and the backstairs to the kitchen. She savored the Sunday meals after church there, and all the holidays; eavesdropping on all the antics of the folks who populated their family. Her grandparents, the second generation, moved from Shaw-LeDroit Park to upper northwest in the second alphabet and been "blockbusters" in the early fifties despite the clandestine and illegal covenants to initially keep Negroes out of the white neighborhoods. Two years before Brown vs. the *Board of Education*, prior to the Gold Coast across Sixteenth Street opening up—and when it did, her grandparents and a few other pioneers refused to move the few arbitrary blocks to the "other side." Persi's parents, then three, predictably moved into the third alphabet—the flowers and trees of Shepherd Park; geranium, holly, iris, and juniper where the Sinclairs lived with their three daughters. Persi's oldest sister, Diana April, escaped to Oberlin College, never returned to D.C., and now lived in Boston with her partner. Her younger sister, Athena June, and her family upheld tradition and moved across Sixteenth to the Platinum Coast of North Portal Estates into more trees at Spruce and Sycamore. By then the black bourgeoise's prosperity outgrew the confines of upper northwest and pushed right up against Maryland into the county of Montgomery. The acceptable excess of upper-crust D.C. flowed over the Maryland line into Silver Spring, Bethesda, and Potomac. Persi May was supposed to buy her house there and had a lovely, all brick, split foyer with a long driveway picked out until Doxie told her that "her house" was for sale.

Since she'd been a child, Persi had loved her house, an all-brick, Second Empire style, Romanesque revival on Logan Circle built in the 1880s. While Diana favored the Seth Phelps house on the corner of Thirteenth Street with the big magnolia for a front yard, Persi preferred the white, four-story Victorian with the mansard roof and Peter Pan dormers. After purchase the high Victorian Gothic stood uninhabitable, forcing Persi to replace the roof, close the fireplaces, install zone heating and air conditioning and address a drainage problem before she moved in. Living in one area, she painstakingly renovated her house, room by room; laying on her back, meticulously hand-painting the medallion around the dining room chandelier and refurbishing the gleam to the original hardwood floors. She'd spent her nights, weekends, and evenings and after sixteen months, like D.C. itself, it was a showpiece. But it was home to her.

Staunch neighborhood purists objected to her conversion of the side yard into a semicircular drive, but with no street parking and the issue of her personal safety, she remained undaunted. This successful modification inadvertently launched a landscape-design business while still a primary researcher at NIH. As the principal landscape company for four architectural firms and freelancing jobs around the metro area, she worked this second job only on weekends and summer evenings. After two years, her landscaping-design business eclipsed chemistry; she left the latter. During the slow winter months, driven more by need for activity than money, she consulted on research teams at NIH, wrote proposals, received grants, accepted speaking engagements in the field of stem cell research and testified at congressional hearings as an expert. She had two jobs; one brand new and the other she'd always felt she'd been in by default. Neither held a candle to her dream career: a perfumer. She'd always concocted her own perfumes in junior high and high school and even today, no matter where she traveled, always visited the botanical grounds expanding her repertoire of aromatic fragrances, preparing for a time when she hoped to use it. The words of George Eliot echoed in her ear, "It's never too late to be what you might have been."

Into this welcomed chaotic mix and convergence of all things possible entered Brad Shelton. At thirty years old, everything she ever wanted was coming to fruition; even a guy she had a crush on in high school who was once out of her league, was now eating out of the palm of her hand.

Persi pulled into her side-yard driveway, cut her engine, and climbed to her front door. *Home*, she thought. The perfect journey; glad to go and glad to come back. She cut off her alarm, unlocked and entered her tiled vestibule before opening her front door. Timers clicked on and off, illuminating various areas of her house and she glanced at the living room and the dining room as she walked her hallway to the kitchen.

A sign *Welcome Home, Aunt Persi*, was propped up on the black granite island in the middle of the kitchen against the basket of mail.

Persi chuckled and looked at the plants that Drew cared for in her absence. *She is such a good kid*, Persi thought, as she ignored the mound of mail, closed her pantry door, and headed up the backstairs to her bedroom. *I suppose if I'm good, one day I'll get a Drew or two*, she thought, pulling off her blouse and turning up the thermostat. The phone rang.

"Hello?"

"Hi."

Persi closed her eyes against the sound of the familiar voice.

"I just called to see if you got home all right," Brad inquired just above a whisper.

"Yeah. Thanks."

"Bruce. We'll figure all this out. You know I love you."

"So you say."

"I've got something really special planned for your birthday. We'll eat at our little place in Alexandria, drive around the monuments—I know how you like them lit up at night—and spend the rest of the evening at the Willard Intercontinental Hotel. How's that sound?"

Persi opened her mouth to speak—

"Somebody's coming. Gotta go. Call you tomorrow."

Click.

Persi stood there with the phone in her hand. The dial tone blared, she hung up.

How could someone who brings you such joy, bring you such pain? she thought with a heavy sigh. She drew her blinds and drapes, walked into her closet, and pulled out a nightgown from the built-in drawers. She cut on the shower faucet, ran the water to the desired temperature, shed the rest of her clothes where she stood, and stepped into the stream of wet, hoping it would wash the travel grime and her adulterous sins away. She loved him and hated herself for loving him. She was a good person. An accomplished and well-respected professional. A great friend, law-abiding citizen, good-hearted. . . she had one flaw. No human being was perfect. When she got to the Pearly Gates would God absolve her of this *one* thing? Forgive her for knowingly coveting another woman's man?

Hell no, she thought. In all the annals of the Bible, she knew adultery was a biggie. The mother of all mothers. She knew her own mother rolled over in her grave every time her daughter rolled in the sheets with Brad Shelton. In all the years her parents were married, she'd never heard anything about outside people. Her daddy mowed the lawn on Saturdays, wheeled his girls to dance or piano lessons, and her parents went out together on Saturday nights—to the movies, a friend's house, and once a month to fraternity or sorority or social club meetings. On Sundays they'd go to church as a family and as they grew, their father slept in, but always had breakfast ready for them upon their return. She knew her father hailed from a different time, but she wondered how a married man got out on a Saturday. Day or night? But once Brad slid his hand up the small of her back, sending shivers in places she'd forgotten about, she didn't wonder anymore. Once he took her chin in his hands, pressed those fabulous lips on hers and parted them with his tongue . . . she didn't wonder or even care anymore. She was single, he was married—it wasn't her problem that his wife couldn't keep him home. Once he pressed that hard, gorgeous body of his against hers . . . there was only him in her world—no one else mattered but the two of them. She had never felt such complete joy as he escorted her to a never-land of carnal pleasures and everything she thought'd she missed in high school, she was getting with him. No other man had ever made her feel that way.

Early on, Persi thought it cute when he checked in with his wife and she'd tell him to bring bread on his way home. Persi would climb on top of him, nuzzle, kiss and flick her tongue in his ear to distract him.

Early on, she liked to listen to him say "Love you too," and thought that his wife was so dumb because she, Persi Sinclair, had him right were she wanted him: under her. They made love after love. Early on, Persi believed him when he told her that he and his wife had an understanding, that she wasn't sensitive to his needs like Persi was. That they had an arrangement and he never slept with her anymore.

Early on, she believed him when he said, "You are number one and I love you and only you." That he loved his wife because she was the mother of his children, but he was in love with Persi. Persi believed him when he declared Brainstorm's "This Must Be Heaven," as their song and he couldn't live without her in his world. She believed him when he said, "If only I had noticed you in high school things would have been so different. You'd have my children now." She believed him when he proclaimed that "they would be together eventually, it'll just take a little time."

And then she, the wife, became pregnant.

That should have been Persi's first clue.

Like when Doxie asked, "How do you know when a man's lying?"

"How?"

"His lips are moving."

But his wife couldn't give him what he wanted—a boy. It was another girl. Persi knew she'd give him a boy . . . after they were married. She did have her standards and a reputation to maintain. So Persi's heart overrode her logical mind and they continued this relationship in secrecy.

Persi stepped from the shower and wrapped her brown body in a thirsty aubergine towel. All that was years ago. She'd justified the hell out of her sordid behavior. What was her excuse now? What could she tell herself now and believe?

She slipped on the nightgown and felt the silk tumble across her clean skin. She opened the drapes of one window, climbed into bed, and cut off her light. She watched the waning moon's illumination paint the blinds' symmetrical pattern on her rug. *How did I get here?* she asked as she prayed for sleep to come. A fire truck blazed by, siren careening, and the flash of lights momentarily lit up her room like twelve o'clock noon. She missed the island's peace, as she tried to ignore that for ten days Brad had been satisfying and lying next to her each and every night and sometimes twice during the day. Now the night called out his name, but she was alone. *He lays next to his wife*, she thought. From heaven to hell in a matter of hours.

She began deep yoga breathing, her body relaxed and finally, she fell asleep. It was the only freedom she knew.

CHAPTER 3

Persi jolted awake from the sound of the bell at her front door. Initially she was disoriented, wondering why she was not in a thatched-roof hut in the South Pacific. She grabbed a robe, descended the stairs, opened the front door onto her vestibule and then the outside door, where a delivery man was hidden by an abundance of exotic, tropical flowers.

"Oh, my!" Persi exclaimed as she took the clipboard from his hands, signed for the flowers, and then accepted the floral bundle. "If you wait, I'll get you—"

"That's okay, ma'am. Enjoy."

"Aunt Persi!" Drew ran up the steps, passing the delivery man and followed by her mother.

"Hey girl," Persi turned in time to absorb her full body hug.

"I missed you, Aunt Persi," Drew said, wrapping her arms around Persi's waist. "Mom made me go to a fashion show. Don't ever go away again. Unless you take me with you."

"That ought to be a hoot. The three of you," Doxie said sardonically, referring to Persi, Brad and Drew as she entered the house. "Nice flowers," she said sarcastically. "What's it been, ten hours? He really can't do without you, huh?"

"Who?" Drew asked.

"Uh! Grown folks' conversation, young lady," Doxie admonished her precocious daughter. "Can't hear when I tell you to clean your room, but you're all up in this."

"Hey," Persi said to Doxie as they shared an air kiss between them.

"Aunt Persi, did you see how I did your mail and watered

your plants?" Drew asked proudly.

"Good job!" Persi slapped five with the ten-year-old girl. "I owe you for a job well done, don't I?"

"Only if you think I deserve it."

"Who is this and what have you done with Drew?" Persi asked playfully of Doxie.

"Oh, Aunt Persi," she laughed with a blush.

"Go on up stairs and get my purse. And there are a few souvenirs as well."

Drew raced up the backstairs, taking the steps by twos.

"There are no condoms, in that purse are there?" Doxie asked.

Persi smirked at her old friend.

"But condoms were used, right?" Doxie pressed.

"Negro, please. I love me."

"Are you sure?" Doxie rolled her eyes.

"Oh! Aunt Persi, can I look at TV up here?"

"Yes!"

"Thank you!"

"Good kid," Persi said as she fluffed and sniffed the flowers.

"Takes after her mama." Doxie eyed her friend and asked, "Good trip?"

"It was." Persi blushed.

"Humph," Doxie commented disdainfully and asked, "Are we going or not?"

"Okay. Let me shower."

Persi went upstairs and picked out jeans and a Howard U. sweatshirt, relishing being back home with folks whose love and motives she never questioned. She'd known Doxie Fitzhugh since the third grade when they'd been joined together by their unusual names. In the fourth grade, they'd postulated that girls with names never shared by anyone else in the world were special, and by the sixth grade, they expanded to become the Fab Four by teaming up with Viviana Hamilton and Nola Rogers. They all transferred to Roosevelt High School in the science pilot program a year ahead of their other classmates, further distinguishing their names to Doxie, the doctor's daughter, Persi-Sin, ViVi-Ham, and Nola-Ro. While others referred to them, not always in a positive light, as the "smart girls" or "brainiacs," privately they called themselves the PVs—professional virgins. Even though they were invited to all the parties and dated, boyfriends didn't last long because they had "too much self-esteem" and reps for not "givin' up nothin,'" having vowed to each other not to just offer their womanly treasure to any old boy.

Only one boy breeched and was admitted to the Fab Four. Desmond "Desi" Fairchild became the plus one"in the tenth grade when his father, the ambassador from Jamaica, moved to D.C. with his family. Desi's test scores and intelligence gained him entry into the science program but his Hershey-chocolate good looks, charm, humor, and dancing ability got him accepted by everyone. Being naturally brilliant and not pretentious, a dufus or boring like other boys in their orbit, Desi-Fair provided a welcomed comic relief in all the Fab Four plus one AP classes. Even though he lived on Colorado Avenue, one block down from Doxie and across from the Carter Baron Amphitheater, he was absolutely, wildly crazy for "Persi-girl" as he called her. Persi missed the attention when he disappeared to Jamaica for the summers and always anticipated his return with great relish, but she didn't want to lose their friendship for a romantic entanglement. Being platonic friends lasted longer than her four-week boyfriends ever had.

After graduation, they'd all gone their separate ways, attending different colleges but remained close in hearts and mind. All expected Desi would return to Jamaica but upon graduation from Stanford, he'd remained in California and was now the premier fertility doctor. Everyone teased that all a fertility-challenged woman needed to do was watch him come toward her in that white coat against his chocolate-dipped skin . . . fertility problem over. ViVi Hamilton also ended up on the West Coast, available mainly during the holidays, and Nola Rogers had gone the route of Persi's younger sister Athena; graduated college, immediately married her college beau, had children, and never used their degrees except to calculate their accounts at Neiman's.

So Persi and Doxie, despite the latter's marriage and divorce, were basically as they'd always been—the two of them. The world knew of Desi's crush on Persi, but Doxie was the only one of the four aware of the love jones Persi had for Brad Shelton all those years. Doxie despised the way the man took advantage of her friend now . . . and Persi knew it. As with all old friends who have different viewpoints, a truce existed between the two women. Each knew how the other felt and no one was changing their minds on the subject.

Doxie felt Brad was robbing Persi of vital years, for as long as her friend dated him she was not going to date anyone else. Brad was a dead-end relationship. Persi felt that she and Brad were destined to be together, as fate had reintroduced them, and if she were patient it would happen. In an unspoken alliance, the three agreed that this surreptitious love affair be conducted in secrecy. Doxie didn't want Persi's reputation trashed as a harlot-jezebel who dated a married man; bad for her future husband, wherever he might be, and bad for women who wouldn't invite her to the necessary social functions, for the untrustworthy pariah they'd surely think she was. Persi knew discretion was paramount for her and Brad so he could make an elegant exit with his name, reputation, and assets intact. These matters were better worked out with clear heads and no unnecessary drama and angst.

So over the last five years she'd dated enough to cover the

illicit romance. She'd had long term relationships prior to Brad and wide receiver Rucker Jackman reigned the longest, but incompatibility and conflicting lifestyles caused Persi to nix him as a viable marital candidate. She'd ended it well enough for them to still to be friends . . . but no sex, as she'd done with a stockbroker and a lawyer who could not hold a candle to the fun and excitement of a Rucker Jackman. It was from this limited roster that Persi pulled necessary dates for the special occasions. With all of her professional obligations, folks assumed that she was simply too busy and career-oriented to cultivate a lasting relationship with one man.

The telephone rang. Persi answered with a "hello."

"Hey, Bruce. How's my lady this afternoon?"

"Fine. Thank you for the flowers," she enthused in spite of her best efforts.

"You got them already?"

"Woke me up."

"I wish it was me doing that," he said huskily. "I loved waking you up in the morning and putting you to bed at night."

She blushed.

"What are you wearing?"

"Actually, jeans and a sweatshirt. Doxie, Drew, and I are about to do our monthly volunteering at the So Others Might Eat soup kitchen before shopping at Pentagon City. Drew needs new ski clothes when she goes to visit her father in a few weeks and we want to pick up some things for the Hannah House."

"Oh. Doxie there already?"

"Yep. I'll tell her you said hi," Persi teased, knowing each equally despised the other. "You coming over tomorrow night?"

"No can do. Sunday with the family especially after being away for ten days."

So I'm free for the rest of the weekend, Persi thought.

"In fact, I'll have to play catch-up at work so I probably won't be able to drop by until mid-week for a few minutes."

"I'll have Drew starting on Wednesday. Doxie is keynote speaker at a conference in Colorado and I get to keep my goddaughter. Picking her up from school, homework, dinner, bath, bed—you know the routine, don't you, Dad?"

"Can't I come over after the little tyke goes to bed?"

"Don't know where I'll be. Their house is nearer to Drew's school and NIH, where I'll be for a few weeks. I'll probably be staying there."

"You punishing me?"

"No. Just making it easier on Drew and me."

"I've made the plans for your birthday. You want to hear them?"

"You already told me. Where are you now?"

"Car wash. We'll dine at our bistro in Alexandria, maybe park near Haines Point and neck before checking into the Willard."

"Isn't that expensive for next-day checkout?"

"The wife is going to see a play in New York with her girlfriends—limo and all. That gives us the entire weekend. I surprised her with the trip and tickets. Part of *your* gift."

"You are such a good boy," Persi said coyly into the phone. When she turned to the side, Doxie stood against the doorjamb, arms folded. Persi's guilt made her straighten up.

"We'd better get going," Doxie said evenly, raised her eyebrow in disgust before turning to check on Drew.

"Listen. I've got to go."

"Love you, Bruce."

"Yep. I know." She hung up. "Is everybody ready?" she sang out.

The trio's day proceeded with them ending up at Nordstrom's in Montgomery Mall and Doxie's house in Kensington. After dinner, with Drew on her computer and Doxie on the telephone, Persi thought of texting Brad but decided not to. She thought of how she knew everything about "the wife" as he called her; where she shopped, when she menstruated or was sick, her doctor's appointments and ailments, where and when she got her hair done, what social clubs she belonged to; Persi knew the girls' activities and their social calendar, mostly so she could avoid the places the wife and family frequented. Persi never understood women who liked being in the presence of the wife at social events and made demands on the man they shared, daring him to mess up. Persi thought that behavior controlling and low-life She needed to show some respect for the institution of marriage.

While Persi knew everything about the wife, the wife knew nothing of Persi. Persi didn't like referring to her by name and the title, "the wife" made her seem less real . . . less of a person . . . less of a human being to be considered. Persi knew if Brad had married a friend or a girl from D.C., she would never never responded to Brad's advances despite her high school crush. Nine times out of ten Persi would have known his wife and her family and upheld the unwritten D.C. sisterhood barring such contemptible behavior. Brad Shelton was taken. But let him divorce or the wife drop dead, then it would be open season on his available butt and consoling casserole ladies at his door. Persi exempted herself from respecting husband, hearth, and home since Brad hadn't married a girl from D.C., but one from South Carolina. Persi had no preexisting relationship or felt no allegiance or particular attachment to Patricia "Trish" Davenport Shelton.

Doxie extended a glass of cabernet to Persi and said, "Here you go."

"Night, Aunt Persi." Drew came in and encircled her with a big hug.

"Night, baby," Persi said.

Doxie turned the sound of the news down and said, "Wanna talk?"

"About what?"

"More like you-know-who."

"Jean-Luc?"

"No. He's an old creepy, coworker guy."

"He isn't. He's brilliant and because he is, he comes off arrogant and caustic. He's a sweetheart if you understand him."

"He's crazy. Who gives up French aristocracy lineage to be in an NIH lab all day?"

"One man's trash is another man's treasure. Research is his passion. I admire him for leaving the family business—"

"And millions."

"And striking out on his own."

"Crazy and creepy. It's because you know how to handle him that he picks you for those grants to augment your design income during the winter months."

"And . . . I'm good."

"And modest."

"I calls 'em like I sees 'em. His wife Claudia is crazy about me too, although she returns to France every chance she gets. Woman wears some bad clothes, girl."

"So when are you going?" Doxie teased. "Take him up on his offer to make the necessary introductions so you can be a French perfumer like you always wanted?"

"Therein lies the rub. I'm not ready to leave D.C. yet."

"We never are. Our hometown. But that's not the 'who' I was talking about. Wanna talk about a black man with honey-sage eyes and a recent trip?"

"No, I do not."

"Sure?"

"Positive."

"Okay."

CHAPTER 4

Frigid February ushered in its first two weeks with gray ghost days and cold nights all perpetually warmed by the effervescent presence of Drew and all her activites. Though Persi loved every minute of it, her appreciation for working mothers grew for those who kept up this pace daily. After Doxie returned from Colorado, the following days filled with birthday parties for Persi's twin nieces, Athena's children, her father and Sylvia's anniversary dinner, preparatory meetings for her sorority's spring fling and the Easter egg roll for the ambulatory patients at Childrens' Hospital. Every three years, Persi gave permission for her house to be featured on the Logan Circle house tour in May, an annual fund raiser for the neighborhood's civic association.

In solidarity with Drew and other school-children in the metro area, Persi wore her pajamas backward, praying for a snow day. When she awoke to the bright-white darkness at seven, her prayers had been answered with a February blizzard; schools, airports, and the government closed. Brad called and they managed forty-five minutes before being interrupted by one of the girls. She hung up, wondering how a wife could ever keep track of her spouse in this millennium; between e-mail, cell phones, pagers, and texting, it'd be an exhausting, full-time job. The prediction of an evening ice storm prompted further cancellations as the metro Washington area suffocated, then became paralyzed by the frozen precipitation. Persi relished working from home and thankful for the free day to address her landscaping business as she reviewed her files and contracts, contacted her guys, ordered supplies, composed the newsletter to her current clients, and sent polite rejections to those who hoped to be future ones. The weather kept Brad home but he promised to make it up to her at the birthday tryst.

"Better take your vitamins, Bruce," he suggested.

"Me? I'm always good to go, old man," she teased as she licked the last envelope.

"Yes, you are," he agreed, thinking of her gorgeous, toned body. Not a stretch mark or sagging breast in sight. "It's been such a long time."

"Over two weeks. Maybe we're already married."

Birthday Friday finally arrived and Persi worked nonstop, looking forward to Brad's exercizing all the tension from her body the way he knew best. She came home, jumped in the shower and then into the slinky gold dress she'd splurged on for her birthday celebration. As she listened to Prince command *"do me, baby,"* she eyed her image approvingly in the Cheval mirror, spinning and stopping in a dramatic pose to view her backless frock that plunged to her waist. "Fierce!"

She slid her bare legs into four-inch stilettos that arched her feet and showcased her famous gams in the most alluring manner. She gazed at her defined calves, then her rounded derriere and liked the firm knot each of them displayed. "Backfield in motion tonight!"

She checked her flawless makeup, her shiny, dark brunette hair and oversized purse for her negligee and fresh undies for the next two days—not that she'd need them. As she cut Prince off, she said, "I will take your advice, my brotha."

When the cab appeared outside her house, she slipped on her fur coat, clicked on her alarm, and cut off her cell phone. She loved her family and friends, accepted their well-wishes all day long, but tonight belonged to Brad; this weekend belonged to them. Persi didn't want family or friends calling her for any emergency—for the next two days and nights they needed to call 911; she'd be igniting her own fires.

She climbed into the cab and gave him the address of the posh, exclusive and private Georgetown restaurant instead of their usual Alexandria haunt. *This is quite a gamble for Mr. Shelton,* she thought. *He's getting a little riskier with the future Mrs. Shelton . . . namely me,* she thought and smiled.

As the cab pulled off, she pointed her key to lock her Audi. Tonight they didn't need two cars as they were going to end up together in the same place. The thought of the next delicious forty-eight hours made her grin with naughty anticipation. On this night, Persi couldn't care less what he told the wife or where she'd be, just so she didn't show up at their door at the Willard Intercontinental Hotel.

Persi paid the cabbie and eyed the secluded restaurant with the serpentine walkway nestled in the shadow of the C&O Canal that Brad selected out of *Conde Nast* magazine. *Impressive,* Persi thought as she sauntered into the welcoming façade, surrendered her Russian lynx to the coat check, and gave her name to the maître'd.

"Bruce."

"Ah, your party has not yet arrived. Would you like to be seated at the table or have a drink at the bar?"

"The bar." Persi wanted Brad to get the full effect of what she wore when they were shown to their table. The front of her dress was a high boatneck cut, but he'd be treated to the curve of her bare back and spine, as it discreetly disappeared into the shimmering metallic gold material gathered at her waist.

"Bellini," she answered when asked by the bartender. All she had to do was shrug out of this designer garb and her breasts would be revealed in all their supple and dark-rung glory.

She perched her body on the cushioned stool, sipped her drink, and admired the decor. Tables for two lined the tapestry-covered walls, reminiscent of the huts in Bora-Bora, insuring privacy by the drapery that hung between them. Like a giant coil, the tables swirled from the walls inward losing their draping toward the middle but still private. She wondered which was theirs. As in many of France's finer restaurants, there were only two seatings, so patrons weren't rushed but encouraged to linger. *Probably the reason their waiting list is booked months in advance*, she postulated.

Persi sampled her drink just as she noticed a small combo playing softly from an almost hidden stage. Despite the elegant and understated ambience of the establishment, it screamed money. She sipped and swayed with the soothing, sexy music, crossed her long, brown bare legs and imagined how she'd run her painted toes up, down, and inside Brad's pant cuffs as they ate and played little sexy pregames before the main event.

The bartender interrupted the sensuous sounds by asking her if she wanted to refresh her drink. As she turned to say no, her eyes snagged on the sight of a lone man sitting at the end of the bar. He was looking at her. He nodded discreetly; Persi gave a noncommittal semi-smile, not wanting to either disrespect or encourage the brother. Even while she listened to the next three songs and eyed her watch, she was conscious that he was still looking at her. She gave no indication of being aware of his existence, despite an odd, magnetic presence, which she ignored until he came over after the fourth song.

"Hello," he said.

Persi glared at him, not knowing whether to be flattered or annoyed. Was it because they were the only two black people here? "I'm waiting for someone," Persi dismissed.

"I think it's me."

"I beg your pardon?"

"Let me rephrase that. Are you Ms. Persi Sinclair?"

"I am," Persi said, wondering if he'd been in one of her lectures or in attendance when she'd testified on the Hill. He didn't look familiar as she would have remembered him.

"I'm Nick Betancourt and I'm here for Brad Shelton."

Persi's face flushed. "Excuse me?" she said and thought, *Just what does that mean?*

"He's had an emergency and won't be coming tonight. He asked me to stop by and let you know."

Immediately pissed, Persi's temper flared; she gritted her teeth as heat warmed her earlobes. She'd waited over two weeks for this night, this special occasion, and someone had ruined it. How many other days and nights had been ruined by other folks? How many times had she cooked dinner for him, only to have him call and say the wife surprised him with theater tickets? The wife's parents had come to town and he couldn't get away. The girls were sick; the dog threw up. The goldfish died. Why was she, Persi, always the causality of a well-planned good time? Why was her life always less impor-tant then theirs? Her eyes flashed, her pulse quickened, she wanted to pimp-slap somebody.

"Are you all right?" he asked with concern.

"Why yes," she lied, an insincere smile frozen on her face. *How much did this man know?* Had he and Brad had a nudge-and-wink before Brad sent him over here? Brad's best friends didn't know about the two of them. Who was this guy?

"He tried calling you but apparently your phone is off."

"Of course." Persi fought to retain some dignity. "Did Mr. Shelton send the papers?"

"Papers?"

"Yes, this was a business meeting and he—I was supposed to sign—" she stuttered, thinking, *Jeez that even sounds lame to me.*

"No. No papers. I'm sure he will be contacting you with the details. To reschedule," he offered amiably.

"Yes," her voice croaked. Embarrassment colored her face as it was obvious that this tryst had nothing to do with business, yet this man was being so gracious about the horrendously awkward situation. "Yes, well . . . thank you." She just wanted to bolt, run home, and curse Brad Shelton out in the privacy of her own house.

"Nick," he reminded.

"What?"

"Nick Betancourt."

"Oh, yes. Right. Well . . ." She summoned the bartender to settle up her bill.

"Allow me."

Persi was an angry wreck. She stopped to breathe. "Thank you again . . . Nick Betancourt."

"Listen, have you eaten?"

"What?"

"If you haven't, you must be hungry. I understand the food here is excellent and the reservations are hard to come by. I'm hungry. Why don't we just stay?"

Persi looked at him—this stranger named Nick Betancourt. It was her thirty-fifth birthday; she was all dressed up and had been stood up by a man who claimed to love her. This Nick seemed harmless and charming enough to spend a few hours with before she caught a cab home; it was too late for her to plan anything else.

"Brad's already paid for it so we might as well have a nice dinner on him," he said, a smile dimpling his cheeks. "What do you say?"

Persi smiled and relaxed for the first time since she'd been reminded again that she was not a priority for Brad. Unless he was on a slab in the morgue, there was no excuse. It would serve him right if she and this Nick ran up an enormous bill. . . then she'd get his attention. Heck, she might even buy drinks for everybody. "That sounds good, Nick Betancourt. Let me go freshen up and then we'll sit."

"Great."

He watched her sashay away from him. Pretty, poised, confident with a thousand Nubian queens rotating her hips; he loved black women to the bone. He'd been asked to come and tell her that Brad couldn't make it tonight. He'd come and sat at the bar waiting for that woman to show, and had noticed this one. Somehow her self-assured posture didn't seem the type who'd be interested in a Brad Shelton. A striking, beautiful black woman with deep nutmeg and ginger–colored skin and naturally shiny, dark sable-hued hair; it shortness gave her long neck a certain fascinating allure. After a drink and a few tunes from the combo, Nick decided that Brad's woman was a no-show, so he intended to introduce himself to this woman in the gold dress perched on the stool. Nick grew intrigued by her and he hadn't been intrigued by any woman in many years. If she were alone, this would be an interesting way to spend an evening. He couldn't believe they were one and the same; Persi Sinclair was an enigma.

Upon her return, they settled into a booth against the wall.

"Have you ever been here before?" Nick asked casually.

"My first time," she said as the waiter laid a linen napkin in her lap.

"A shared adventure." Nick commented.

Persi ordered seared lobster bisque, a Caesar salad, and sea scallops in an apple glaze dolloped with caviar to his curried corn chowder, grilled asparagus, and lamb chops infused with rosemary-mint stuffing. At the suggestion of the waiter, they also ordered the chocolate soufflé for dessert as it required two hours of preparation.

Despite their meal choices, Nick selected a Shiraz from the wine list and made a sophisticated production of tasting the offering from the sommelier before giving his approval. She liked that his choice bucked convention, which dictated white wine; Brad would have ordered a chardonnay on principle.

"Persi is an unusual name for a lady."

"It's really Persephone—"

"Ah, daughter of Zeus and Demeter, goddess of spring. Someone was into Greek mythology."

"You have no idea." She found it refreshing that he knew the origin of her name yet was thoughtful enough not to mention that Persephone was taken by Hades, lord of the underworld. Speaking of the devil, she asked first, "So. How do you know Brad Shelton?"

"Brad and I were at Columbia together."

"MBA program."

"Yep. I was MBA-JD. He was there when I came and there when I left."

"I suppose he was in no hurry."

"I didn't have that luxury. My scholarship was very specific about how long I had," he chuckled without arrogance. "And you?" he shot.

Persi almost choked on her wine. "Actually, I knew Brad in high school."

"You are not that old."

Today's my birthday, she thought longing to tell him, but said, "I went in the ninth grade. A special science program and he was a senior."

"Oh. And you kept in touch?"

"No. I was reintroduced to him about five years ago." She didn't like this conversation at all. "And you? You all good friends?"

"Not exactly. Brad is older. We belong to the same fraternity. I lived in the frat house for awhile but it really wasn't conducive to studying. I ran into him downtown on K Street today. He invited me up to his office."

"Where are you from?"

"Originally, Baltimore."

"Really?"

They talked about everything and nothing and, during the next three hours and forty-five minutes, the conversation never returned to Brad Shelton. She explained that she was a chemist and landscaper, and he countered with being a musician and organizer of karate tournaments for inner-city boys across the country. His main address was a Chicago condo, but he traveled a lot and was thinking of settling down in this area near the water, so either the Potomac or Severn River were likely candidates. The couple hadn't run out of topics to discuss but they had completed dessert, coffee, and their after-dinner drinks.

Before she knew it, Persi was being helped on with her coat. The bitter cold air swirled off the C&O Canal and assaulted her thin dress. She pulled her small-dotted lynx about her.

"Where's your parking ticket?" he asked, giving his to the attendant.

"Oh. I didn't drive. I'll catch a cab."

"Nonsense. I'll take you home." He watched the rental car approach, tipped the attendant, and asked, "Where do you live?"

"Mount Vernon," she teased as she got in and watched his face split into a wide smile. "You should have asked first." She laughed. "I live on Logan Circle."

"I would have driven you to Mount Vernon," he counter-teased. "Can't have you traipsing around D.C. in the wee hours of the morning alone."

As he made a right turn, she thought of how many nights she'd left Brad in those wee hours, driven home, parked and scurried up her steps to safety, and the most she got from Brad was a call when he got home. If something happened to her in the street, Brad would have read about it in the paper the next day. As it was, he always took a cab to her house—day or night. With his vanity plates, neither he nor his car could chance being consistently seen in her neighborhood, but it was perfectly acceptable for her to risk flesh and limb to have an amorous assignation any place in the metro area.

With the two o'clock traffic down to nil, in seemingly minutes they'd stopped in front of her house.

"You live here?" Nick asked.

"Yep."

"How many of you all live in here?"

She giggled; she was getting used to his humor. "Just me."

He let out a long whistle. "I guess a landscaping-chemist must do pretty good."

"Thanks for the evening. It turned out better than I expected."

"My pleasure," he began seriously. "Want me to walk you up?"

"No. I'll be fine."

"Flick the lights when you get in your vestibule."

She chuckled again before becoming lightly conflicted. This was all it would ever be between her and Nick, but there was Doxie. *He'd be so good for Doxie*, she thought.

He looked around the quiet circle and said, "You can walk to U Street from here."

"Yep. Just up the block."

"I'll let you know when I come back to town and play at Balzac's." He decided to let her off this awkward hook. No pressure. "You know it?"

"Yeah. Nice club. That'd be great. I have a friend I'd like you to meet. You aren't married, are you?"

The question hung out there like a water-soaked diaper . . . full and stinky.

"No. I'm not," he answered evenly.

"Do you like children?"

"Love 'em. Want a passel of my own one day."

"Good." She needed to quit while she was ahead. "Thanks again, Nick Betancourt. It was great meeting you." Persi stuck out her hand for him to shake. When he did, she smiled, opened, then closed the car door and walked up her steps, reaffirming that this would be her first, last, and only personal encounter with this guy . . . but Doxie could really use a Nick Betancourt.

When she entered her house, she flicked on the lights. She heard him toot lightly and she smiled.

"Easy come, easy go," she said, reengaging her alarm.

As Nick rounded the circle to P Street heading back toward Georgetown, he thought of Persi Sinclair; her physical presence, quiet dignity, classical elegance, and smarts whose company he had truly enjoyed. *How did Brad Shelton pull her?* he wondered, as he sailed though the blinking yellow light. A single, self-sufficient, simply gorgeous woman who could not only captivate but hold his attention and leave him wanting more. When was the last time a woman had piqued his interest? Brad Shelton? It did not compute. But Persi Sinclair was as complicated as her situation, and Nick had no place for crazy drama in his tranquil life. He knew there were three sides to every story: his, hers, and the truth. But Nick didn't want complications . . . his life had been complex enough and at this stage he only sought serenity.

Too bad, he thought as he rubbed his lip absently and passed M Street.

CHAPTER 5

A blanket of gray clouds lay over the skyline of the District of Columbia as Brad filled Persi's answering machine and voice mail with inane apologies. She erased them all. If he was alive and well, there was no excuse for missing her birthday. The flowers and jewelry he'd sent were refused and marked *returned to sender*. Doxie was elated and Persi was resigned, but of course, Brad, like the comfortable habit he was, squirmed his way back into Persi's good graces. After two weeks, she'd finally agreed to see him at her house.

"C'mon, Bruce. It couldn't be avoided. Her best friend got sick so she'd canceled her trip and got tickets for us to the symphony at the Strathmore as a surprise. What could I do?"

"Coulda told her you had other plans."

"I see you've never been married."

Her head jerked in his direction. Was he stupid or arrogant? She couldn't quite figure out which. Nonetheless, she fought the urge to slap the mouth that just spoke the ridiculous statement.

"And you couldn't at least come and tell me yourself. Sent your flunky," she spat.

"Flunky?" he chuckled. "Nick Betancourt might be a lot of things but *flunky* isn't one of them." He laughed at the absurd notion.

Persi was infuriated at Brad's cavalier response.

"What did you all do? Discuss me? Think you could pass me around like a frat hoochie? What did he do? Volunteer to come and tell me the bad news?"

"Are you kidding? I practically had to beg him. He was staying in Georgetown and I asked him to go by and let you know I'd have to miss our . . . meeting. I couldn't come and couldn't get you on your cell. He was on his way someplace else. I figured you'd rather it come from him than the maître d'. I was being considerate."

"Where was he going?"

"I dunno or care. Probably to a hotel to bed. He's a very . . . disciplined man."

Persi cut her eyes at him and put her juice in the fridge.

"He was always a strange one," Brad mused. "Don't know why he really pledged the fraternity. He never seemed to partake of the female, fringe benefits of being a frat man."

"You are a pig."

"A pig in love with you, Bruce. Oink. Oink. C'mon, you know we belong together. These things happen from time to time. You're not going to be this way once we get married, are you?"

"Not so sure I want to marry you," Persi scoffed.

"Ugh!" He grabbed his chest. "You wound me, Bruce. Hurt me to my heart." He began staggering around her kitchen like Redd Foxx in *Sanford and Son*. "This is the big one!"

Persi smiled despite her best efforts.

"I see my girl's smile." He went over to her. "I'll make it up to you. I promise."

"It was my thirty-fifth birthday, Brad."

"I know. C'mere." He gathered her in his arms. "I thought about you the whole time. I don't know what I'd do without you, Bruce. Please don't make me find out."

Persi sighed wearily.

"Let's go upstairs. Let me start making it up to you now."

***

Persi agreed to accompany her old beau, Rucker Jackman, to the Kennedy Center Honors for Sidney Poitier. The Heisman Trophy winner, wide receiver with Super Bowl rings for each finger was a smash-hit success, thanks to the tweaking of his date Persi. Although she and Rucker were now just friends who enjoyed a good platonic relationship, these dates with him were dangerous as she could easily recall their phenomenal loving. Always a one-man woman, his loving caused her to drop the other contenders at the time: a stockbroker and a lawyer. Rucker Jackman remained the best lover she'd ever had. His lithe, powerful body, his skillful hands and, with each rhythmic thrust of his talented love muscle, he'd coax her into the wildest, orgasmic ecstasy she'd never known.

"Persi May, Persi May, Persi MAY!" Persi smiled, remembering his loud professtations as he rode to their mutual climaxing. The first time it happened startled her as she wondered how he knew her middle name. When asked, he'd said, "I didn't know. But where I come from in Mississippi, May just goes naturally with Persi. Like you and me go together real natural-like. Know what I mean?"

Back then, the sex had been supernaturally unparalleled and they shared an inexhaustible thirst for one another, but once their feet it the floor, they had little in common. From two different worlds, she couldn't appreciate or fit into his constant party-people mode, and he thought her world interesting but largely square, although he aspired to that lifestyle in the distant future. To his credit, with all his millions, he had only one baby's-mama and the baby was almost seventeen. Also to his credit were the Jackman Joints Cineplexes he'd opened across the country as well as Jackman Joints BBQ Shacks. Persi realized he had potential but she did not have the patience or inclination to work with him, though many women would. Money and class are not mutually inclusive, but Persi knew she continually fascinated Rucker Jackman.

A fine, smart, independent black woman who didn't want or expect anything from him was a refreshing anomaly to him.

Persi liked her men strong, confident, and on the verge of arrogance. The fact that Rucker hoped that he could eventually win and keep her interest disqualified him from being a serious contender. So he toted her out to impress folks, always noting her title of doctor; leaving her to explain it wasn't a medical degree but a Ph.D. in chemistry. In the old days before Brad, she'd reciprocated and kept him around for extraordinary sex and perks—he'd flown her and her friends to two of his four Super Bowls. Now as friends he agreed with Persi's directive of no seriousness and no sex, but their friendship drove Brad Shelton nuts; an unintended delight.

She and Rucker always had a great time and when he'd walk her to the door he'd try to steal a kiss as she'd playfully push him away. "If you become Mrs. Rucker Jackman, we could just go and do what we do best."

"You crazy man. I'll watch you back to your limo," she dismissed.

"One day Persi May. You and me," he said, descending the steps. "For good. 'Till death do us part. I love you, girl."

"Bye," she said and closed her door. She did love Rucker Jackman, a good, honest man but opposites attract, then repel, and while the present was fun it did not lend itself to a lasting future. It wouldn't be until death do us part but more of until our lifestyles really clash and we aren't having fun anymore. Even if he didn't know it, Persi did.

Finally, the long, protracted harsh weather ushered in longer days and warmth that nudged the dawning of spring daffodils, lilacs, azaleas and, the anticipated pink buds of Japanese cherry trees that rung the Tidal Basin. Like a superhero, Persi reveled in her transition from winter grant chemist to spring landscaper. Now, busy and smelly most of the time, she tried locating the three giant black and orange koi in time for a client's garden party. Preparing her house for the Logan Circle spring tour, she placed her valuable collectibles in the upstairs hall closet when her high school scrapbook fell down on her head.

"Damn!"

Old, grainy, monochromatic pictures of Brad Shelton splattered across her highly polished hardwood floors. *Look at this. Jeez, girl you had it bad,* she thought as she began picking them up. Inside a black-and-white composition notebook—two pages were devoted to writing Mr. and Mrs. Bradford Myles Shelton. Persi and Brad Shelton. Persephone and Bradford Sheltonin all sorts of fancy and plain handwriting combinations. Persi knew that only Brad could lure her from her scruples. Besides not attending Howard University and being a perfumer, he was the only thing she ever really wanted in her life and didn't get.

Persi, the middle daughter, did everything her parents wanted and expected of her, except being a debutante and coming out, as her mother had. The archaic tradition made no sense to Persi. She put her foot down, which had been such a heady experience. Her older sister, Diana, obliged before promptly going to Oberlin College and now was eligible for tenure in the music department of Boston University. The compliant Athena wanted what her parents wanted. The one tradition Persi wanted to perpetuate—Howard University, where her grandparents and parents had met and married—and a career goal—to become a perfumer—both denied her. Once test scores identified her for the science program, they fast-tracked her into chemistry, thinking she was the second coming of Dr. Shirley Jackson, also a Roosevelt High School graduate. Persi didn't have the interest, aptitude, or attitude of Dr. Jackson, the first black women to earn a masters and Ph.D. in physics from MIT. Her parents' pride was evident when MIT offered Persi a full scholarship. Her mother lived long enough to hear the announcement at graduation in June, but by her fall dorm check-in, only her father and aunts escorted her; her mother had died that August. An emotionally numb Persi successfully and rotely ambled through the MIT program—undergrad, grad, and then completed the Ph.D. program. Once she graduated, she took the position at NIH, more out of convenience than desire. Opportunities always came to her and from them she selected the path of least resistance. Not once had she set out to get anything on her own . . . except Brad Shelton.

As Persi stacked the scrapbook and yearbooks back into the closet, she thought how her younger sister, Athena, got to Howard U, got her man, Bernard, and four children: a boy, twin girls, and another boy. Persi smiled, both happy and envious of her baby sister who'd never worked, had a nanny, housekeeper, and a man who thought life didn't begin until Athena woke up. He'd looked at her with such love and admiration, and Persi wondered if any man would ever look at her like that. She closed her closet door.

"Must be my time of the month," she said out loud as she gathered some of Drew's books. "Lucky girl to be on her way to Disneyland with her father and his family."

Persi thought of her own father who'd married too soon after her mother's death. Two and a half years. Disrespectful. Until Brad, she hadn't wondered if her dad and Sylvia knew each other while her mom was alive and sick. Few things were more heinous than a married man who cheats on his wife while she was either pregnant or sick. What about the vow, for better or worse. In sickness and health?

Yeah. It must be my time of the month. Chocolate. I need chocolate, she thought.

Persi never liked Sylvia; she tried too hard. Diana was already out of the house when their mother died and Persi was on her way, but Athena was caught in the cross fire between Dad and Sylvia, though her younger sister seemed to have managed. When her father and his new wife began having children—it was just too weird a notion for Persi to warm up to. As she matured, Persi had gotten better about her half-siblings, but Sylvia never seemed to bring much to the Sinclair table. Being seven years younger than her father wasn't an issue, but Sylvia wasn't educated like the women in her family. Persi's mother had been an elementary school teacher before she stopped working to take care of her children; her father, an U.S. Post Office administrator. Sylvia . . .what did she do? A clerk at the post office from Kentucky.

Snob, Persi self-proclaimed, but it was natural to gravitate to folks like you; good, bad or otherwise. Everyone had a comfort zone. She was only snobby when it came to her dad. Sylvia made him happy. *So be it; they're grown-ass people*, she thought.

Persi went into her freezer and popped the lid of Haagen-Dazs Amazon Valley chocolate, drove a spoon deep inside and licked it clean. Orgasmic. Persi pondered the first objection to Sylvia's cluelessness revolving around their names: Diana April, Persephone May, and Athena June—all Greek mythological mavens, testament to her father's love of literature and her mother's penchant for the months. Although her mother was relieved that they'd never had that boy . . . Ajax July Sinclair, as her father thought Jax Sinclair sound like a jock.

As she plunged her spoon into the cold confection again, she thought how Sylvia would have nothing to contribute to the Sunday dinners they had as youngsters at her great-grandparents'. Persi loved hearing the stories around the Gospel bird about segregated Washington. Her parents, who had Rock Creek Park as a backyard, frequented the Hot Shoppe at Georgia Avenue and Gallatin Streets, the Polar Bear frozen custard further up on Van Buren, Carter Baron Amphitheater for twenty-five cent double-feature movies with cartoons and previews and stayed all day, and slept with their doors unlocked. A time when D.C. public schools were like private institutions and Roosevelt, Coolidge, and Western high schools ruled, where excellence was the norm and students rushed to get to homeroom before the first bell. But her grands and great-grands had the famed U Street. The Black Broadway. The social and commercial mecca in the shadow of Howard University, the educational center of bourgeois black America. Their generation fashioned their own self-contained and sustained universe despite a hostile world that wouldn't have them or their money. In their cultural enclave, owned, operated, and enjoyed by its residents, black folks pleasured themselves with their own movie houses and the Howard Theater, almost ten years before Harlem's Apollo, where black royalty like Duke, Count, Sarah, and Nat "King" Cole shared their talents then relaxed at the Bohemian Caverns or Club Bali. As streetcars clanged down U on tracks, normal folk conducted business at Industrial Savings Bank, Standard Drug Store, Thompson's Dairy, the Whitelaw Market and, since 1858, worshiped at St. Augustine Catholic Church. In response to black folks complaining about discrimination at the main post office, the T Street post office was opened. Their proudest family moments captured by Scurlock Studios and displayed on fireplace mantles in their homes. Baseball games at Griffith Stadium, formal dances at the Whitelaw Hotel and Lincoln Colonnade where her grandmother, a debutante, came out in the 1945 Bachelor Benedict Cotillion. The first YMCA for blacks in the United States was on Twelfth Street, and the pride of attending Old Dunbar High School; the next stop was college . . . a potpourri of clothing haberdasheries, dress shops, millineries, hair salons, and barbershops to keep everybody looking clean as the board of health or sharp as a tack.

She chuckled, remembering her granddaddy's sayings, and wondered what made her rehash all of that.

The phone rang. "Hey professor," Persi said to her sister Diana. "How goes it?"

The two sisters spoke for almost an hour, catching up with one another's lives. As Diana spoke of heading over to her house in the Vineyard for most of the summer, Persi thought about the Shelton home on Martha's Vineyard where the wife and girls disappeared for a few weeks out of each summer month and she got to play with Brad in D.C.

"Remember when the cottage at Highland Beach was the best fun we had all summer? We could leave when the sun came up, stay out all day, come home when the sun set and our parents never worried," Diana mused.

"I sure do. Now Dad's put in heat, air-conditioning, and enclosed the side porch."

"What's doing with you this summer? Playing with dirt?" Diana chuckled.

"Yep. After Disneyland, Drew's off to Camp Mawavi and Doxie'll be lost until ViVi comes to town. We'll get Nola and the Fab Four will ride again."

"Oh Lawd, watch out!" Diana said. "You know what today is?"

"Mom's birthday," Persi answered with reverence.

"I think she is proud of all her girls."

"Spoken like the oldest one," Persi said and thought, *Not me with my married man.*

"Athena's next. She always had it made."

"Yeah, she was the lucky one."

"I've got to go but I'll talk to you soon. Take good care. Love you."

"Love you too," Persi said and hung up.

She glanced outside and noticed how the traffic slowed and jammed around two cars and a policeman. Absently, she continued her chores, reflecting on how different her two sisters were. Diana had been her rock after their mother died. While at MIT, Persi visited her frequently because going home to the house where they'd lived with their mother proved too difficult. On the holidays when Persi had forced herself home, Athena seemed to have adjusted flawlessly while Persi had not, another source of pain, so Persi stopped going home. Diana graduated and began her own life and Persi threw herself into her classes. Then her father married Sylvia and Persi was through with him and the house. Upon graduation, carried by her intellect and what would make her mother happy, Persi just continued into the master's program, forestalling any need to make a definitive decision about her life. When she did visit D.C., she stayed with Doxie until she married, then spent some nights with ViVi and her folks until ViVi stayed on the coast. The one time Persi returned to the family house, her mother's house, with the same address but different decor, she felt like an orphan. With no homestead, she applied and was accepted to the Ph.D. program and upon graduation accepted the position at NIH. Instead of planning and building her life, she was carried with the tide, not steering it. Not a bad life at all—but not one she designed.

Persi marched her nieces up the steps and into their house.

The nanny took them up immediately for baths as Persi plopped on the couch.

"Bye Aunt Persi!" they sang out, "And thank you!"

"You're welcome." As they disappeared upstairs she jokingly added, "Next time I'll make sure Drew goes with us."

Athena chuckled.

"My hat's off to you, sis. I dunno how you do it." Persi

rested for a few beats and then sprang up. "Well, let me go. Got to make it back downtown." She went to kiss her sister on the cheek and headed for the front door. "Where's Bernard and the boys?"

"Still out. They'll come in late and smelly."

"Manly men huh?" She noticed Athena seemed tense. "So what's up?"

"I'm thirty-one and I feel like I'm missing out on life."

Persi looked at her evenly.

"I mean, you're going home to do and be whatever you want to. Sleep till noon tomorrow. . . go nude. Hop a plane and go someplace exotic. You have the perfect, sweet life."

Persi let out a loud cackle. "Who knew I'd be bitter from the sweet?"

Athena looked quizzically at her older, accomplished sister.

"Every now and then I think it's human nature to want what you don't have. I'm thirty-five years old, heading fast toward thirty-six, and yes, my time is my own. My money is my own. My house is my own. There's a good chance I'll live out my life. . .on my own. Maybe alone. I'm all right with that, but sometimes I look at you and think you have it all. A man who loves you free and clear. Sure, he's a pain in the ass sometimes . . . that's his job. But he's there to bring you soup when you're sick, run out to the store. Takes the kids out so you can read a book. I've seen wonderful Christmases here with your children around. Unless I find a really special man in a few years, I can only dream about unborn children who may have made my life complete. You have four. Doxie has one." She stopped. "What I'm saying is that everyone wonders what would have happened if they took one path instead of the other; turned right instead of left. The trick is to be happy with the road you've selected. To make the best of it. See the glass half-full and thank God everyday for your health and the health of those your love. That's the key."

Persi touched her sister's hand, knowing that losing their mother at an early age played a part in their bouts of collective family melancholia. "The time to be happy is now. The place to be happy is here."

Athena's face broke into a wide grin as the twins ran downstairs in their pajamas, clamoring for ice cream.

"Aunt Persi's leaving. Say good-bye and thank you," Athena directed.

"Good-bye and thank you," the distracted girls said as they hopped to the kitchen.

Persi started down Sixteenth Street, got caught by two red lights, cut a left on Whittier Place, made a right on Fourteenth, left on Missouri Avenue and right on Thirteenth, and relaxed. Now she'd be able to cruise home. She passed Roosevelt High School; the brick edifice with pillars sitting atop a hill had been an absolutely beautiful, college-like campus. Now a former shadow of its regal self, it saddened Persi greatly.

She sailed down the single lane of Thirteenth Street and at U, and contemplated stopping at Ben's Chili Bowl but decided she didn't feel like finding a parking space. For the next few blocks she thought that once Athena got a good night's sleep, awakened in the arms of a man who would be there in the morning, that night and the next morning and tomorrow and all the tomorrows to come, she'd realize her good fortune. Persi swung around Logan Circle into her driveway and supposed everyone's life looked perfect to outsiders looking in. *But life is a crapshoot*, she admitted, cutting her engine. What you do for a living and who and if you marry can make or break your world. Despite outward appearances to the contrary, Persi admitted her life was ethically fragile. But it could be worse, she justified as she disarmed her alarm, walked the hallway to her kitchen, flipped on the television, pulled out the last of her Chinese food, dumped it on a plate, and stuck it in the microwave. She started to call Doxie and remembered she was visiting her parents and wondered if she decided to take her current beau. They'd been dating for over a year but, according to Doxie, he was convenient but no sparks. Persi began rifling through her mail. The phone rang.

"Hello."

"Hi. Persi?"

"Yes. Who's this?" She stopped shuffling through her catalogues.

"The man who helped you celebrate your thirty-fifth."

"I guess there's no sense in me telling you it was really my thirtieth?"

They both chuckled and Persi couldn't recall if she'd told him it was her birthday or not.

"No, that ship has sailed. Although you do look good," he teased.

"Don't say 'for my age.'"

"Wouldn't dream of it. So how have you been?"

"Fine—" she hesitated.

"Nick. Nick Betancourt."

"I remember. I'm not senile. Are you calling from Chicago?"

"You do remember. I am, but I have a gig in D.C. for four weeks beginning on Saturday and I wanted to invite you to opening night."

"Oh." The microwave chimed and she removed her plate. "This Saturday?"

"Yep. Up the street from you on U. Balzac's."

"The place to be in D.C. when you want great live jazz. You must be pretty good."

"I can hold my own. I'll put your name on the list."

"May I bring a friend?"

"Sure. Just one?"

"Just one. What instrument do you play?"

"The sax."

"Of course. So you're leaving your club in Chi town?"

He laughed at her reference to Chicago. "Just for a short engagement. Gotta give folks a chance to miss you."

They talked affably for a few more minutes before ringing off. "See you this Saturday."

"Looking forward to it." Persi immediately called Doxie at her parents'. "You're busy this Saturday. We're going to Balzac's. You can park here, we'll walk up and you'll spend the night unless something else comes up."

"What are you talking about?"

"Trust me. I may be bringing that little 'sparkle' to your life you've been wanting."

"Oh, really? I don't need another evening dress—"

"More like undress if you play your cards right. Details later. Tell your folks hi. Bye."

CHAPTER 6

The following Saturday Persi and Doxie compiled and mailed a care package to Drew at Camp Mawavi in Maine and Persi got a text message from Brad in the Vineyard.

"Time to get dressed," Persi told Doxie.

"Do we have to go? Let's see what the HBO movie is."

"No. Go on. Put on that red number." She shooed her friend to the guest room.

When Doxie reemerged an hour later, Persi let out a long wolf whistle. "You look good, kiddo. Sexy, not sleazy. Leaving something to the imagination but showcasing those signature big boobs."

"I do look good, don't I?" Doxie enthused. "You don't look half-bad yourself."

"Well, I had to tone it down so as not to outshine you."

"Excuse you?" Doxie teased. "Ready?"

It was hell-hot. Washington D.C. hot with the summer humidity closing in around you and hanging over your head like a thirsty, yet-to-be-wrung-out towel. All matter of people populated Thirteenth Street as they headed for U Street, the most obvious were folks walking dogs and picking up their poop in plastic bags. "I just don't get it," Persi said after passing a white couple with a huge Great Dane.

"That's a lot of poop over the years," Doxie said.

They chuckled. "And we haven't even started drinking yet."

They turned right and the line to Balzac's stretched up the steps and down the street.

"Wow. He must be good. You heard of him before?" Doxie asked.

"No. Jazz isn't my genre so I couldn't tell you. He is easy on the eyes. You'll like him."

The pair threaded their way up the stairs, gave their names, and were escorted in to a reserved table for two up front. "Well, excuse the hell outta me," Doxie said.

Persi offered an impressed expression as the waitress took their drink orders.

By the time they'd completed the first round of watermelon martinis and ordered again, they'd become friends with the women at the next table and clapped vigorously for the female vocalist's first three numbers.

"Why don't we do this more often? This is fun." Doxie snapped her fingers and danced in the chair as the vocalist belted out a bluesy "Your Husband's Cheatin' on Us."

After a few more songs, the slender lady with the big voice thanked everyone and announced she was taking a break but the Chip Benoit Trio featuring Nick Betancourt was up next. Their new friends at the neighboring table squealed at the mention of his name.

Persi knowingly eyed Doxie. "Told you."

"Umm. Competition, huh?" Doxie teased.

They ordered buffalo chicken wings and an artichoke-and-spinach dip with pita chips to accompany their next drink order.

The trio took the stage and the crowd immediately hushed. Last out, Nick wove his body though the packed tables like a shark fin cutting through a rough ocean . . . smooth. As he climbed the few steps to the stage he took the rapt attention of the female clientele. So furious with Brad at the time, Persi hadn't remembered much about her "date" the night of her non-birthday. Now Nick's tall, slender, well-built frame caught her by surprise as his jacket hung open, revealing an imported knit clinging to his solid torso. A symphony in all black, his milk-chocolate complexion vibrated under the dim lights as his cheeks collapsed when he placed his firm, kiss-ready lips on the reed of his sax. He blew into the instrument a couple of times and sent the most beguiling smile to the audience.

"Well, well, well," Doxie intoned. "Thank you, my friend. *This* is who you spent your birthday with and I'm just seeing him? Umph. Hallelujah."

A mesmerized Persi didn't respond.

At the edge of the stage, Nick casually perched on a stool and aimed his dark obsidian eyes on the two women at the front table he'd reserved. He nodded, winked and smiled at Persi.

Persi couldn't define the unidentifiable shiver that went up her spine. *Okay, I must be drunk.* She crossed her legs, took a celery stick, drug it though blue cheese dressing, chomped down on the vegetable and blushed.

"What is this?" Doxie asked, noticing her friend's eyes riveted on Nick's body.

"Tsk. I got a man," Persi said defensively.

"You got a *piece* of man," Doxie retorted.

Persi blew out the steam Nick generated within her. *Maybe I miss my man,* she thought. *Yeah, that's all this reaction to Nick is.*

As the trio took their repertoire though musical paces, the crowd went wild. When Nick Betancourt rose and began jamming with his sax, the experience was apocalyptic. He removed his jacket and the black knit clung across his broad shoulders and down his svelte upper body. He remained in total control as his hands executed furious licks, drawing out hot, magical notes from the cold gold brass. A thin veil of sweat coated his manly face, his movements like harnessed power, and those lips; firm, kiss-ready lips devoured the reed . . . he oozed sex from the stage. Nick and his sexy sax. He slowed it down and played "Song For You" and Persi placed her face in her hand, her eyes shining sheer admiration as she smiled.

Doxie was as enraptured as the audience until she looked over at her friend. Doxie smiled. Other than Brad, Doxie had never seen Persi enthralled by any other man the way she seemed to be with this Nick Betancourt. Was he the savior Doxie had been praying for the past five years? Was he the one to finally draw Persi away from Brad the cad? She scrutinized Nick as he performed and, when he finished his solo, the way he let his sax dangle and hang casually between his legs as his eyes combed the audience. *Confidence, that's what he has, Doxie thought.* When the trumpeter finished his solo, Nick clapped for him before resuming his playing. And kindness. *A rare combination,* Doxie surmised. After Nick finished his last song, he looked directly at Persi. They held each other's gaze and Doxie wanted to whoop for joy. *Thank you, Jesus!* she exclaimed to herself.

Persi glanced at Doxie and asked, "Isn't he good?"

"Exceptional," Doxie agreed. She knew not to push or coax her friend. While Doxie had waited for an opportunity like this, she was unprepared on how to assist in it. Persi Sinclair was willful, goal-oriented, and one of the smartest women she knew and admired with two great careers already, a gorgeous house, a paid-for car, healthy stock portfolio, a year's salary in savings, and no credit card debt. Persi was solid, grounded, and not into ostentatious jewelry or only designer clothes, although she owned three full-length fur coats, (one had been her mother's), and a short coyote jacket. Besides splurging on her house with the fifteen-year mortgage and her car, Persi lived below her means. Practically solvent. Suppose this guy was a ne'er-do-well. A player. A gigolo?

As Nick launched into another song, Doxie decided on caution. She knew too little about this guy to promote him and risk her friend getting hurt by him as well as Brad the cad; jumping from the frying pan and into the fire. She'd wait and observe.

At the break, Nick mopped his brow, sauntered offstage, and Doxie asked, "Tell me about him? What does he do?"

"Well, he plays sax—"

"Yes, he does. No question about that . . . what else?"

"Goes around the country setting up karate tournaments for youth, I think."

"That explains that body and the way he moves," Doxie said. "Umph!"

"I need to leave some things for you to find out about as you date him," Persi said, giggling.

"Hey, Persi," Nick said, approaching from the side.

"Hey," Persi said and braced herself awkwardly. "You are *really* good. I had no idea!" Not knowing what to do with her hands she began pulling her short-cropped hair down on her neck.

"Thanks." He smiled, his eyes never leaving hers.

"Ah-hem," Doxie said feeling like a third wheel.

"This is my friend, Doxie Fitzhugh. Doxie, Nick Betancourt."

"Pleased to meet you," he said evenly as he shook her hand.

"The pleasure is all mine. Believe me, you'll never know." Doxie smiled, showing all thirty- two of her pearly-whites. "So how long you been playing that sexy sax, Nick?"

"Long as I can remember. Picked it up seriously in middle school and never put it down."

"It shows. You're exceptional," Doxie said.

"Thanks. It helps pay the bills."

Persi smiled, looking at the two as if she had made the match of the century.

"And you're a karate man?" Doxie continued.

Persi looked horrified. She didn't know what the proper term was, but she was sure it wasn't *karate man*.

"Yeah. Got into that about the same time. Maybe a little earlier."

"I guess that accounts for the way you move. Like a panther. Like a cat. Rrrrr," Doxie roared and Persi held her head.

"Nick?" A man called him from the bar.

"Excuse me," Nick said.

"Okay, no more for you," Persi said, removing Doxie's drink from arm's reach.

"No. What? Why? You wanted me to get to know him."

"You are growling at him."

"We're Googling him when we get home."

Four AM found the three of them at the club's front door. "I'm glad you came, Persi."

"Me too."

"And it was good meeting you, Doxie. Where'd you park?"

"In my driveway. We walked."

"What?" He laughed.

A charming chuckle, Persi thought, which dimpled his cheeks. "I'll take you home. And you, Doxie?"

"Oh, we're staying together. A little pajama party. Do you have sisters?"

"No. Only a brother."

Oh, Lord, what the hell does that mean? Persi thought. *He's going to think she's a lesbian.* "Well, this way, ladies." He opened the car door for both of them.

Persi climbed in the back so Doxie could sit up front.

Nick drove the few blocks and when he reached Persi's house, said, "Here you are."

"Thanks again," Persi said. "We really enjoyed it."

"We don't get out much," Doxie offered. "But we make the best of it when we do."

"Great. I'm here for a few weeks. I'll give you a call, if that's all right." He looked at Persi, then Doxie, then back to Persi again.

"Fine. Good night."

"You know the drill," he said to Persi with a smile.

Persi said, "Yes. I remember. Night." She turned and walked right into Doxie.

"Night, Nick," Doxie said, leaning in for her own goodbye before following Persi up the stairs to the front door.

We must be the most dufus women he's ever encountered, Persi thought as she started up her stairs.

Just like the first night he'd dropped her off, he waited for her to get inside her vestibule. She flashed the light. He tooted and drove off.

"Well, well, well . . . knew where you lived and you all got this little horn-tooting ritual going," Doxie teased. "What else did you all get going that night?"

"Okay, my friend, do you want coffee or to go straight to bed?" Persi asked Doxie.

"I ain't mad at you, girlfriend. In fact, I have a new respect for you." She kicked off her shoes and followed Persi to the kitchen. "That brother is f-i-n-e! In that rugged, masculine kind of way. He could hold me any night of the week." She grabbed herself. "I do want to fire up the computer and Google him. Did you see that tore-up car?"

"I'm sure it's a rental. But I'm glad you're interested. He seems like a nice guy who, if you haven't chased him off with your less-than-attractive behavior, could put sparkle in your life."

"Razzle-dazzle is more like it." Doxie stopped at the newel and looked soberly into Persi's eyes and said, "But it's not me he's interested in."

"Of course, not in your current state, but he'll succumb to that Doxie Fitz charm in no time."

"He's not looking at me, Persephone May Sinclair," Doxie pronounced as she sashayed up the backstairs to the guest room. "Baby, it's you!"

Persi set her alarm, cut off her lights, and headed upstairs. It would be daylight in a few hours. She hated when Doxie imbibed too much; it only happened when Drew was out of town and Doxie was on her own. Besides, Doxie was drunk and wrong. Nick Betancourt could not be interested in her. He had to know that she was Brad's girl. Right? Surely he must know that there was no business meeting set for the night of her birthday. Monkey business, maybe. How could a man like Nick be interested in her, knowing that she was. . . not available? "Pst," Persi scoffed and dismissed as she changed into her pajamas.

She slid into her sheets and had to admit she'd never known a man who could play an instrument like that. In the last remnants of the night she wondered what else he could play.

"Is the gazebo already in place?" Persi asked into the phone and listened at the explanation. "I was there yesterday and marked it off." She listened again while rubbing the door-jamb free of grime put there by her visiting nephew. "Great, then cut and lay the stone around that. Okay. Call me if anything else comes up."

She looked out over Logan Circle at the flow of traffic. Waves of heat rippled up from the asphalt like a waterfall in reverse, as D.C. was in full-fledged summer. Tourists-laden buses, mosquitoes, and heat . . . suffocating, unrelenting heat that begged for a rainy relief that afterward would render the Nation's Capital the largest sauna in the world.

"I love the smell of D.C. in the summer," Persi paraphrased aloud. She went into her office off the kitchen and filed an invoice. The phone rang. Absently, she yanked it up and said, "Dr. Sinclair."

There was a chuckle. "Persi?"

"Yes." She stopped to indentify the voice. "Nick?"

"Yes. Sounds like both Dr. Sinclair and Persi need a break."

Persi chuckled. "You got me." She hadn't seen or heard from him in over a week. Neither had Doxie. Persi supposed he had other women to work through before he got to either of them again. "So how's D.C. treating you?"

"Hot. And you? You sound a little preoccupied."

"It's that time of year . . . when my two jobs collide. Nothing I can't handle."

"I'm sure. How about taking a ride with me? Either today or tomorrow. I have a house I'm thinking of buying on the Severn River and I'd like you to look at it."

"Why?" *This is an invite for Doxie,* she thought.

"Well, not only could you use a ride out of the city, but you're into architecture, right?"

"Hat number two—landscape designer."

"Great. I need a professional to factor what I need into the cost of the property."

"Today's not doable." Brad was coming home and over tonight. It had been over three weeks and she was beyond horny.

"How about tomorrow? In the afternoon?"

Brad would be long gone and she'd be ready for a distraction as her own house chaffed her after one of his quick visits. "Sure. That'd be nice."

"Great. Then I'll see you tomorrow, Persi."

That evening, Persi waited up well past the appointed hour. He finally called, whispering that he wouldn't be able to get away tonight, but tomorrow afternoon was perfect. "I'm dying to see you, Bruce. God, I missed you."

Persi hung up, slipped out of her gold teddy, kicked off her high heel sandals, and blew out the candles for the elaborately set table. Persi thought after roughing it for three weeks on a family vacation, she'd give him an elegant fantasy. As usual, the joke was on her. She put the lobster salad and the chilled champagne in the refrigerator along with the cake celebrating his belated birthday. She went upstairs to bed.

That morning she was awakened by a thunderous rap on her back door. She pulled on her robe, flew down the backstairs, pushed back her curtains, and stared into honey-sage eyes.

She looked a fright but all Brad was worried about was her opening the door before anyone saw him on her back steps. "I couldn't wait to see you, Bruce."

"Wait!" she screamed. "I haven't showered or brushed my teeth. I look a mess."

"Hey, it's just like when we get married. Right?" He was removing his clothes.

"Let me go freshen up, at least."

"Your funk is better than most women's perfume."

"You are full of it, Brad Shelton. Give me twenty minutes."

"I don't have that kind of time."

They made time and love, and fell asleep. The phone rang.

"I'm on my way," Nick said.

Persi bolted from the bed, next to a sleeping and satisfied Brad. She watched him scratch and turn over as she scurried to the guest room.

"I'm *so* sorry, but something came up," Persi said to Nick. It wasn't a lie; it was Brad's gi-normous hard-on.

"Oh?"

Persi hated this; she felt if a person committed to something, they ought to do it. She could hear the disappointment in Nick's voice. As a visitor to D.C., he was probably looking forward to something other than the club scene.

"Can we go tomorrow?" Persi suggested into the empty silence.

"I've got a karate tournament practice in the morning but we can go in the afternoon."

"Great. Okay."

"I'll pick you up at eight."

"In the morning? I thought you had a karate thing to go to."

"I do and you're going with me."

"Oh. Okay." She chuckled. "Eight it is."

"I'm not calling first thing tomorrow. I'll be there at eight."

"That's fine."

"Have a good evening."

Persi climbed back into bed beside Brad and glanced at the clock. The alarm would go off in fifteen more minutes and he'd leave her to go home. She lay nestled against his chest, playing pretend; pretending that she was his woman—his only woman. She was with him now but would be alone for the rest of the evening, while Mr. and Mrs. Shelton attended a charity function and danced the night away with family and friends. Declining an invite from Jean-Luc and Doxie out with her sparkless man, Persi would be home with movie and a pint of Ben and Jerry's for company. She rationalized that her life was still better than most . . . most of the time.

The alarm sounded and Brad looked into her eyes.

"Don't be sad, Bruce. I'll be back. I always come back, don't I?"

"Maybe one day, Brad, I won't be here."

"What? Don't even play like that. I'd stay and talk it out, but I got to go." He climbed into his clothes. "No time to call a cab. I'll walk down to M Street. If I get a chance, I'll text you. Love you."

And he was gone, taking most of her pride with him.

Leaving her with perplexed wonder, she questioned why she stayed with him. Why, where professionally she'd always been number one, she put up with being relegated to third, fourth, and fifth priority in his life. Was she an undercover masochist? She looked out of her window and watched his image fade away from her and disappear down to M Street to hail a cab back to his car parked in his office garage downtown.

She had no answer. No intelligent, soul-soothing answer. She only knew that, after they made love and he held her in his arms . . . she was a teenager again, she was in high school again when her world was upright and ordered; her mother was alive, cooking dinner in the kitchen, her father read the paper in his den's easy chair, Diana listened to music, and Athena was on the phone. When he held her in his arms, she knew her place in a secure world.

CHAPTER 7

The sun peaked over the Nation's Capital, dousing the city in its scorching, golden glow. Nick double-parked as he ran up the steps to get Persi. Seeing him pull up, she locked her front door and met him on the concrete steps.

"Good morning," she said brightly, actually glad to be going somewhere new and not semi-waiting for Brad to call and recap his splendid evening with the wife before asking to come over for a quick visit.

"You look great!" Nick said, eyeing her white slacks, colorful tunic top that grazed her hips, and thong sandals, revealing perfectly manicured feet.

"Oh!" Persi exclaimed and giggled, seeing the vintage 1965 burgundy GTO convertible waiting at the curb. "What fun!"

"We'll be tearing up some road today, so I thought, what better way to travel on a hot summer day than with the top down?"

"My mother would have loved this. She went to her prom in this car."

"Her date had taste and money. Your dad?"

"No. She did have a life before him. Her class was the first black class to have their prom at the Washington Hilton Hotel."

"A little D.C. history."

He opened her car door; she sat and swung her legs around as he closed it. Persi watched him round the hood of the car, dressed in tan slacks and a charcoal-gray knit that clung to his form. Despite how good he looked, she decided not to comment on his attire. He was just a friend and was to remain one. Complications ruled her life, besides—this was Doxie's man.

Nick up-shifted and sped away from the curb as they zoomed toward the Baltimore Washington Parkway. Persi thought, *When Nick picks up Doxie at her Kensington house, they'll take the Connecticut Avenue exit onto the Beltway to 95 North into Baltimore.* In seemingly minutes, she and Nick passed the Inner Harbor, then John Hopkins, into the hood, stopping in front of the Ulysses Thigmont Boys and Girls Club. Nick parked, grabbed his black jacket from the backseat, and opened her car door.

"My hair must look a fright," she said, running her fingers through her short do.

"You look fine." He smiled.

"Mr. Nick! Mr. Nick!" an excited boy yelled and set off the other youngsters.

"Wow. Rock-star status," Persi said.

Nick roughed the boys' heads and patted them on the back as he entered the building and settled Persi in the first row. He spoke with an official-looking man and strode to the microphone and said, "Good morning!"

"Good morning!" all chorused enthusiastically back at him.

"I'm proud to be here this morning in the presence of you fine young men-in-the-making and your families and friends," he continued.

They clapped and Persi joined in.

"Having grown up in the neighborhood, you all know how importantly I feel about the young men who live here. . . and the women, like the women here, being a part of their lives. I know that in this neighborhood, it is difficult for the young-men-in-the-making to adhere to the five tenets of Tae Kwon Do. But if I can. . .you can!"

The crowd thundered applause.

"What are they?" Nick asked, cupping his hand behind his ear.

The entire assemblage chanted, "Ye-Ui—courtesy. Yom-Chi—integrity. In-Nae—perseverance. Guk-Gi—self-control, and Baekjul-Bool Gool—indomitable spirit!"

"Yeah!" Nick turned, gesturing proudly with his fist. "You make me proud!"

An inspired Persi recognized that the gym's bleachers were filled with mostly single mothers with their other children and a smattering of fathers, brothers or uncles coming together for one child in the karate class. She watched Nick galvanize the crowd and felt remiss that she did not know these five tenets.

"I know it's hard, but are you living them everyday. . . to the best of your ability?"

"Yes!"

"That's all I can ask of you. That's all your parents can ask of you. Always do your best! Thank you for inviting me! Good luck to all of you."

The audience clapped vigorously and, as officials and local reporters staged pictures, Persi felt humbled by this saxophone-playing karate man.

"Are you Mr. Nick's girlfriend?" a little boy asked and several women leaned in to hear Persi's answer.

"No. Just a friend."

"A girl friend?"

"Jamal, are you bothering my guest?" an approaching Nick asked playfully. "Ye-Ui."

"Courtesy," Jamal proudly defined with a grin.

"How's school? Remember our deal."

"Yeah."

"What?"

"Yes," Jamal corrected.

"That's better. Where's your mom?" Jamal pointed and she waved. "Let's go see her."

"Aw, man."

"I'll be right back," Nick told Persi.

"Take your time," Persi said, stretched and walked toward a glass-enshrouded case. She noted the trophies therein: karate, basketball, and baseball. She looked up toward the rafters and saw pennants and banners toting championships both local and regional. Why did she believe that Nick Betancourt was responsible for these Thigmont Boys Club victories?

He came toward her, asking, "Ready?"

"Yes." She walked with him to the car and felt the presence of an extraordinary man; an important and respected man. He opened the car door for her, waved at some of the guys who followed him out, got in and drove away. No fanfare, no showboatin', just doing what he'd surely always done. . . with courtesy, integrity, and self-control.

"Stayed a little longer than I had intended. Sorry about that."

"No. I really enjoyed it. They surely admire you."

"And I them. I *am* them."

They drove a few blocks in the depressed area. "See over there? Second floor back? That's where I grew up. My mother, brother, and me."

Persi looked at the handsome, urbane, sophisticated man who played an exquisite sax, graduated from Columbia, and was worshiped by the locals. Maybe that was the reason why— he got out. But he came back. By example, he showed them possibility.

"You've come a long way."

"I played in the park there, stalling the time when I had to go inside. My mother worked constantly, so she wasn't home. That was before the Boys Club was built. I went to school there." He pointed. "Eventually. I was an angry young boy for a lot of years."

"I find that hard to believe. You seem to have such control."

"Appearances can be deceiving," he said, glancing at her as he turned left.

Their eyes met only momentarily and she felt he could see right through her—despite her polished veneer, her education, upbringing and privilege, when you got down to the nitty-gritty, she was sleeping with a married man; she knew it . . . he knew it.

"I'm trying to be the change I want to see in the world," he said without conceit. Not liking the serious tone of the conversation he asked, "You hungry?"

"Oh, yes," she answered, relieved by the change in topic. "Past my feeding time. This is your territory . . . where do you suggest?"

"I know just the place."

He swung the car back on the parkway; the hot summer breeze tousled her hair as he aimed the auto toward the Severn River. "Hot Fun in the Summertime," played on the radio and they sang along with Sly and the Family Stone, their voices riding the wind. They pulled into a nondescript joint; the kind locals knew and swore had the best seafood in Maryland.

"You want inside or out?" he asked her.

Her eyes were drawn to the umbrella picnic tables perched on a weathered pier. "Out. Air-conditioning is for sissies."

"Great."

After being seated and given menus, Persi absorbed her setting. Slow, so quiet she could hear the water lap lazily against the seasoned wooden posts, smell the salt, and feel the sun on her skin. Boat slips rung the establishment on one side near the upstairs bar. She saw the houses across the river, dotting the other side. "This is nice. Come here often?" she teased.

"Not as much as I'd like but maybe that will change. If I buy this house, it'll be nearby. When I don't want to cook, I can either drive or sail down."

"Going to buy a boat too?"

"Maybe." He smiled and the waitress came to take their order. "You like crabs?"

"Is water wet?"

He eyed her and challenged. "D.C. girl can't outdo a B'more guy in the crab department."

"Try me."

"We'll start with jalapeño pepper poppers. Bacon-wrapped scallops," he said to the waitress then asked Persi, "You're not a vegetarian, are you?"

"Not at all."

"And an order of shrimp to start. Then a dozen hard-shell crabs and keep them comin' until we yell 'uncle.'" He snapped the menu shut. "Thanks," he said to the waitress.

The waitress returned and spread a layer of newspaper before setting down the beer and first appetizers.

"Now this is a classy joint," Persi joked. "They might just know what they're doin'."

"But will you?"

"Oh, yeah. When I was growing up, a trip to the Seventh Street wharf to buy live crabs was the way we began many a summer day. Cook 'em with plenty of Old Bay. . . lay the newspaper, spread the red-hot crustaceans with a couple of mallets and it was on!"

"Got to have those elegant mallets." His phone rang. He looked at the number and said, "I'm sorry. I have to take this."

"Sure."

"Betancourt," he answered and listened.

She looked at him in the light of day. Not in the seductive darkness of a club, where he played a smoky sax and she was tipsy on drinks, but in the impenitent starkness of afternoon daylight. He wasn't a pretty boy but his presence superseded looks and held a certain charisma, which commanded respect and admiration and, unlike looks, would not fade in time. Still, visually, he was a pleasure to behold. The richness of his brown complexion seemed to have intricate under-layers of color and intensity, but once reaching the surface, emerged smoothly. Like I don't-even-shave smooth. A strong jawline, defined cheekbones, and last but not least. . . those full, kiss-ready lips. When he glanced over at her piercing see-through-to-your-soul eyes absorbed hers and were crowned with a flux of thick, tamed eyelashes.

"Just go with the asphalt. The macadam won't work there," he was saying.

Persi noticed that, when in deep contemplation, he had a habit of taking his thumbnail and drawing it from a corner of his luscious bottom lip across to the other side. Just once. That gesture was followed by him then holding his chin in the cradle created between his thumb and index finger. She noticed it first at the club, and depending on the depth of his thoughts, it could be done quickly, or slowly, like now; a manly gesture, like a cowboy. *Whoa, I am noticing too much about this brother*, she thought as she peeled another jumbo shrimp, bit it in half, and tasted its yielding flesh.

"Go with that. Let me know if there are any more problems." He snapped the phone shut. "Sorry about that," he apologized again and cut his phone off. "That's the call I was waiting for. Now—" He stopped. He almost said, "I'm all yours," but that would have been inappropriate. "I can get down to brass tacks." He grabbed a bacon-wrapped scallop and popped it into his mouth.

"So, you were telling me your life story," Persi said.

"No. I don't think so."

"Let me rephase that. How did you get from the inner city of Baltimore to buying a house on the Severn River?"

"*Contemplating* buying a house," he corrected.

"Are you quibbling with me, Betancourt?"

The fragrant, steaming crabs made their entrance on a tray, dusted with Old Bay seasoning and accompanied by small cups of drawn butter. "Oh, baby!" he clapped his hands together joyfully. "This is what I miss most while living in Chicago."

"Nothing says summer like Maryland's blue crabs steamed red," Persi agreed and they each grabbed one, pulled on the legs, releasing the succulent meat and sliding it joyfully between their teeth.

They laughed out loud at the carnal bliss of it. He grabbed a mallet to attack the claw while she turned the crustacean over and popped it down the middle.

"I see we have a difference in technique."

"It's all good!"

They laughed, talked, ordered another dozen, and switched from beer to soda. After forcing coleslaw and hush puppies upon themselves, they devoured another half dozen and yelled uncle at the same time.

Laughter erupted from the couple sitting at the picnic table by the river. For just a millisecond Persi thought of how they looked to other people. Of how nice it was to be out in the open, enjoying the company of a man who had no place else to go or no one else he had to be with later. Of having a man all to herself.

"I think we've done enough damage. You can take the rest home."

"I can make a great omelet—" She stopped, thinking that sounded suggestive as in "after our night tonight I can makes us eggs tomorrow."

"Or crab salad," she amended quickly.

"Or just eat them cold in front of an old movie."

"I suppose I should just say thank you before you renege on your offer." She stood. "Going to the ladies' room."

"I'll settle up and meet you out front."

"Let me pay half," she offered.

"You can get the next meal."

"Deal." Persi liked the sound of that. *I have a new friend,* she thought, *at least until Doxie takes him over and I won't see him again until their wedding.*

When she came out he was standing out on the pier. Her father and grandfather had a penchant for those Greek names, and if Nick's father had one also, Nick's name would have been Adonis. There was just something about the physicality of the man that was exceptional and indescribable. There he stood fully clothed, whittled against a water canvas, but he elicited in her a desire to see him with less on.

He turned and smiled at her. The smile that dimpled his cheek.

He's smiling at me? she thought curiously. *That's not right.*

He began walking toward her and she enjoyed his approach . . . a long, strident swagger.

"Ready?" he asked.

"Yes. Where to next?"

"The house."

"Ah, yes. And why do you want me to look at it?"

"I bought you lunch. Now you'll tell me if it's worth it, and about its landscaping potential and cost. It's a fixer-upper."

"Horrific words when buying a house, you know."

As Bill Withers sang "Ain't No Sunshine When She's Gone," Nick and Persi joined in on the *I know, I knows.* With the top down, the wind in her hair, the sun in their faces, they epitomized a happy black couple having the time of their lives as they sped along Route 50. Alicia Keyes's, "No One" spun next and the couple lent their voices to the chorus *Oh. oh, oh, oh, oh.* They pealed into laughter at the song's end and it was late afternoon when they crossed the Severn River. Stately houses perched atop a hill while boats dotted and bobbed on the smooth currents of the river below. The sun, having shone brightly all day, began its wane.

"Isn't that just beautiful?" Persi asked absently, recognizing that the scene was eons away from the traffic-laden circle she called home.

"Tranquility at its best."

"It just screams sleeping late in the mornings and going to bed early at night," she mused, carelessly.

Nick did not comment. Finally he relented. "It certainly says peace."

They turned off of Route 50 onto a two-lane highway before taking a left through a meandering neighborhood and a final left through a cul-de-sac into an expansive grassy area on the side of a huge edifice. When Nick cut the engine, Persi opened her own car door and headed directly for the Severn River in front of her.

"Oh my God—this is absolutely breathtaking," she enthused like a child who'd just received the only Christmas gift she'd ever wanted. "Look, we are atop the hill looking down. These are the houses you can see from the bridge."

"Not really. The bridge is around that bend."

"Quibbling again, Betancourt?" She moved closer to the edge and saw how the property tumbled down a slope, until it reached the bottom bank with a private pier and a place for a boat. She laughed. "You weren't kidding!"

"Well, what do you think?"

"I would terrace this slope—no mountain—and make this first part plants, seasonal flowers, the second terrace a gazebo or wisteria-laden pergola with hammocks or Adirondack chairs perched come-sa, and the third plateau nearest the water down there, maybe prickly vegetation to discourage any little critters or uninvited guests from climbing up for a closer look. We'd widen the pier, add steps and lighting and—" Persi turned. She put her hands akimbo and looked at Nick, then to the house looming behind his back.

"Is this some sort of joke?"

"No. What do you mean?" Nick asked sincerely.

"This," she pointed impatiently and began climbing the steep hill, "is no house. What is it?"

"If I buy it. It'll be my house while I'm here in the area."

Persi passed him and hiked straight to the top and stopped in front of a small swimming pool, beyond it five stone steps and double-glass doors. "And what will it be when you are not here? A bed-and-breakfast?"

Nick laughed. "I hadn't thought of that, but it's a good idea." He walked ahead of her. "Let me show you inside."

"Where's the Realtor?"

He answered by dangling the keys to the house.

Apparently, he is a more successful sax player than I had imagined, she thought as he opened the door for her. *Maybe he's buying it with other investors.*

"It was built in the 1920s by a bootlegging gangster. The family owned it for years until the matriarch died without direct heirs."

"She died here?"

"No, a ritzy upstate sanatorium. Family was so wealthy, they didn't put this house on the market for years. It's not as large as it looks. The rooms and people were smaller in the twenties. You'll see it's quite homey."

"And formidable. Like a fortress."

Persi stepped into and was immediately dwarfed by a two-story center hall with a fireplace. She realized they'd come in the back way, as she was staring at the front entrance and a beautifully carved wooden door with beveled glass. She stood there, paralyzed because she didn't know where to go first.

Nick remained behind her and let her take in the house at her own pace.

To the left of the front door, flush against the outer wall, steps led to the second floor; the risers short and wide enough to comfortably accommodate folks going up and down simul-

taneously; the balustrades, as richly carved as the front door
and the catwalk above them. On the first floor nestled under
the steps in the hall, a guest powder room. Without moving,
Persi swayed to the left where there was an open room.

"The old library," Nick identified.

Persi silently confirmed this when she walked in and was
surrounded by the built-in mahogany bookshelves. Through
another opening at the other end, an exquisite gem of a room
with all beveled glass windows, where the sun threw colorful
prismatic splashes on the stone walls and beamed ceilings,
summoned her. She walked slowly toward the shimmering
kaleidoscope of nature's colors.

"The music room. It's got great acoustics. My sax sounds
like Gabriel's trumpet in here." Nick smiled, remembering
his second visit to the house. "Let me show you this." He
urged her back though the library into the hall and into another room behind the music room. "This is the playroom. A
pool table. A bar. A jukebox. Can't you see it?"

"And I thought my house was big."

"It's not that big. That's the whole of this side. Follow me."

Nick led her pass the steps, the front door back to the center hall into the dining room; a magnificent, regal room with
high ceilings, crown molding and space for a table that could
seat sixteen comfortably. The back window displayed a view
of the Severn River and the setting sun; the side windows
formed a wall of the beveled beauties that led into a butler's
panty the size of most bedrooms.

"Built-in cabinets for all the dishes, silverware, place set-
tings, tablecloths. A microwave. A sink and dishwasher right
here. Guest bathroom," he pointed as he walked into and
identified, "Family room and separate kitchen."

Persi looked at him. "Why do you need all this?"

"I don't. I want it. It's not that big. Really."

"You keep saying that but it isn't getting any smaller."

"The kitchen is pretty small."

"Well, you got everything you need in the butler's pantry."

"That's the first floor. Come on upstairs." He began walking again and said, as he passed an alcove, "Those are backstairs, but let's go back out front so you can get the full effect."

Persi followed Nick around past the front door to the mammoth steps and thought that a man who'd grown up in the inner city of Baltimore and never had anything, may want a house like this; have a hunger for a house like this. And if he was able to afford it. . . why not?

"Is this zoned heating?" she asked, her voice echoing in the grand foyer.

"Yep, two downstairs and one up for the bedrooms," he said, walking slightly ahead of her.

"You may want to consider a geothermal heating system, as well as solar electric and water heating systems. You may be eligible for a two-thousand-dollar credit green-energy tax break for each one."

"Really? Sounds good. I'll look into it."

As she ascended the steps, to the right, she looked though the gorgeous, two-story stained glass windows onto the front of the house they'd skipped by coming in the back; a small circular courtyard and a four-car garage made of the same stone as the house laid out before her. *It's exquisite*, she thought. Doxie'll love this house, reminiscent of the one she grew up in and where her parents still resided; with its stained glass window ensconced in pink stucco with green ivy and crowned with red, Spanish tile roof. Persi recalled her first visit to Doxie's house and how, as she'd approached the long driveway on her bike, she thought it was a church. Drew would love the pool and fill the house with friends and sleepovers in no time. Persi decided to just be happy for Nick and share in his excitement, as long as he did not ask her to invest.

Persi reached the top of the stairs and cater-cornered, yet straight ahead, a picture window beckoned her from the hallway. Nick went over to the immense window and waited for her arrival.

"Oh, Nick!" Persi looked at an uninterrupted vista of the Severn River. Painted in striations of gold, red, and fuchsia, the setting sun spilled though the clear panes of the expansive room. "This view alone would be worth the price of the house. Can you imagine waking up to this each and every morning?"

"Even in the snow. It's got to be glorious."

"Priceless."

They stood in the window, basking in the last solar rays, captivated by the world beyond the first simple pane glass window in the house.

"It's a big room but cozy," Persi said. "Put his-and-hers chaise lounges here so you can witness the view. A king-size bed against this wall—"

"Too far away. Queen is big enough."

Persi eyed him and looked beyond his shoulder. "I missed the fireplace." A stone fireplace flanked by two elongated windows, looked down on the car they'd parked on the grassy side yard.

"The closets have built-ins, so you don't need much furniture."

Persi walked into the separate room and thought again, *Doxie will love this.* "Her" closet, almost the size of her current bedroom, had stationary shelves, armoire, wardrobe, and a vanity next to a single window for natural light. Persi proceeded through the next door.

"His closet," Nick identified, as Persi looked at the superb built-in furniture.

She meandered through yet another door. A sleigh bed and chest were anchored to the floor and another single window provided a soft glow. She looked at Nick for an explanation.

"Snore room. If the husband gets too loud. Two rooms and three doors away. *Better homes* had them and the men decorated them in masculine motifs, including humidors and a bar."

"I guess there's no sleeping on the downstairs couch for him."

Persi opened another door and they were back into the hallway on the other side of the main staircase. This wing housed an office and linen closet next to the door that led to the attic. The end of the hall had a storage room.

"Well," was all Persi could say as she walked back down the hall past the main staircase and the open master bedroom. "A master bath?"

"Oh, yeah." Nick reentered the master bedroom and behind the door was a walk-through closet and the master bathroom.

"I didn't figure you'd have to go downstairs and use the one under the steps," she teased. "I love these walls."

"Plaster," he said proudly. "Some people like new houses with humongous rooms and no character."

"This house oozes character, and old world elegance."

"Let me show you the other bedrooms." He guided her through the other five rooms that lined the hallway with built-in seats against the balustrades so you could sit and look down the stairs or out the stained glass windows to the front courtyard. Each of the five bedrooms had the same unobstructed view of the river and shared a bathroom with the next room. When they rounded the corner of this second-floor wing, over the kitchen there were three other rooms; one for laundry-ironing and two smaller ones for the live-in help.

When they took the backstairs down to the family room and kitchen area, he noted, "the elevator doesn't work."

"Well, then. No sale," Persi teased.

"What do you think?"

"I think this is a great house. Solidly built with lots of potential." She walked to the kitchen and looked out of the door that led to the front courtyard, surely so "the help" could unload the groceries and not traipse though the house. "You're right. It is large but I think once you move in and decorate. . . it'll be a cozy place you can call home."

"That's what I was thinking."

He looked around proudly as he envisioning himself living happily ever after here.

"Growing up, I never dreamed that I'd ever see a place like this, much less own it."

"You've worked hard. Now there is a place for your mother and brother too."

"My mother has a place of her own and my brother lives in Hawaii."

"Hawaii? You Betancourt boys must really be something."

"I almost wasn't," he said softly. He stopped and looked at her, wondering if his secrets would be safe with her.

"Why was that?" she tested.

He did that thumbnail gesture with his bottom lip and leaned against the granite island in the middle of the kitchen. "My dad left us when I was five and my brother nine. It took me four years to figure he wasn't coming back. My mother worked two jobs, doing the best she could but I was a child and only knew she wasn't home when I left for school or when I got back. By that time, my brother found the gangs and I was left to fend for myself. Unlike the boys of today, I found solace in school, which became the best part of my day until I ran into the sixth grade; mother not around, brother not around. The school janitor, who lived in a basement apartment across the street, told my mother that I was heading for trouble if somebody didn't pay attention to me. He'd see me at school about to commit mischief and just eye me. Look at me like 'boy, don't even think about it.'"

Nick chuckled and continued, "I'd followed him home

once because I was going to do him harm for always riding me, but when I saw how close he lived to me, I thought better of it. When he saw me the next day at school he said, 'Boy, next time you come to my house, knock on the door.' I swore he had some voodoo powers. I stayed away for months until one day my brother got hurt and I didn't want to go home. So, I knocked on his door, and we struck up a friendship. He told me things like 'Boy, shouldn't be no struggle to do what's right.' Or, 'That's no way to be a man. Ain't no man who does that; a scared boy acts like that.' Turned out he was a Vietnam War vet who got a raw deal. He loved the Drifters . . . always had them playing. 'See how smooth they play? First R&B group to use strings.'" Nick smiled imitating him. "Ulysses Thigmont," he concluded with a chuckle.

"The name of the Boys Club. You did that?"

"The least I could do. I give those boys some of what he gave me. Pass it on."

"Whatever happened to him?"

"Died . . . an unhealthy death. He did have a military funeral." Nick smiled.

"Because of you," she surmised.

"I helped. What goes around comes around. He helped me mature and told me that my mama worked two jobs and volunteered for extra shifts because she didn't want to be on public assistance, and the best way to show I loved her was to stay out of trouble. 'When she misses work to come to school after you—she don't get paid.'"

"Hmm."

"After my brother joined the gangs I would be left totally alone. I begged him to take me along but he refused. I thought he hated me; later I learned that he joined so I wouldn't have to. When he got old enough, he got out. . . went into the service, then college. School is the way out. I want these kids to see that. I am their example that it can be done if they just believe and work hard. Like Henry Ford said, 'whether you think you can, or think you can't—you're right.'"

"You're a fine example. And now you'll have a fine house to further prove it."

"Will you come and see me?"

The question surprised her. "All the way out here?" she joked, but knew that once he and Doxie got married she'd be spending some nights in one of those five rooms upstairs.

The sun finally set, plunging them into a comfortable, light gray-black darkness. She knew if Brad had called, she'd missed it, but this was so much better than sitting and hoping and praying. "Welcome home, James?" Persi teased.

"We've got one more stop to make. Got to check on my mom's house in Annapolis."

"Where is she?"

"In Hawaii visiting my brother and his family. She goes two-three times a year; stays about a month or so—in the summer when her grandkids are out of school and the other times in the winter. Let's leave by the front door." He led the way and when he got to the threshold he turned to her and said softly, "Thanks for coming."

"Sure."

Then he bent and kissed her. It happened so quickly Persi didn't know how to react. She felt those firm, warm, kiss-ready lips ever so gently upon hers. Startled, confused, and happy, she challenged, "What are you doing?"

"I think it's called a kiss." He straightened back to his full six feet plus. "People do it all over Europe."

"We're not in Europe. Don't let it happen again."

"Why? Are you seeing someone?"

She was glad it was dark. She was glad he couldn't see the timid shame in her eyes. Did he really not know about Brad or did he think after more than six months their affair had run its course?

"Listen, Nick. I think you are a nice guy and I like your company but I am not in the position—in the market for—at liberty—" She stumbled, stopped, and breathed. "If you want more than friendship, then I am not the girl for you."

Quiet claimed him.

She held her breath. She didn't think now was the time to tell him that he and Doxie would make a terrific couple; she'd be the perfect mate for him and this house.

"All right," he finally said.

She exhaled.

"I appreciate your telling me. That shows integrity."

Integrity? Persi thought as he opened the door and she followed him down the steps. His characterization made her feel like crap; like the biggest liar-hypocrite that ever walked the face of earth.

When she got to the car, she stopped and absorbed the tranquil scene, like this might be her first and last visit. She sat in the car and offered him a weak smile.

"Listen, my word is bond," he said, starting the car, not wanting to ruin anything between them for the rest of the trip. "I promise I will not make any advances on you. I am getting to know you and already value your friendship. And I'm not in the habit of forcing myself on women."

I know that's right. They're lining up as we speak, wondering what's keeping you, she thought.

"It's your call. If friendship is all you're offering—so be it." He pulled out through the cul-de-sac. "But if you ever change your mind, you let me know," he teased, dispelling the tension.

"Deal," she agreed as he turned back, heading for Route 50.

Absently, she found herself touching her lips that he had just kissed, the taste of him still on them.

"Look at that moon," he directed. "Hungry?"

"It has been hours since we've eaten."

Nick found a space in Annapolis near Anchor Inn, his mother's favorite restaurant. When they went in, the owner greeted him warmly with "Your mother gets more beautiful every time I see her."

"What's good here?" Persi asked.

"Everything."

Persi perused the menu and decided on fish chowder to start—and the grilled grouper. When the waitress came and engaged in what Persi defined as flirty banter surely working on her tip, Nick settled on a Caesar salad, steak—medium, baked potato, and mixed veggies.

The waitress brought hot bread and a wink to the table with two glasses of red wine. They ate and talked leisurely, the table's candle flickering in their faces.

"Dessert?"

"Why not? Something chocolate."

After they devoured their desserts and cups of coffee—his black, hers with lots of cream—he checked his watch.

"We'd better get going."

"You play tonight?"

"No. I would have been long gone." He waved for the check. "Basically, I had today off for the tournament. When you couldn't go yesterday, I made other plans for today."

"My turn to pay. Friends take turns."

"I'd hate to deny you the pleasure of being an independent woman."

"Don't patronize me."

"Wouldn't think of it." He liked that she called him on it. "I'm going to make a pit stop."

He rose as she paid the check, laying the money with tip on the tray.

Persi checked her cell phone for missed calls; nine from Brad. A perverse pleasure caused her to smile.

They drove through the sleepy town and down a dark lane to a little house with the front light on. Nick pulled around the drive, got out, and before he could open Persi's door she was out of the car. "Friends can't open the door?" he asked.

"Not if I'm capable. Isn't getting to know me fun?"

"Hysterical." He smiled and ushered, "This way."

The outline of the house against the night presented a well-kept one-story rambler; antithetical to the one they'd just left. As Nick opened the screen door and then the main door, Persi could see the vacant expanse of water to the left and hear a soothing ebb and flow on the shore. The door whined opened and Persi stepped into a homey, comfortable cottage house. "It looks like someone's here," she said.

"That's the idea," he said, walking past the dining area to the kitchen door before disappearing into one bedroom and then the other. When he returned, Persi was looking at the pictures on the mantel piece. "How much for you never mentioning these again?"

"Is this you?" Persi asked. "You were a cutie."

"Were?" he teased. "School pictures. We didn't have much use for a camera back then."

"Who is this?"

"My brother and his family. Her grands."

Choreographed timers clicked on and off. From the dining room to the bedroom then to the bath. Persi giggled. "Your mother is good."

"Synchronized."

As Persi walked along the portrait gallery she wondered if Nick's original master plan was to bed her here. He'd fed her a couple of times, showed her the big house, then brought her to the cozy little one, make a fire, make love in front of the roaring flames, spend the night and drive her home tomorrow afternoon.

"Ready?"

"Oh. Sure." But she'd been out of the game so long that might have been the furthest thing from his mind. She walked past him and got into the car as he locked up and reengaged the alarm. He sauntered past the lamppost light and she saw his features again—those lips again. She admitted that he was a man of his word; not a touch or a hint of impropriety since the kiss. He got in, his features briefly illuminated by the overhead light before tumbling into night's obscurity again. Perhaps she wished he wasn't so gentlemanly.

They whizzed back and parked in front of her house far too soon, the traffic lights blinking yellow in the early morning hour. She got out and closed the car door. "How did it get so late?" she asked, leaning in from the passenger side.

"Time flies when you're having fun."

"I had a great time. Thanks for inviting me."

"Next time I go check on the house, I'll ask you to go again."

"Sounds good."

"You want to come in for—"

"For what?"

She supposed she'd never get used to his directness.

"No. It's late. I'm tired," he said, surely not the night he had planned. "You better get on up to your door before we are arrested for soliciting."

"Ah, good point. Good night."

"Good night, Persi." He watched her go up and walk into her vestibule. She flashed her lights and he tooted quietly.

Gone. But not forgotten.

CHAPTER 8

The phone's shrill awakened her early the next morning. Persi fumbled for the phone.

"Hello?"

"Where were you all day yesterday?" Brad assaulted.

"Good morning to you too."

"I was going to come over for a while."

"Oh. Sorry I missed that," she said sarcastically.

"Are you alone?"

"What?!"

"Is Doxie there with you?"

"No."

"Did you tell me you were going to be out all day yesterday?"

"I can't remember. Probably, but you didn't listen because you knew you couldn't get away anyway." She knew the drill.

"It turns out I could have. Plans changed."

"In my favor, for once."

"Okay, I know you're not a morning person. I'll call back when you're in a better mood."

"Are you coming over today?"

"Probably not."

"Bye Brad." She hung up, scooched down in her sheets. "Can't wait for my girls to get here," she whispered dreamily, as she turned over and went back to sleep.

The Fab Four, together again, if only for a week before

ViVi Hamilton returned to the coast. Of the chemist-landscaper, the psychologist turned government administrator, and the housewife, ViVi won the prize as the ultimate success of the group. She'd used her mathematically ordered brain to dissect and reconstruct stories and had four successful screenplays made into movies, and was now the writer-creator of two award-winning televisions shows. The Fab Four rotated between the three houses and ended up at the Fitzhugh house at Highland Beach extolling one anothers' virtues and reliving all the boys—crushes, peaks, and valleys—of their lives. Old times waxed fresh and new—the bond as deep and steady as ever. They spilled more apple martinis than they drank, played their music loudly, and danced with wild abandon. ViVi, denying that she'd succumbed to L.A.'s cosmetic culture and despite obvious evidence to the contrary, asked, "whatever happen to that guy you were mad about, Persi? Brad Shelton?"

His name hung out there in midair as Doxie took another sip and raised her eyebrow, waiting for Persi's answer.

"I guess he's around," Persi finally said.

"I wish the plus one, Desi-Fair, could come. He was crazy about Persi-girl," ViVi teased.

"I was crazy about him too," Persi said.

"Got you all a trip to Jamaica in the eleventh grade," Nola reminded.

"We were all invited," Persi said smiling.

"He'd do anything to get you alone," ViVi said. "Even invite your three girlfriends."

"We had big fun," Doxie recalled, "and Persi-girl was the epitome of decorum."

"But you, on the other hand," Persi teased her friend.

"Hey . . . love those Rasta boys—man," Doxie toasted and sipped again.

"All I know was that four of us were invited and only two went," Persi said.

"Luckily, your mother believed the world should be seen and experienced. Not my mama," Nola said.

"Well, we all missed the boat. That brother is doing it in L.A.," ViVi said. "He told me to tell you all hi. He's as rich as Cootie Brown."

"Still unmarried. There's time, Persi," Nola teased.

"We have a pact. If we're unmarried by forty, we'll marry one another," Persi jived her friends, changing the age.

"What's happening with that fine Rucker Jackman?" ViVi enthused. "Oh lawd, just looking at that man makes me cum."

They continued to discuss their love lives, the married Nola relegated to a listen-only status. ViVi admitted to dating voraciously as part of establishing her L.A. rep and maintaining her routine G-spot shots. Doxie spoke of Mr. Sparkless and Persi confessed that Rucker Jackman remained the best love she'd ever had, testifying to his prowess and proficiency —"the man has skills on and off the field."

"That brother we saw at Balzac's was fine," ViVi said. "Had that certain something."

"Who?" Nola asked as Persi and Doxie eyed each other.

"That sexy, sax player," ViVi intoned as she poured a refill. "I might be able to use him in an upcoming movie."

Persi recalled the Fab Four sitting at a ring-side table while Nick played an instrumental version of Phyllis Hyman's, "Nobody's Wanted More Than I Want You." The audience completely submerged in the darkness as a lone, amber glow shone on Nick's handsome face. He seemed oblivious to there being a crowd as he folded those long lashes over his eyes and put those perfect lips on the mouth of that sax and blew full, sexy, undulating tones into that brass instrument. He exuded an intimacy like it was just the two of them at Balzac's.

"That's Doxie's man," Persi teased, to break her train of thought.

"Don't start," Doxie warned.

"They would be so perfect for each other," Persi continued. "And the house he's buying reminds me of the Fitzhugh house with the stained glass window. Drew would love the pool—"

All eyes were on her.

"What are you talking about?" ViVi asked.

"He's thinking about buying this house and I could see Doxie and Drew there," Persi said and thought, *Damn—I am talking too much. I never could drink.*

"So you've been there and Doxie hasn't?" Nola asked. "But he's Doxie's man?"

"It's a surprise," Persi pressed on. "That I've just ruined so let's change the subject."

"Yeah. Let's," Doxie said drolly.

After two more days and what seemed only minutes, their week ended and Nola-Ro was driving ViVi-Ham to National Airport with a promise to return for her holiday hiatus.

"Love you girl," ViVi kissed Persi and Doxie in turn.

Persi and Doxie ate at a good local dive, walked the beach, watched the sun set, and returned to the beach house. "I loved coming down here with your family. Your beach house was the bomb," Persi said.

"I preferred yours. Mainly because my parents and brothers weren't there," Doxie said with a chuckle.

"Now your baby's coming home."

"Persi, I miss that little girl. Glad to see her go and ecstatic to see her come home."

"You think she'll ever outgrow Camp Mawavi?"

"I hope so," Doxie laughed. "I was hoping she wanted to decrease her time there but instead, each year she wants to stay longer and longer."

"You done good. Raising an independent woman. Anyone else you want to invite to her welcome-home barbeque?"

"No. I've just been trying to decide whether I want to have it at your house or Nick's new house with the pool," Doxie said sarcastically.

Persi smiled like the cat that swallowed the canary. She should have known her friend wouldn't let it slide. "He called and asked me to ride down and take a look at this house he was thinking of buying. He wanted my professional ideas on the terracing."

"Um-hum."

"So I went and saw you and Drew all over the place. You two—it's kismet. Don't get your butt on your back. It was innocent enough."

"Didn't have to be."

"He's your man."

"Nick's no more my man than Brad is yours."

Oh Lord, Persi thought, *I hope she doesn't start in on Brad. Here I am sequestered down here all night with Doxie.* She hadn't had the "you're wasting your time with Brad" speech in over a year. Persi'd hoped they'd just maintain their silent truce and retain fundamental differences of opinions. . . in politics, religion, and married men.

"Well, it was nothing and that's that."

"No, it isn't."

"Doxie, don't go there."

"I'm driving, Persi."

"Jeez, Doxie. So you say I should have slept with Nick and keep Brad on the side?"

"What? I thought you said it was innocent."

"It was! I'm just a simple, one-man woman. I just picked the wrong man; a slow man."

"Retarded is more like it." Doxie sipped, then said, "Wait a minute." Doxie sat up from the wicker couch. "So does this mean that you *wanted* something to happen with Nick, but stayed true to Brad the cad?"

"I've asked you not to call him that."

"Okay. You prefer his childhood title—Brad the spoiled brat? Five years older, he should've set the example but if he couldn't get his way, he always took his ball and went home."

"Are you still mad at him for that?"

"I'll tell you what I'm mad at."

"Oh, Lord." Persi held her head.

"I'm raging mad that he is stealing the best years of my girlfriend's life."

"Fair exchange is no robbery. I am *giving* them to him."

"And why is that, Persi? That makes no intelligent sense." She rose on her knees. "You know if it hadn't been for Brad, you would be knockin' boots with Nick."

"I know no such of a thing."

"Ha!" She slipped back down on the couch.

"And if you recall, I do date."

"The three blind mice?" Doxie asked sarcastically, referring to Rucker Jackman, the lawyer, and stockbroker. "And when was the last time you had sex with anybody but Brad the ca—"

Persi shot her a disapproving look.

Doxie admired her girlfriend for many reasons, especially for bypassing the proposal of Rucker. The NFL player loved her smelly armpits but Persi had declined, as she wanted more for herself and her children-to-be. Doxie knew of women who'd marry the player in a heartbeat, have a couple of kids to seal the deal, and move on—after securing their and their children's future. But not Persi. But Persi's morals, values, and standards had taken a holiday with Brad Shelton, her one Achilles heel; the chink in her armor. Doxie couldn't figure out why. With any other guy, Persi would have told him and his wife what a crush she had on her husband in high school, and that would have been the end of it. But not Brad Shelton, who must have put a voodoo taint on her. He had an emotional noose around her neck as he slowly choked her spirit and chance at true happiness. *If I could just get her away from him*, Doxie thought. Persi exhibited totally out-of-character behavior and Doxie couldn't make sense of this nonsense; like her friend had arrested development at age fourteen. As empirical people, they believed in cause and effect and formulas and this was not going to work out in Persi's favor.

Employing her scientific training, Doxie likened Persi's "love" for Brad to a latent, defective gene for a disease that left alone remained recessive until death. But Persi saw Brad, he pursued her, and she turned around and let him catch her. That triggered the diseased gene alive, to malignantly grow into some maniacal fixation . . . a cancer that could ruin Persi's life. For Persi, Brad in his shining armor on a white horse represented everything she ever wanted . . . except he was married, a detail Persi seemed apt to overlook. Doxie couldn't get her friend to recognize what she was doing to herself; she didn't give a flying fart about Brad.

As Doxie drained her glass, she admired Persi for two things: she had never given Brad a key to her house, and she kept their relationship on the down-low as much for her own reputation's protection as his. In her practice, Doxie counseled women who relished confronting the wife when the husband failed to. Not Persi. Deep down, perhaps her friend knew that eventually this wasn't going to work so she better make sure she survived with her good name in tact. *If I could just tap that deep down part of Persi so she'd kick Brad the cad to the curb, I'd rest easy and Persi could get on with the life she deserves*, Doxie thought.

"Persi," Doxie began. "I've known you since we could pee straight. We were in and out of each other's houses like they were our own since we were eight . . . you know I love you . . . and I hate what you are doing to yourself. You have some odd, emotional, adolescent attachment to him."

"But I love him."

"It's not."

"Yes. Love, Doxie."

"You don't string somebody along for years if you *love* them. Love is a verb based on mutual respect, admiration, and caring about the other person as much yourself. He cares about, what? At least four other people and a dog before he gets to you."

"That's going to change."

"You seriously can't believe that? C'mon. If he was going to leave, he would have left. It doesn't take five years for a grown-ass man to make up his mind whether he's going or stayin'."

"It's complicated."

"And in another five years—when you're forty—what adjective will you use to describe it then?"

Persi sighed and cut her eyes impatiently.

"It's not who you lie *with* but who you lie *to*," Doxie continued. "You are lying to yourself if you think Brad is leaving his wife and you two will live happily ever after."

"I have faith."

"God? Seriously Persi, you're bringin' God into this? Prayin' for another woman's husband? *If* it happens it won't be God's doing—it'll be the devil's work for sure."

When Persi slammed the cabinet door, Doxie stopped, knowing her decisive and obstinate friend was about to shut down and not let anything in. Doxie softened her stance.

"Brad, men like him and the women who love his type are the reason I left private practice. The women with their non-existent sense of self were both arrogant and stupid; arrogant to think they had the right to lay with a married man and stupid for accepting being low woman on the totem pole, while making him a priority."

Doxie got up and poured the last of the martini in her glass. "Women should be *offended* when a married man approaches them. The audacity of it. He's saying 'I'm married and have a wife who I have no intention of leaving, but I want you too. I'm auditioning women for the number-five spot in my life. What do ya say?'"she mimicked in a deeper voice as she sat back on the couch. "What he's saying is, 'I'm married but I'm greedy and immature, screw my vows and you if you let me.'"

"It isn't like that," Persi defended wearily, regretting being trapped in this beach house and willing that Doxie have her say and shut up. "But I love him," Persi said just to irritate her friend.

"You think you do," Doxie sighed.

"I know you are not going to tell me how I feel."

"He's different,'" Doxie continued undaunted. "You are different. Suppose," she posed. "Suppose after another five or ten years he leaves Trish and three children for you. You get no prize. You already know he's a cheater. What he does *with* you, he will do *to* you. 'Cause the fresh and new will eventually turn old and comfortable and—oops—there he goes again."

Persi went over to the window with her drink in hand.

"There's an old saying 'before you seriously envy anything, look into the happiness of its current owner.' Even the *prize* is no prize. It's a lose-lose proposition. There is no relationship with no trust. Only suspicions when he goes to walk the dog . . . a dog walking a dog." She chuckled humoreslessly and sipped. "I think we ought to stop referring to men as dogs. Dogs are loyal and always there when you need them."

Doxie glanced at Persi's back as she stared out the window. *At least she hasn't cursed me out or left like she usually does*, Doxie thought.

"In my practice, the women were bad but the men were the worse," Doxie continued. "They sent me screaming to my good government job. On occasion, I felt sorry for the women, whose men expected me to take their side; that Y chromosome is a rationalizing genius. The most loathsome are those who felt justified in cheating on their pregnant or sick wives. She's carrying your baby and not meeting his sexual needs, he feels he has the right—no, the duty—as a man to go out and satisfy his horny self.

"And by *sick* I don't mean the flu. I mean chemotherapy-fighting-for-your-life-cancer sick. Maybe while she's puking her guts out and losing her hair, having sex just isn't a priority. He steps out with a little guilt, but not enough to keep his peter in his pants. How selfish and immature can a male—not a man—be? I wanted to bitch-slap them and yell Grow up! Get some balls and be a *real* man who takes his vows seriously—better or worse 'til death do you part, you sorry excuse for a man."

Persi chuckled; at least she was off of the subject of Brad, whose wife was quite healthy. Persi went over and took the empty martini glass from Doxie.

"At least be man enough to go to your wife and say, 'This is not working. I think we should split up,' so everyone can date—not just him. So everybody can satisfy their neglected needs accordingly. Either work on the marriage or leave it."

"Equal opportunity."

"Exactly! Okay, I digressed," Doxie admitted. "But I still know from what I speak."

Persi looked at her friend patiently.

"I am not drunk. Maybe feeling no pain, but we aren't going anywhere."

"Unfortunately."

"*In vino veritas.* I speak the truth and I'm trying to spare you, Persi. Seriously."

"I know."

"No, you don't, because I've never really discussed it with you or anybody. Not in detail. If I was going to tell anybody, it would have been you."

"Thanks." Persi handed her friend a glass of room-temperature water. She went and sat across from Doxie, watching her drink the glass of water and waiting for her to exhaust the subject; knowing neither would change their minds, but Doxie would feel compelled to share.

"It's just like if Drew were going down the wrong path. I'd want to warn her."

"I'm not your daughter."

"But you're the sister I never had. I guess I've tried to give you the benefit of my dubious knowledge." Doxie's voice cracked.

Persi look over at her and watched her friend grab the afghan and start fingering the fringed edges.

"I've been on both sides of that situation," Doxie began quietly without looking at Persi. "I'm not proud of either side. I've been that married woman with a child sleeping in the next room, laying in bed at three o'clock AM, when you feel your husband silently slip into bed beside you with the smell of another woman."

A surprised Persi stared at Doxie, who still wouldn't meet her gaze.

"Or worse. The smell of a freshly showered body. It's a wrenching, inexpressible thing when you know you've done your personal best and still. . . You ask him why he's late and cringe when he tells you a business meeting ran long, or the game ran over; any old thing he throws at you, expecting you to believe him. So you stop asking, knowing it'll be lie after lie. Slowly, you watch your Prince Charming disintegrate and morph into Mr. Lie and Deny. 'Cause when you went to do the laundry you find a condom in his pocket. After a really bad day at work, you beg him to stay home with your sick child and he goes to the game anyway. Then he disappears for an entire weekend and tells you when he returns on Sunday he had car trouble. Or every time you walk into a room he switches the computer screen. Or you see the last part of an e-Valentine card—not from you. Or the hushed, cell phone calls. He's texting somebody at a wedding reception and you ask who, expecting a lie, and you are not disappointed. And you wonder. *Does he think he is slick or that I'm as stupid as whomever he's dating?*" Doxie looked over to the side, out the window, then back to her hands fidgeting the fringe. "It turns your stomach every time he reaches for you because AIDS kills, or he wants to kiss you and you wonder where else those lips have been. On what woman, on how many other women? On what parts of another woman? And you've got no place to go," Doxie's voice choked and tears slid down her face.

Persi went and sat beside her on the couch.

Doxie opened her mouth but nothing came out. She finally said, "See, that's the look I wanted to avoid."

"I'm sorry." Persi handed her a tissue.

"You didn't do anything. But I did. I decided what was good for the goose was good for the gander. So all the attention and flirting I was receiving—"

Doxie blew her nose and continued. "You know I never quite got how women get propositioned by guys all day long, but we don't cheat. We all have an opportunity to throw our vows away, but most women never do."

"We're more grown up. Our word is our bond."

"Yeah." Doxie shook her head and noticed how Persi had teared up. "So, I try to follow though. I wanted to be with this one guy. Whew, he was fine. I got close, but in the end, I just couldn't. Two wrongs don't make a right, you know? I needn't stoop to my husband's level. But every time I looked at that man I married I felt both betrayed by and superior to him—I was the more evolved. One of us ought to keep the vows sacred. I didn't sleep with the other guy because I loved my husband; all I could think of was me losing Drew in a court of law. He'd be sure I was declared an unfit mother . . . and that would kill me.

"So I watched the way my innocent daughter marveled at her dad—like every word he spoke was gospel and I didn't want her hurt. So we did that dance people do when you live together, but have no life together. I never thought I'd be one of those clichéd martyr parents who stay for the sake of the child. I used to hate those women until I became one. He'd broken my heart; he didn't have to break Drew's too. So I lowered my expectations and dealt with him. Anything goes, when everything's gone; there was no right or wrong 'cause no one gave a damn anymore." Doxie cleared her throat of emotion. "A husband ought to honor his vows whether his wife is with him or not. It's not the wife's duty to police her husband's fidelity; if he's any kind of man, you ought to be able to trust him to uphold his vows himself," she mused.

"But I did mess with his mind. I realized that he was snooping on me. Imagine? Now that's a case of projection and displacement if I ever saw one. I'd move my diaphragm around. Take it with me. But one day I went into his briefcase to get the stamps he kept clipped on the inside flap and found a letter from one of his women accusing him of seeing another woman. A married womanizer? Oh, hell no! I put on Chrisette Michele's "Blame it on Me",—*say it's my fault just so it's over*, called a lawyer, and filed." Doxie blew her nose again and said, "The rest, as they say, is history."

"I had no idea."

"What could you have done? The first divorce in my family—bad. But it had to be done."

"It certainly did." Persi wondered if she could be as magnanimous as Doxie was with Drew and her father knowing the background. "You never speak against him with Drew."

"No. Because I'm grown up. I know how important the father-daughter relationship is and I don't want her to judge all men unjustly because her father is an asshole."

They both laughed.

"But if need be, I'll tell her, like I'm telling you because I'm trying to save her from pain and heartache."

Persi smiled sadly.

"So I know what it is to be the wife. Trish may or may not know. Maybe she knows and doesn't even care; maybe she'd love to send you a thank-you Christmas gift, saying *Keep up the good work*. But don't think she has it all sunshine and roses."

Persi shook her head.

"And don't think I'm all that grown-up and perfect because I know the flip side too. I'm not proud, but I dated a married man after my divorce. I figured I was free and clear, he's the one with the vows. So I know what it is to put your life on hold, waiting for his call. Never having him with you all day on holidays, birthdays, always leaving your bed to return home, maybe getting an occasional trip. But the kicker for me was when I saw him with his wife and children at the Annual Black Family Reunion on the Mall. The realization hit me that I was doing to this woman what had been done to me. And I thought, *I am better than this*. We, as women—vaginal America—on some level, ought to stick together; do unto others for a change. The wife hadn't done anything to me, yet I was stealing her happiness, leaving a void in her marriage by being available to her husband—like a receptacle for all his immature wants and desires, waiting to be discarded at some later time. So I took charge of my life, my choice, and opted out—I'm sure he's gone on to cheat with someone else many times over because, unfortunately, there are always women willing to open their legs. But the next time he cheated . . . it wasn't with me."

Persi hugged her friend, knowing how difficult it must have been for her to disclose this painful history. "Doxie Fitzhugh. You are some kind of woman."

"If just one woman can benefit from my story," she teased and they both laughed.

"Drew is one lucky little girl."

"I swore that I would never introduce a man into our relationship. She will never wake up and find a man in my bed and there will be no this is Uncle the-man-I'm-dating-right-now. I concentrate on her and my career. This might not work for every woman and I'm not preaching or judging—this is *my* choice and what works for her and me best."

"She'll be gone sooner than we think," Persi said.

"Then I'll get my freak on."

"'Get my freak on?' Okay, I'm sure that's not current slang."

"What is it then?"

"I didn't say I knew, but that ain't it."

"Oh, Persi," Doxie laughingly said. "The reason I can be so moral and upstanding is that I have a great friend like you who takes Drew for weekends at a time so I can handle my business—personally and professionally, and you don't have a child that I have to exchange time with later."

"Gee, thanks."

They chuckled. "Drew's not getting married until she's thirty, when her prefrontal cortex is fully formed and she can make sound decisions. I was young . . . what's your excuse?"

Persi cut her eyes. "We're done with that topic and good luck with Drew marryin' at thirty; she has a mind of her own."

"I'm surrounded by strong, smart-ass heffas," Doxie conceded quietly and blew her nose again.

"Aren't you lucky?"

CHAPTER 9

At three o'clock on a hot afternoon, Persi lay in bed with Brad making plans for their next getaway trip. "I'd really like to cruise the Greek islands."

"No can do. Too risky—too visible. Maybe a honeymoon trip later on."

Persi smiled at his reference to a honeymoon and said, "The honeymoon list is really growing." She snuggled down on his chest. "I'll stick with Paris. We'll stroll the Champs Elysees . . . and people watch, climb Notre Dame, Arc de Triomphe, Sacré Coeur. Make love in the shadow of the Eiffel Tower."

The alarm went off.

"Got to go, Bruce." He kissed her on the forehead and hopped out of bed and into the shower singing "If Loving You Is Wrong I Don't Want To Be Right."

The phone rang.

"Hi Persi."

"Oh, hey, Nick." Persi sat straight up in bed; she didn't know why. He couldn't see her reclining on the bed of sin. "How are you?"

"Fine. Been busy. ViVi get back to L.A.?"

"Yeah. You were quite the hit with her. She says she's going to use you in one of her episodes."

"Oh, yeah?" He chuckled. "I'm glad you all stopped by. I know the Fab Four had fun at the beach and my buddy, KC, surprised me."

"That's great. Hope you had as much fun as we did. The time went too fast."

"It always does when you're having fun," he said. "Speaking of time. Can we get together this weekend before I head back?"

"To where?"

"Chicago. It was nice of Balzac's to extend my engagement for a few weeks but the Blue Note wants me back."

"So loved. So wanted."

He only responded with a chuckle.

"What's going to happen when you buy the house on the Severn?"

"Go to settlement on Saturday."

Persi heard the singing stop and shower shut off.

"Want to join me for the final walk-through?"

Persi recalled the kiss at twilight on the threshold's front door and touched her fingertips to her lips.

"No can do. That's Drew's welcome back from camp, birthday celebration, and sleepover. It began with just her grandparents, relatives, and a few friends getting together but has turned into an annual end-of-season barbeque with family and friends."

"Sounds like fun."

His comment just hung there and Persi heard Brad begin to hum again. Surely he was lotioning up now.

"Would you like to come?" Persi asked graciously.

"Sure. Can I bring a friend?"

"Friend?" *Male or female,* Persi wondered–then wondered why she wondered and dismissed the thought, "The more the merrier. Any time after noon will be fine."

"Can we bring anything?"

"Just your appetites. Listen, I have to go. So I'll see you on Saturday," she said brightly.

"Great."

"Bye." She hung up just as Brad flung the bathroom door open.

"Who was that?" Brad asked casually as he entered the bedroom.

"Jean-Luc and Claudia with an invite to lunch."

"That cat is always trying to get you to France to work in his family business."

"Wrong again, *mon frère*. He's the brother of the guy who's always trying to lure me to France into the family business." Persi stopped and posed seductively in front of Brad. "Jean-Luc just told him that I am a gifted chemist. Jean-Luc left the business and doesn't want me to go." She let her robe hang open, revealing her pert, taut breasts with raisin-rung nipples. "He doesn't want to lose me to France."

Brad's eyes were glued to her mammeries and drifted down to her hairy triangle. She walked over to him so he could touch. "What about you? You want to lose me to France?"

"Lawd, Bruce, down start nothing we can't finish."

"Me?" Persi teased innocently. "I got all day."

His hands felt her satiny skin and she moved in to kiss him. They kissed as if they'd just come together for a tryst, not at the end when he was leaving. "I am so addicted to you, Bruce, you know that?" He rubbed his hands across her derriére and she felt his nature rise again. "Will I ever get tired of this?"

"I don't know. Will you?"

"I got to go." He strong-armed her by pushing her away, holding her at the shoulders. "Stay," he said as he grabbed his shoes and bolted down the backstairs.

Persi laughed.

"Bye Babe," he yelled upstairs as he put his shoes on at the back door. "You know I'm crazy about you."

She didn't respond but listened for the door to shut as she went to the window and watched him jog toward M Street to hail a cab. Her window was like the widow's walk that crowned old Victorian houses where fishermen's wives waited for their

husbands to return from sea. Only she watched her man leave
her . . . again. Always moving away from her.

"But I love him," she told her nagging heart.

The house on Logan Circle teemed with folks and the back
deck, shrouded in a cloud of fragrant smoke, was in full barbeque mode. Drew and her friends claimed the top floor's
recreation room playing video games, the jukebox and, when
not hoisting food up the dumbwaiter, making reconnaissance
runs to the first floor for refreshments. Younger children stayed
with their parents, scattered over the living room, dining
room, and in the kitchen. Music played, a balloon popped,
and the doorbell rang. Persi made her way to the vestibule as
her niece and nephew encircled her every step. "Here, take
this to your daddy on the deck. Tell him we need more." As
they scurried off, she laughed and opened the door onto an
engaging, beautiful brown face.

"Yes?"

"Hi. Are you Persi?"

"Yes."

"I'm DeDe and Nick—"

"Of course. Please come in." Persi moved aside for the woman to enter, an attractive woman in her mid-forties with an in-
fectious smile and luminous presence. Who was she? He had
no wife or sisters—he'd said "a friend." Was she his woman?
Why not? If Nick liked an older woman, he'd date an older
woman and not be concerned about what people thought.

"Welcome to my home," Persi continued as DeDe looked
around.

"It's lovely. And so big."

Guests looked at the stranger who'd come into their midst.

"I like it. Everyone—this is DeDe," she introduced to which
everyone nodded hello and waved, as children surrounded
Persi again.

DeDe offered a lilting laugh and asked, "Are these yours?"

"In a manner of speaking. My nieces and nephew. Please, the bar is over there, make your pleasure known and yourself at home. I'm going to check on reinforcements from the grill."

"Alrighty," DeDe said as she sauntered off confidently.

Persi joined Bernard, testing the state of a cheeseburger when Doxie came out.

"Who is that?"

"Who?" Persi checked the readiness of the toasting buns.

"DeDe. Is that his sister?"

"Doesn't have any sisters."

"Is Nick married? Is he coming?"

"Why ask me? Ask her. She's right in there and very friendly." Persi tore off pieces of lettuce. "Are you finally admitting that you're interested in Nick?" Her eyes glinted in the sun.

"Not for me, you nut."

"Oh jeez Doxie, I told you we are just friends."

"Um-hum. So you're telling me if that is his wife, you don't have a problem with that?"

"It's not his wife."

"Oh really? And you would know this how?"

"Aunt Persi, could you send more sodas upstairs?"

"For the birthday girl? Anything." Persi followed Drew into the kitchen and took sodas from the refrigerator and placed them on the dumbwaiter. "Can I get anyone anything?" she asked on her way upstairs. "How are you doing, DeDe?"

"Just fine, Persi."

"Great," Persi said as she rounded the stairs for the two-story climb to the top.

She seems very nice and pleasant, Persi thought. But of course Nick would only deal with someone who was nice, pleasant, and fun; she was happy for him—for them. Even with the age difference, they seemed suited for one another. But if he intended to fill that Severn house with children, they'd better hurry. "How are you all doing up here?" Persi said as she went over to the dumbwaiter and removed the sodas to the refrigerator. "Drew, you need anything else?"

Drew came up and grabbed Persi around the waist. "Thank you, Aunt Persi. This is the best party ever."

"You're welcome, sweetie." She kissed the top of her head. She and her mother should be in that house on the Severn River with Nick. But so be it.

When Persi came back downstairs Nick was introducing himself to folks in the living room. She watched him move easily, confidently, to each person, shaking hands, looking them in the eye, surely committing their names to memory, making them feel special and important; he excelled at that. DeDe came up beside him from the other room. As she touched his arm and kissed his cheek, he embraced her and Persi felt a prick in her heart. She couldn't identify the sensation and was perplexed by any reaction at all. Nick turned and saw her. His face split into a welcoming grin.

"Hi," she said simply.

"Hi." A smile dimpled his cheek and they both became immediately aware that all eyes were on them.

"I'm glad you could make it. Are you hungry?"

"Yes, I am."

"Well, good. We have plenty."

He followed her to the dining room spread and through to the back deck with hamburgers sizzling on the grill. "You look great," he said, his eyes piercing her reserve.

"Shorts and a T-shirt?"

"You wear it well. I like the Asian-inspired top with the giant red-orange poppy," he said but thought, *And the way those lovely shaped, ginger-snap-cinnamon-hued legs are crowned with the tailored, white Bermudas.*

She blushed as her brother-in-law returned to his post. "This is Bernard, Athena's husband and grill master; ribs are his specialty."

"Nick Betancourt," he introduced with the shake of a hand. "Smells great, man."

"Taste good too," Bernard said. "What can I get you?"

Persi excused herself to check the music and talked with guests, not trusting herself to chat with Nick right away. With a full plate, Nick meandered his way over to where she talked with Doxie's parents. He complimented her on the food and she ran down a list of what everyone brought. "I like your home," he said.

"She's always loved this house," Dr. Fitzhugh offered.

"Whenever we were anywhere near it she'd say 'Please, take me past my house,'" Mrs. Fitzhugh said with a chuckle.

"It's nice to get what you want," Nick said, looking at Persi.

"Nick went to settlement on a house on the Severn River," Persi offered just as Doxie came over.

"Oh. It is so lovely down there. You have family moving in with you?"

"No. Just me," Nick said, chomping down on a piece of jalapeño cornbread.

"What about DeDe?" Doxie asked.

Nick laughed, and Doxie waited for an answer while Persi inwardly cringed.

"I think my brother would have something to say about that."

"She's your sister-in-law," came out on a relieved gust of wind from Persi.

"Yep. For over fifteen years now. She came back with my mother and has been here for a couple of days. My brother meets her here tonight and they're flying back home."

Persi stood there with a frozen grin on her face and Doxie eyed her.

"Oh, where's home?" Dr. Fitzhugh asked.

"For them, Hawaii," Nick said.

"We spend some time there. We honeymooned there years ago," Mrs. Fitzhugh said. "And home for you?"

"Chicago, mostly. As of today, a house on the Severn River, which will need some TLC before I can make it a real home."

"What's your field?" Dr. Fitzhugh asked.

"Dad, this is Nick Betancourt. He's been at Balzac's for over a month," Doxie said.

"The Nick Betancourt?" Dr. Fitzhugh asked as Jean-Luc joined the discussion. "But I thought you'd be a much older man."

"Sometimes I feel like it."

Persi, Doxie, and her mother looked at one another with questioning eyes, preferring to remain silent than show their collective jazz ignorance. When asked, they listened to Nick recite the jazz greats with whom he'd played. Some names they recognized, but only Dr. Fitzhugh and men of that generation who read liner notes could really appreciate the discussion on Nick's session players and accompaniments.

Dr. Fitzhugh and Jean-Luc seemed enthralled with the conversation but Nick would rather talk with Persi since he was leaving town soon. He remained polite and focused on the manly conversation until Alicia Keys's "No One" came on.

Persi and Nick looked at each other and burst out laughing.

Doxie stared at her friend in wonderment. Neither Nick nor Persi stopped to explain their singing in the convertible on their way to the Severn house.

When Persi excused herself and went into the kitchen, Doxie followed. "Okay, what is going on?" Doxie asked. "No. Actually, I don't want to know. I am just happy for you."

"What are you talking about?" Persi said as she began putting the candles into the cake. "It's me that is happy for you. She's his sister-in-law, which means the position of wife is still open."

"I told you once, I'll tell you again. It ain't me he's interested in."

"Whatever. You'll see when I dance at your wedding, Doxie-Fitz."

"You've already done that. It didn't take."

"This one will. He'll see to it. C'mon. Time to sing 'Happy Birthday' to Drew."

After the cake had been cut and the self-service ice cream bar destroyed, the phone jangled.

"Hello?"

"Persi-May! Persi-May . . . It's me!'

Persi's face split into a smile at his voice and identified, "Rucker Jackman."

"In the flesh!" They talked, catching up for a few minutes, until he said, "Okay Persi-May. You know I love you but if you're not going to marry me I'm gonna marry this other woman."

Persi laughed.

"I thought I'd give you one last chance to become Mrs. Rucker Jackman before I proposed to this other babe."

"Is she worthy of you, Rucker?"

"Well, she's no you, but she'll do fine."

"I'm going to decline, but thank you for asking."

"Okay. Now this is it. Won't be no 'Rucker I made a mistake and I love you and want you back.' Once I'm married, I'm married."

"As it should be. She's a lucky woman."

"Who you telling?" They both laughed. "I didn't want you to hear it from the tabloids."

"I appreciate that."

"I'll let you go, I know you got a houseful. I'll send you a invite or two. It's gonna be a party, Persi-May!"

They said their good-byes and Persi hung up the phone with a smile on her lips; she'd miss her buddy Rucker. "Aunt Persi, where are the game prizes?" Drew asked in passing.

By three o'clock in the morning, the girls finally settled

down and Persi slipped upstairs and cut off the movie. Only the light from a street lamp cut across the dark room. She adjusted the thermostat and peered out at the sleeping Logan Circle.

Her mind flitted across the whirlwind of the last few days with Drew's return from camp, all the preparations for the party she had at her Kensington home and the big BBQ she'd just hosted. Too keyed-up to sleep, and with Doxie on her own sleepover with Mr. Sparkless, Persi thought that now would be a nice time to have a man help expend some pent-up energy and relax. Now would be a good time to make love and engage in pillow talk, recapping the days' events. Now would be a good time to go downstairs, raid the refrigerator, race each other up stairs, and make love again before falling into a deep sleep. Then tomorrow, he'd get up with her in the morning and help her make the pancake breakfast before sending the girls on their way with Doxie to the Rock Creek Stables.

I have a man, Persi thought, but he's not here with me this night or any other night when I could really use him. She chuckled at her final proposal from Rucker Jackman, but at three AM, he'd still have a houseful of people here. On the occasion when she'd spent the night at his huge Prince George's County home in Fort Washington, the next morning his entourage waited in the kitchen for him to get up. Persi relished the quiet and privacy of her life. She focused on a police car as it silently rode by, red light flashing. She really didn't want to think about Rucker or Brad now; the latter who didn't help and couldn't come.

But Nick came and that was pleasant. He seemed to have a good time talking jazz with the guys as the women guests asked, "who was he and where has he been?"

"You all are married so what's it to you?" she'd joked. "Besides, that's Doxie's man."

Drew got up and stumbled toward the night-light in the bathroom. She flushed the toilet, rinsed her hands, and came straight for Persi, hugging her tightly before wriggling her body back into her sleeping bag. Wordlessly. But the sentiment rang loud and clear, clearer than any spoken words. Brad spewed words all over her, in and out of bed. But his actions told the tale.

Persi couldn't think about Brad if she intended to get any sleep tonight. Family occasions, holidays, and just plain being out in the open usually got Persi's goat. His words and actions seldom lined up properly.

"I had a really good time. Why don't you join us this evening? I want you to meet my husband," DeDe Betancourt spoke genuine words at the door when she and Nick were leaving.

"Oh, I'd love to," Persi answered. "But I have a houseful of little women to tend to and a pancake breakfast tomorrow."

"You're a good woman," Nick said to an echoing DeDe. Nick's gaze held hers; he frequently unsettled her with his penetrating eyes, and she didn't know why. Again, a wordless transmission of the unknown bypassed her mind to her very soul. *What did he mean by that?* Persi wondered. "Yes, I know you sleep with a married man but you are still a good person." Or simply, "you are a good woman to do all this for a child not your own." But he knew about doing for children not his own.

"Thanks," she'd said, trying to remember what philosopher penned, *a guilty conscience needs no accusation.*

She walked down a flight of stairs to the second floor, climbed in-between the cold, crisp sheets and envisioned a man's form beside her—waiting for her. She couldn't make out his face, only his warm body shielded her from the edge of the mattress beyond. "Pssh," she scoffed. Too tired to fantasize but not to wonder if she would ever have a complete, committed 24-7 man of her own, or was she destined to have a very full, complete, and happy life without a male of her own in it? She could cope with either, but she did have a preference . . . like every woman, hers was the same as theirs.

CHAPTER 10

The winter sun filtered through the window like a giant spot-light, past the Christmas wreaths hung in each, and bouncing off of the clear twinkling lights that outlined the exquisitely decorated Victorian home on Logan Circle. *Showtime, Persi* thought as she fidgeted like a girl waiting for her prom date. *The culmination of all my hopes and dreams are about to come to fruition. There is no other more heady feeling,* she thought as she checked her makeup again, fluffed her hair, and went to the bathroom for the umpteenth time since Brad called. *This is it, the mother of all Christmas gifts; the perfect way to begin her New Year . . . their New Year.* He was coming with astronomical, life-changing news; she could hear it in his voice and feel it like champagne bubbles in her veins. A Thursday night visit; he seldom came over on a weeknight; they were more afternoon delight people. How would he tell her? That they could take that honeymoon trip to Paris in the spring. She speculated wistfully: he'd left his wife. Perhaps he sensed Persi's pulling away and decided to make his move or he was going to lose her. "I wanted to know if I could have a key now, since I'm leaving Trish and moving in with you," Persi imagined him saying. "Life is too short for us not to be together, Bruce."

Persi giggled out loud, then calmed herself. She promised she would not gloat and vowed to be respectful of the time he needed to resolve and dissolve his marriage. Persi would be completely supportive of him while he went though the di-vorce and promised to embrace his three daughters by being the best stepmother alive. She hoped Brad wouldn't want to move. She loved her house, which had enough space for the girls when they came to visit every other weekend. She vowed to cook more and be sensitive to his needs for however long it took for him to transtition from being Trish's husband to hers. In a respectable time, they could now go out in public to a restaurant, a movie, to the Consorts on New Year's Eve, the Hellions for Valentine's Day, the Guardsmen in the spring, and the What Good Are We in the fall. They would hold hands, dance and cuddle for all to see; he'd check her coat, get her drinks, slide back her chair, retrieve her coat when the dance was over and she'd wait with him for the valet to bring the car. They'd talk about people on the drive home and when they got there—here, they'd make love, sleep in each other's arms all night long, rise late in the morning, and run errands. Like normal folk. Ordinary folk.

Persi's first call would be Doxie. She wouldn't do a "na na na na na," but she'd revel in telling her the inevitable news. Perhaps Persi'd ask her, "Are you available this fall? To be my maid of honor?" Divorces don't work that quickly but Doxie would get the idea, apologize for ever doubting them, and all would be right with the world. She and Doxie would plan her wedding to Brad; nothing outlandish or lavish, a discreet and elegant event. Maybe at the Decatur House. Or maybe a destination wedding in Paris, where she and Brad could begin their honeymoon immediately. Location didn't matter but the ceremony must be performed by a priest or clergy-man; an unholy alliance becoming a holy bond of matrimony to last for always. Then she'd be forgiven all her trespasses because she and Brad would be legally and spiritually married and absolved all her sins . . . their sins. The means justified the end. A spring or an autumn wedding . . . she didn't care when, just that it was finally going to happen. She and Brad had beaten the cheating odds statistics on couples who had affairs that actually lead to marriage. A personal victory, as Persi still didn't want folks to know they'd dated while he was married. During the acceptable waiting period, Persi would win Brad's three girls over. So excited, she couldn't hold a complete thought in her head as she anticipated all types of scenarios. She didn't want to have a heart attack before he came. It was finally happening; her Prince Charming was going to be her husband. She'll tell ViVi, "know what happened to that guy I had a crush on in high school? We're getting married. Boo-ya!"

She heard the familiar knock at the back and took the steps by twos to open it. She glanced outside and swung open the door with wide anticipation. "Hey, handsome," she intoned.

He walked in and turned around.

He looks awful, Persi thought.

"Bruce, Bruce, Bruce," he whispered, grabbing and holding her fervently like they were in the throes of passion.

"Hello. Aren't we getting a little ahead of ourselves," she teased into his left ear. "It took me awhile to get all dolled up and you want to undress me right away." She undid his hands and headed for the backstairs. "So be it. I'm anything but inflexible." She seductively posed and playfully stood at the newel. He didn't follow. *Okay he's not ready to play*, she thought and asked, "What's the matter, Brad?" He twisted toward her and she could see him struggling with words.

"Has something happened to one of the girls?"

"Not exactly. Well, yes. . ."

"What? Are they all right?"

"The girls are and I want them to stay that way, but Trish—"

"Did something happen to her?" *Will I have to raise the three girls?* Persi wondered.

"There's just no easy way to say it, Bruce."

"Say what?" She braced for the news of her lifetime, unsuccessfully suppressing a smile.

"It's over. We can't see each other anymore," he blurted out, seemingly briefly relieved.

She stopped breathing and the smile dripped from her face. "Say what?" Persi asked, inclining her ear, watching his lips move to make sure she heard every word correctly.

"I've been up for hours trying to figure out the best way to tell you, so that you wouldn't get upset, Bruce. You know I love you, but we both knew this day would come eventually . . . maybe not this way."

Her inner voice bypassed all her controls and told her, *Here comes good-bye.* Here comes the beginning of the end. Here comes the start of sleepless nights, but Persi shook her head clear of such nonsense.

But Brad kept talking. The more he spoke the worse it got. She grabbed her stomach as if someone had just punched her in the gut. Her head reeled, her heart cracked, then burst into a million little pieces while her soul abandoned her body completely, leaving no remnants. Every breath a struggle, she felt like she'd been submerged underwater and all she saw was Brad's lips moving—flapping with more lies. Or perhaps for the first time in their relationship, he spoke the truth; the truth that he was dumping her . . . for his wife and family.

Persi struggled to maintain control and wondered why he was still talking. What could he be saying? There was no justifiable explanation. She wondered where her gun was. In a lockbox. By the time she went to get it, he would be gone. A knife. A butcher knife. Over on her drain, she could slit his throat, and then there would be no more Brad to lie to her or his wife. He'd be gone, but her problems would just begin. The blood could easily be wiped off her granite island and counters, but it would stain her ceramic tiled floor; she would always see the faded red splotches in her cream-colored stone. Then she would be locked up and Drew, Doxie, her sisters, family, friends would all know what a class-A fool she'd been all these years, and to add insult to injury, she'd killed the bastard and now she was going to jail. *I can't do jail*, Persi thought lucidly. Maybe they'd send her to an asylum for the criminally insane. *I can't do insane asylum either*, Persi thought. But I can do this.

Persi lunged for and struck Brad's face once. "Get out!"

A shocked Brad grabbed the side of his cheek; the force so hard it made his eyes tear and shook a tooth loose. "Bruce—"

"My name is Persephone. Persi to family and friends," she seethed lethally. "You are neither. Do not ever call me again." She opened the back door.

"I think you broke my jaw—"

Persi glared at him in a way he'd never seen before and never wanted to see again. He wanted to ask if he had to fear for his life or the lives of his children, but thought better of it.

"Maybe when this all blows over we can resume—"

"Get the hell outta my house and life! If you *ever* call me again, I will kill you."

He looked at her like she was a multiheaded Medusa. A wild woman he didn't know and wanted to leave far behind. Brad bit his tongue and tasted salty red blood. He held his jaw and walked though the door just as it slammed behind him.

Persi's world stopped, then slid off its axis. Somewhere in her mind's ear she heard the opening bars of Aretha Franklin's "Never Loved A Man The Way I Love You," *you're a liar and a cheat...* Persi held on to the corner of her kitchen island as she felt herself being pulled from a tranquil tributary into a floodwater maelstrom, feeling the edges of her contained existence begin to fray. She sensed herself sinking into an unavoidable physical and mental meltdown. With one stroke of her arm, she sheared her countertop of dishes and silver with a loud crash. She screamed at the top of her lungs and tore around her house looking for pictures of him—them—to destroy. By the time she reached her bedroom, she realized there were none. He was married and they hadn't taken any pictures. That realization made her laugh uncontrollably, hysterically. The sheer lunacy that controlled her life over the past five years: constantly checking her cell or text messages, never venturing too far from home so that, just in case he could steal a few hours away, she could race home and be there to open the door for him—ready, willing, and able.

Stupid, stupid, idiotic little girl, she self-chastised. Faithful to a man who was routinely unfaithful to her. Making him a priority when she was his horny afterthought; a sport to fill his free time. Had Trish found out or did he get tired of her demands for Paris? Persi didn't know and didn't care. No matter the reason why—the outcome was the same—it was over; the charade had run its course from good to gone. She had nothing to show for it . . . no marriage, no children, no dignity. What had she left? A gigantic, shattered, and tender-to-the-touch heart and a mountain of used condoms—enough foil to make a space shuttle. All this time she thought she'd be the exception to the rule; instead she was just another pathetic cautionary tale. A big, dumb cliché; an educated idiot.

She felt sick to her stomach and bolted to the downstairs powder room and threw up as anger tumbled from her mouth. She flushed, rinsed her mouth, and let out another primal scream, which did little to make her feel better. She went back upstairs, removed her clothes, and got into bed. She cried, thrashed, beat the pillows and, when physically and emotionally exhausted, finally fell to sleep. She awakened in eerie darkness. She couldn't tell the time but the digital clock read six. Six in the morning or six in the evening? She didn't know. The solar Christmas candles flickered in each window. She sank back into the refuge of sleep, later opening her eyes to pitch-black. Her answering machine winked red. She hit it. Jean-Luc asked where she was. She hadn't come to work.

What day is it? she wondered. How long had she been in bed? The next message from Doxie asked if she was joining them for Christmas at her parents or going to her father's? Nothing from Brad.

Why did she even care? Had she hoped it was all a mistake that he would call and apologize or check on her? "It's over. We can't see each other anymore." His words stung in her ears, pierced her eardrums and made them bleed. She was out of tears, or so she thought. But when she asked herself honestly that if he called right this very minute, would she take him back? She had no answer—she cried all over again.

The light of day and the time on the clock finally collided and Persi, darting out into humanity, called Jean Luc and told him she had the flu. She told Doxie who was ready to bring Soup the same lie, until Persi reminded her of the annual mother-daughter Christmas and New Year's ski trip and how Drew would never forgive her mother if she got sick. Persi called her sisters with the same story, covering with anyone who'd be concerned by her absence over the holidays, and staggered back to bed. The grandfather clock chimed, the timers clicked on and off, the cold, brittle sun shone, set, and sent out the moon for days until the next thing Persi remembered was being awakened by the loud sound of car horns blowing, accompanied by vocal jubilation. Apparently, the New Year dawned. She'd missed her favorite week of the year, Christmas to New Year's. Brad had stolen five years. She wasn't going to give him anymore; "don't throw good time after bad," her mother used to say about moping, and, "when you point your finger at somebody, three others are pointing back at you." Deep down in the recesses of her soul, Persi knew she was doing wrong and didn't care because she and Brad were different. "Well, no, little girl," she could hear her mother say. "When you choose the behavior, you choose the consequences. Take your lumps, learn from your mistakes, and move on."

Reluctantly, Persi accepted some responsibility for the Brad debacle; it takes two to tango and she wasn't raped. Serves her right, her dream hadn't been deferred, it had run amok. She should have aimed higher for herself. Persi felt hollowness in her chest, like her bruised and battered heart losing its shape and melting into a meaningless mass of errant tissues and cells. She absently massaged her chest but felt her heart irrevocably, irreversibly broken. Never to love, trust, or be vulnerable ever again.

After two weeks Persi deemed it time for her to reintegrate into the world. A world without Brad. In the depths of her mind she agreed with Nancy Wilson's "I Can't Make You Love Me If You Don't." Thankful that this affair had been surreptitious, Persi had been spared the whispers, the gloating, innuendos, or the sad-eyed looks. Jean-Luc suspected, but never said; he was French, after all. Persi couldn't bear to hear, "I told you so." Or, "Thank God!" Or, "It's about time" from her best friend, who'd she'd eventually have to tell—or maybe she'd just let Doxie discover the breakup. She could hear Doxie's advice, "Best way to get *over* somebody is to get *under* somebody else." Even in absentia, her friend made her smile.

Persi got out of bed, stripped the wet, soggy sheets and put them in the second-floor laundry room on her way to the bathroom. She peeled off the clothes she wore and stepped in a stream of warm water. She washed and washed and scrubbed as if exorcising her body of any place ever touched by Brad Shelton. She looked at her fresh, clean face and wrapped her mango-scented hair in a terry turban. She drew on the robe that hung on her bathroom door. Having eaten very little in the last week, she was ravenous and went downstairs. Opening her refrigerator, she began cleaning out the spoiled and furry food and took out a Marie Callender's chicken potpie from the freezer. She popped it in the microwave on her way to the front door and shoveled in the mail dropped in her vestibule through the front door slot.

"Jeez. I must have been Rip Van Winkle."

With the ding of the microwave, she removed her food, sat at the kitchen table, and began opening all the Christmas cards she'd received. "I missed the entire season," she realized. "Pathetic. You've let a man steal your good time. It won't happen again. I promise you that, Persephone May Sinclair."

As she pulled on sweats, started the wash cycle on her sheets, and began to make her bed anew, she listened to her messages, full of the usual suspects with the where-are-yous to we just decided to. . . so come overs. A couple from Doxie and Drew checking up on her and three from Nick. She heard his voice and stopped just as the sheet fluttered above, then settled on her mattress.

"Happy holidays. This is Nick and I'm in town. Thought we could get together. Maybe take a ride out to the Severn house and see how it looks in the winter's light." He chuckled as she smoothed out the sheet and tucked in the side. "Let me know." He left his number.

"Hi, Nick again. Is it too late to ask what you are doing New Year's?"

Persi retrieved a fresh blanket from her linen closet.

"Thought you'd like to go to Ben's Chili Bowl for a chili half smoke with everything."

He laughed and so did Persi. She imagined his piercing eyes and those kiss-ready lips. "If you don't have a better offer, give me a call."

The third and final call was "Happy New Year, Persi. I'm heading back to Chicago and then to the coast for awhile. Sorry we couldn't connect. You're probably out of town. Maybe we'll have better luck when I come back. Feel free to call anytime. Hope all your dreams come true this New Year. Take care."

Persi placed her comforter and arranged her pillows. No call from Brad. She hit the erase button and sat on her newly made, showroom-decorated bed. There was nothing left for her to do. She wouldn't pine or ponder; she'd proceed. This new year and the ones to follow would be Brad-less so she better get used to the idea. She'd work and play and stay away from Phyllis Hyman's song, "Old Friend." So pissed at Brad, but more so at herself; she hated that even now, if he came contritely to her back door . . . she'd take him back in a heartbeat.

Persi abhorred the slate-gray D.C. days of January and February. Dreary, cold, and damp, folks shrouded themselves in wool coats, plunked knit hats down securely on heads and ditched sunglasses. The morning drive, like the evening—dark, all you wanted to do was get to your destination; the anticlimactic, dog days of winter in the District.

With no reason to hurry home or to check for messages twenty times a day, Persi worked long hours at the NIH lab with Jean-Luc Etienne. When Doxie traveled with her job and Persi took care of Drew, there were no discussion as to why she remained in suburbia. When she left work at seven, her pattern had become to drive down Cedar Lane, make that right on Beach Drive across Connecticut Avenue, and make a left on Old Spring Road right up and into Doxie's driveway in time for dinner, Jeopardy!, and Alex Trebek.

"Still time to get to New Orleans for Mardi Gras this year," Doxie suggested.

"Once is enough. We can go after," Persi suggested half-heartedly.

"I love D.C. but it sure sucks during these monotonous, sunless winter months."

"Amen to that. Your parents and friends have the right idea."

"Snowbirds. But I don't want Florida either. Now, the Caribbean . . ." Doxie smiled broadly and then stopped, realizing that this was the time that Persi and Brad the cad usually made her tropical birthday trip. Unless . . . "So you going to Paris this spring?"

Persi looked at her friend with surprised wonder. "Did Jean-Luc tell you?"

"What? Why would I talk to that creepy old man?" Doxie shivered and screwed up her mouth. "Now Marius—is another story." Doxie grinned, then caught herself. "Tell me what?"

"I am thinking of going to Paris in the spring. To live for awhile."

"Say what?" Doxie sat up and looked at her friend. "Brad left his wife?"

"No. It's got nothing to do with him. I'm thinking of a career change."

"Perfumer," Doxie identified.

"Close," Persi said, warming up to the idea slowly. She liked to think things through before discussing them with her friends. "Thanks to Jean-Luc, I've been in touch with Marius. I won't be a perfumer but he's excited about my ideas."

"Well, you were the only ten-year-old I knew who used to dab vanilla behind her ears."

Persi laughed.

"And then those concoctions in junior high." They slapped five. "Wait a minute. You're doing all this discussion with strangers without my input?"

"Of course."

Doxie cut her eyes playfully.

"Nothing's final yet. I'm still thinkin on it.'"

"If you're thinking on it—you're going."

"It would be a place for you and Drew to visit. From there we could jump off to any European country."

Doxie beamed. "Yeah, make up for the stick-in-the-mud you were on our senior trip."

"I had other things on my mind," Persi said, referring to her sick mother.

"Speaking of sticks-in-the-mud, how does Brad feel about this?" Doxie tested.

"I don't know or care."

"Really?" Doxie said sarcastically.

"Really. I'm ready for a change in venue—new place, new people, new career. It's very appealing to me."

Doxie didn't want to seem too encouraging as she didn't want to jinx it. If Doxie attacked Brad, Persi would defend him. But Doxie's heart was doing cartwheels. "Would you keep your house?"

"Of course. I need some place to live when I come back. I'd like to leave my car in your driveway."

"No problem. I got a two-car garage with only one car and Drew doesn't drive yet. You *will* be back before Drew learns to drive?"

"I only plan to stay a year or two."

"Does anyone ever really come back from living abroad?"

"I will. The people I care about most are here."

"Hell, once you move over there the people you care about most will be visiting your butt like crazy!"

"Promise?"

"Oh, I do. Where will I be staying?"

"According to Jean-Luc and Marius, the main Etienne laboratory and company is in the French country-side, outside of Paris, amid lavender fields. It's an ancient chateau that has been converted into labs, showroom, museum, and a restaurant open only in the spring and summer. The family lives in their own chateaus on the surrounding acreage, but there is a fully furnished, two-bedroom flat in Paris that I can have while there." Persi glanced over at Doxie, who had tears in her eyes. "What?"

"You're leaving us."

"You just promised to come."

"I know, but there won't be nights like this when you stop by after work. Drew is going to have a cow."

"You can always send her to Paris," Persi said weakly.

"I am so happy for you, Persi." Doxie hugged her friend. "I really, really am. Finally," she began and wanted to say "you got rid of Brad the cad." "Finally, you are moving on with your life. Finally, you are going to do something you always wanted do. "Finally," Doxie repeated. "You are getting the life you wanted and deserved."

"Well, I'm almost forty. It's about time."

"Hey! We are only thirty-five and rising. Don't rush it." She looked at her friend. "Who knows where you'll be or what you will be doing by forty. You could marry a king or a prince or count. Countess—"

"Not unless he's black—"

"He can be from Africa." They laughed.

"I tell you. Honestly, right now—I don't have a man. And I don't want a man. I just want—me. To concentrate on me. Only me. I've never really had that before."

"I hear you. My girl's going to live in Gay Paree!"

CHAPTER 11

The hum of the plane droned in Persi's ears as the anticipation and excitement kept her mind aflame. She'd closed all five fireplace flues, cut the thermostat to fifty degrees so her pipes wouldn't freeze, secured the alarm, put her car in Doxie's garage, and given her house keys to Doxie and her sisters at the farewell party; quite the Parisian-themed birthday bash. Thirty-six. She purposefully took an early-evening flight to avoid a teary good bye scene at the airport. *A new chapter, a new adventure,* she thought as the flight attendant brought warm nuts and a glass of pinot. The last time she'd flown first-class was on the way back from Bora-Bora—after ten days with Brad. She sipped the wine as a distraction—it didn't work. As a musical conspiracy, Phyllis Hyman's voice crooned "Old Friend" through the headset. Persi made no effort to change the channel. Maybe while trying to work it out with his wife, he'd discover they belonged together. Maybe he would come to his senses soon and follow her to Paris. "*Welcome back into my life again . . .*" Phyllis sang and a single tear fell from Persi's eyes.

What fairy tale are you conjuring up now, Persephone. Get over and on with it, she self-admonished, thankful folks could not read her mind. They'd be as disappointed in her as she was in herself. *You are free, black and over twenty-one. Live it up. You're going to live in Paris!*

A driver and limo picked her up at the airport and drove her out to Château Etienne. The impressive ancient castle loomed over thousands of dormant acres like an enchanted kingdom lit by the cold February sun. The convivial and gracious Etienne family showed her around the stone fortress with traditions older than the United States of America, and asked her which room she'd like to call home. She was gratefully relieved when Marius rescued her and offered her the second-floor quarters over the storage building, explaining that "Persi likes her privacy. N'est pas?"

The first few weeks sped by like the candy-factory conveyer belt in an old *I Love Lucy* episode. Between resurrecting her high school French to fluency, meeting staff, acclimating herself to the bucolic environment, and eating nightly with the Etienne family, she fell into bed each night over fed and exhausted. A real rooster crowed to announce morning early each workday and unfortunately on weekends as well. If not awakened by the loud fowl, two Etienne children smitten by "the pretty black woman" loved to knock on her door early in the morning. Their mother caught them too late, after they'd destroyed Persi's sleeping late on weekends by at least an hour. On Saturdays and Sundays, she was expected to become part of the family by attending their chapel on the premises, lunching, walking, recreating until dinner where the menu included lively discussions, a musicale, and another walk before bed. Persi enjoyed the work immensely but the demands on her private life were killing her; she had no time to herself.

In the fourth week, Persi caught a ride to the city. Although April in Paris proved to be cooler than the standard song suggested, she meandered through the streets, looking at the lovers and imagining that she was one part of a couple—any couple, fighting thoughts of Brad. Marius had blessedly given her keys to the flat and suggested that she take a look while in town. "My family can be overwhelming, I know," he said in his thick French accent. "We keep to ourselves because, of course, no one outside the family is good enough and then we wear each other out. It's my family so I know how they can be. Why you think Jean-Luc moved to America?"

Persi strolled the Champs-Elysées from the Louvre toward the Arc de Triomphe and could hear the classic accordion music with each step. After only a few blocks sadness seized her like a cloying, panic attack and she left the main boulevard. In all her dreams and imaginings, she was not supposed to be alone. She was to have been Mrs. Bradford Shelton with her husband on their honeymoon as they walked the famed eight-laned concourse. The fact that she walked by herself, while everyone else seemed paired and in love, pierced her heart and she made a mental note to avoid the Champs. It only reminded her of her failure to have the man she wanted; reminded her that she was dumped like sewage from a barge in the Potomac River. Taking a self-guided detour, she ended up walking along the Seine and began warming up in the spring sunshine. She meandered up to Notre Dame and over toward St. Germain de Pres and the Latin Quarter, the part of Paris that most spoke to her. She bypassed many of the familiar places, preferring to wait until Doxie, her sister, or some friend came over to enjoy it with her—she figured over the next few years she'd see a lot of these landmarks. She walked back to the other side of the right bank along the Seine and found the apartment building owned by the Etiennes; a formidable, three-story edifice with the flat in question on the second floor. Once inside the exquisite lobby with a spectacular chandelier dripping above the stairs, Persi realized that the building consisted of only six huge apartments, two on each floor, which ran front to back for ancient ventilation.

Persi climbed the marble stairs, worn smooth by thousands of feet, and inserted the antique key into the keyhole. With one twist, the door sprang open and Persi stepped in.

"Oh, wow," Persi said as she closed the door behind her.

She stood on a platform in an enormous room with ceilings as high as those she had at home. This mammoth, elegantly appointed room screamed old world money. Directly ahead stood an ornate fireplace, above its mantel, a flamboyant, gold-gilded mirror that kissed the ceiling, stripped with roughly hewed beams. In front of this focal point was a conversation area composed of formal settee, two matching chairs, and one big leather lounge with an accompanying ottoman built for comfort, an afghan carelessly tossed over its back. Persi sauntered down the two steps, her feet landing on a heavy, hardwood floor just before stepping onto an intricately woven Abusson rug on which the furniture sat; a massive table in its middle, accessible to all four seats. To the left, two-floor-to ceiling French door windows flooded the apartment with the rays of a setting sun, and between them, a table, lamp and two chairs. Two more sets of the same massive windows flanked the fireplace; it was an impressive, casually elegant room made more so by the tapestry that covered the four windows and complemented the well-worn silk damask upholstery of the settee and chairs. Persi already heard the leather lounge call her name—now and in the winter, when she lit the fire . . . she could live right there.

To her right, one long room ran perpendicular from side to side. The ceiling, not as high as the living room, hung above a long table with eight well-spaced chairs. At this dining room's center, another fireplace, the entrance to two rooms at either end. Persi walked toward the back room and noted a door tucked off to the right, near the two-step entrance. She pushed it open onto a small, galley-like kitchen; functional with a refrigerator, stove, sink, oven, a little window, a door, and a bistro set with only two chairs. When she walked over to the door at the end, it opened onto a minute balcony that Persi supposed was for ventilation or putting a pot of basil on its rod-ironed base. There were compact pantry-type shelves and very little cabinet space.

So French and definitely not for cooking big meals, she thought.

She left the kitchen, crossed through the dining room and passed a credenza, old and discriminating enough to be in the Smithsonian, into the door beside one end of the fireplace. To the right, a small powder room; a basin with a mirror, towel rack, and commode. To the left, an alcove with a stack washer and dryer. She walked into a small bedroom with the basics and one French door window, which overlooked a scene of connecting backs of properties and a festoon of washed laundry hanging out to air dry—clearly Parisian. Persi left that room, back into the dining room, passing its fireplace again, and looked at the only window that seemed to be especially scaled, as it was walled up by four feet before the unadorned windows commenced. Persi stepped into the bedroom, where the same windows continued, uninterrupted, straight across the length of this room until the next door, a bathroom. This bedroom shared the dining room fireplace and the ceiling remained low, to keep a steady temperature in both summer and winter. A bed dominated the room. An armoire sat in the corner next to the fireplace and a dresser with a rectangular mirror against the wall on the other side of the bed where a shallow closet appeared, seemingly more of an afterthought then a mainstay. Persi looked out of the bedroom window to the street below. Although only the second floor, the flat seemed much higher as she could see the Seine River a few blocks away and the top part of the Eiffel Tower in the distance. The square on the cobblestoned road below reminded her of the circle outside her home in D.C., but not nearly as busy. Across the street, another apartment building entrance was visible, but the rest of the buildings faced the other street. *It must be nice and quiet here at night,* she thought, and no darling Etienne children to wake you early on a Saturday and Sunday.

Persi was hooked and she hadn't seen the bathroom yet.

She followed the same windows to the next door, which revealed a very ordinary bathroom. Pristine white tile wrapped itself around a commode, a bidet, a shallow tub with a hand-held shower, and a small window. She looked at the thick towel rack and noted, "Heated. I'm in heaven."

Persi laid across the bed, spread out her arms then curled up into a ball. *Yep. This'll do fine,* she thought. *Once I get my body pillow,* it'll be just like home. She turned over on her stomach and looked straight through the fireplace to the dining room and into the living room beyond. She could see the front door from her bedroom.

When Persi returned to the chateau, Marius asked her how she liked the flat. "I'll take it."

"I thought you would. You Americans do like your privacy."

"Yes, we do. Do I get a car or does a driver escort me back and forth?"

"Well, there is a lab in Paris. You can do some days there and some here. It's up to you. You Americans do also like your freedom."

"*Absolutey.*"

By May, Persi felt like a true Parisian, firmly ensconced in her flat on the Rue TreMarquis. The Etienne family was pleased with her proposals for introducing a new fragrance line and updating the tried-and-true staples of Etienne Parfums, older than and as popular as most Parisian brands. The Etiennes proudly displayed the original perfume recipes for Marie Antoinette and Empress Josephine in their museum as well as those mixed especially for Louis XIII, XV and XIV and all of Giacomo Casanova's women in Venice. The Etienne name and fortune solidified in a century when *parfum* was used in lieu of baths and long before the advent of deodorant. Persi realized that the Etiennes were rich hundreds of years before her family came into existence as slaves picking cotton on a Tennessee plantation, giving the term old money a brand-new perspective.

Persi curled up in the tufted leather lounging chair, and thought up mixes and variations on formulas for *Joie de Vivre*, as she named the new line. Besides the usual lavender, rose, sandalwoods, and bergamots, she pioneered mixing fragrances with exotic combinations: tiare flowers with gardenia, jasmine and tea leaves or fig, palm, cyclamen and sandalwood. Into a base of coconut, she added ruby guava and pomelo—with plans to name it Hawaiian something. She explored opposites to the flowery aromas with earthy nutmegs, almond, cinnamon, vanilla and chocolate. . . naming it Mexican something. She was fascinated by the scents of hyacinth and ylang-ylang with lilac. Intrigued with unique, yummy aromatics of edibles like mango, peach, apricot, pineapple, and grapefruit. Or intoxicatingly intimate ginger and patchouli or the bold, magical romantics of Madagascar spices like clove, black pepper, vanilla bean, and blood orange. Infinite ideas and combinations reeled in her head to present to The Nose, whose trained olfactory senses approved the feasibility of all fragrance compatibilities. With only three hundred perfumers in the world, France boasted of having half of them and Etienne had one première perfumer: the Nose.

Persi shook her head free of any probable intimidation from him and thought of the other projects she'd tackle after the success of her *Joie deVivre* line. In an elegant, keepsake box, she envisioned packaging vials of pure perfume oils so that young girls as she once was, or sophisticated ladies could mix their own signature fragrances; a practice done all over France but not in the United States. In this exchange of cultures, she'd give Europeans the scent of a U.S. beach, maybe with lemon, flowering angels trumpet and sweet, salty fragrances and call it Beaches or Pacific Ocean or Malibu something; any would surely sound fabulous in French. *Fragrances first, names later,* Persi thought, trying to harness and order her mind.

Besides conducting market research, reviewing statistical analysis, and working tirelessly at the lab and at home, Persi held testing parties with the Etiennes and other focus groups at their shops to grasp the preferences of the Parisian women. She also initiated the American concept of body butters made of all-natural ingredients and shea butters from Africa. Eventually, she'd introduce the Etiennes to hand-poured soy wax candles with lead-free cotton wicks; handmade soaps with natural biodegradable, paraben-free vegetable bases—but these ideas were after the Malibu fragrance and keepsake chest.

By June, The Nose approved of her line and Persi was ready to proceed with first runs and have a little well-deserved fun. Before her summer classes, Diana April came and went, followed by ViVi Ham, her visit a complete antithesis to her scholarly sister's. Doxie and Drew flew in for Bastille Day celebrations. Persi was elated that the almost eleven-year-old was willing to give up part of her Camp Mawavi stay to come to Paris; the chance of a lifetime as her mother and Auntie Persi had to wait until high school graduation.

Upon sight of one another, the three black females squealed and screeched as they ran toward one another; very un-Parisian. When Drew ran ahead toward baggage claim, Doxie turned to Persi and said, "Damn girl, you look good! I ought to move to Paris! I don't have to ask how you've been."

"I am so happy, Doxie. For the first time I really feel like . . . me. The me I knew I could be. The me, I am."

"Good for you. Perhaps you need a little something to round out those hectic days you have," Doxie broached. "Know who called me looking for you?"

"Who? Not Rucker Jackman. His marriage over already?"

"I wouldn't pass that one on, honey. I'd keep him to myself. He's all wrong for you."

"Thanks, Mom."

"Nick," Doxie offered.

"Oh really," Persi lamented.

"Yeah, I think Paris scared the brother off."

"I'm done with scaredy brothers." They went to the luggage carousel as Drew watched intently for their bags.

"Who are you dating?"

"No one. No time. Working. I got a body pillow and a vibrator. Most nights I'm too tired to even use them."

"Oh. So sad."

"Oh? Seems to me you have their twins. And just how is Mr. Sparkless?"

Doxie grinned. "Actually, he's beginning to get a little glitter 'round the edges."

"Do tell?"

The transplanted trio, anxious to settle into Parisian life, spoke mostly French until they got to a difficult word and just substituted in English. To fight jet lag, that Friday night they joined the Paris Skate, a three-hour Rollerblade view of the city but they cut it short after one and a half hours at the Eiffel Tower. The next few days, Persi and Doxie retraced their teenage steps to the Eiffel Tower, the Louvre, Sacré Coeur, and Notre Dame, climbing the steps and posing beside the gargoyles. They stood before the *Mona Lisa*, still not getting what the hoopla was about, but came to near tears as they basked in the genius of the Impressionists, especially Monet. They walked and subwayed all over the city and ventured down to the Rodin Museum. In the garden, Persi anchored herself in front of his *Gates of Hell* and told Doxie, "I was on my way, girl."

"Well, you got hold of yourself and repented."

They walked over to the Claude Monet House and dined at a neighborhood bistro. None of them could get used to dodging the dog poop in the streets or the way restaurants welcomed the little precious canines. The quiet, furry pets sat at the table with their masters and ate along with other patrons.

"The French and their dogs," Persi lamented. "Truth is, Fifi lives and eats better than a lot of us in southeast D.C."

"Don't know which I hate more . . . the dogs or the smoke," Doxie said.

"That's why folks prefer to eat outside. Fresh air."

They spent two days at Disneyland and one at Versailles, Paris. When Persi went to work, the visitors went to the Pompidou, followed by shopping, and met for ice cream at Berthillon before taking a dinner cruise down the Seine. After eating, a bored Drew and third wheels Persi and Doxie realized that river cruises were best reserved for lovers. With renewed energy the next day, Persi drove them to the Etienne Château where both visiting D.C. tourists were duly impressed. "It's an enchanted palace," Drew proclaimed.

"Great setting for a wedding," Persi told Doxie. "Even Mr. Sparkless could rev up a few luminations here."

They walked through rows of fragrant lavender fields where Drew found a resident cat to chase. "This is heaven, Persi," Doxie said quietly, looping her hand through her friend's the way most Parisian women did. "You're never coming home, are you?"

"Of course I am."

"No. I don't mean for a visit." Doxie took a deep breath and looked around, overwhelmed by the calm, serene beauty of the French countryside. The pace, the order of the rows of flowers. The sun casually setting into colorful hues of fuchsia and gold. "I could live here forever."

"Ha! Not D.C. Doxie." They walked a few steps and watched Drew turn the spigot on for her feline companion. "It's nice. It's just what I needed."

"Still think on him?" Doxie asked. The name *Brad* dangeled between them, unspoken.

"Everyday, but not in the way you think. He's there, in the back of my mind; sometimes my thoughts focus on him and sometimes they leave him alone. But it's good here. Time and distance are the key. As long as I don't see his lying, cheating face—I'm good. I do wish . . ."

Doxie stopped. "Wish what?"

"That he'd want me back so I can tell him no, thank you. I am so over you."

"Ha!" Doxie began walking again. "Every woman wishes that about an ex-beau or two."

Persi took one Friday and they spent almost the entire day in one of her favorite haunts, Evangeline's on the Rue Faubourg Saint Honore where she found Chanel, Valentino and other haute couture designer clothes at fifty percent off, forcing Doxie to purchase another suitcase to carry her fashion booty home. That weekend they drove further into the countryside, stayed overnight and returned to the Château Etienne for Drew's birthday barbeque, where the family was jubilant, the food exquisite, and the time sped by much too fast. They were at the airport saying their good-bye.

"I tell you one thing, I won't ever be in use or loose category ever again. I'll be back," Doxie promised.

"Me too, Aunt Persi."

"Next time we'll have to go to Italy or Spain. Train to St. Tropez. And maybe this Christmas you all can ski at St. Moritz."

"I have a good government job. But it ain't that good," Doxie joked as their flight was announced. "Bye, Persi-Sin. Love ya."

"Love you too," Persi said, embracing them in turn. "Safe flight."

Persi returned to her quiet flat that wasn't the same without the pair. She looked out of the window of her bedroom and watched a returning dinner cruise on the Seine and laughed, recalling how out of place they were. She looked over at her neighbors across the square. A few weeks ago, while making her half-asleep nocturnal trot to the bathroom, she'd noticed the couple, a man and a woman, so in love that they had no time to notice anyone else . . . typical in Paris; folks cuddling, fondling, kissing all over the place without regard to anyone who wasn't a direct participant. *And why should they?* Persi thought. She wondered if the man had a night job as he frequently left in the wee hours; he could be a baker, butcher, florist, chef—someone who rose early to get the business started before Paris proper woke up. Tonight he was leaving earlier than usual and she, Collette, as Persi had named her, draped herself over him as he reluctantly pulled away. *Easy girl, he'll be back,* Persi scolded. *You're a lucky woman.* Her mind volleyed back to Rucker Jackman and Phyllis Hyman's song, "You Know How to Love Me," popped into her head. *I could use him about now.*

Persi fell back into her comfortable and rigorous routine, preparing the *Joie de Vivre* line for a Christmas launch. Athena and Bernard rounded out the end of her summer guests, but Persi hardly saw them as they were just glad to be childless in Paris. Persi entered her apartment to a ringing telephone. It was Labor Day back home and Drew had surely laid out all of the Parisian frocks Persi had sent her to wear before the school uniform dress became required attire.

"*Bonjour,*" Persi sang out, placing her briefcase down by the table.

"*Bonsoir,*" a male voice corrected.

Even after all this time, the familiar sound of his voice caused her heart to lurch. She couldn't believe she remembered its timbre.

"Persi?"

"Yes. Nick."

She could hear his grin through the phone line.

"You remembered."

"Of course. How have you been?"

"Just fine and you?

"Fine. Working hard—"

"But loving it."

She smiled into the phone and agreed, "Yes. Loving it. So you called to wish me happy Labor Day?" She rifled though her mail, trying to decide if she'd see him if he were to come to Paris. *Why would he come to Paris?* she thought.

"Happy Labor Day. I also want to invite you to the club."

Persi stopped shuffling mail, chuckled, and said, "You're good but a little too far away for a quick trip to Balzac's."

"Actually, I'm only a few blocks. At Bricktop's on Rue Ciel-Etoiles."

Persi was speechless.

"Hello?"

"Yes.You're in Paris? France?"

"Yes, I am. I go where they want me . . . and this is it. It'd be nice to have a friendly face from home in the crowd."

Oh, they'll be plenty of friendly faces looking up at you, she thought but said, "You sure do get around, Nick Betancourt."

"The nature of the beast. So you'll come this Saturday at eight?"

After seven months in Paris, she had a date. "Sure. Where is this again?"

"How long have you been here?"

"Since February."

"And you haven't been to Bricktop's? Well, you are in for a real treat. It's only the best jazz enclave in Paris. You might even run into tourists from the States."

"Are you kidding me?"

"Would I do that? It's a must-see. It's named for Ada 'Bricktop' Smith, an expatriate chanteuse and nightclub owner in Paris in the 1920s up to the sixties. Cole Porter wrote 'Miss Otis Regrets' for her to perform. Her niece runs the club now."

"The sobriquet Bricktop because . . ."

"Her red hair and freckles."

"Of course. You are just a wealth of knowledge. Well, how can I refuse historical, educational, and fun."

"Absolutely. I'll leave your name at the door. You're going to have to push past the crowd to get in. You want to invite anyone else?"

"Not right now."

Nick grinned, happy she didn't want to add any name, especially a male one. "Great. I'll see you in two days. Take care."

He hung up and smiled. After all this time, he'd given up and given in. There was no denying his interest in Persi Sinclair and he had to play it out once and for all. A man of his maturity knew what he wanted in a woman and knew it when he saw it. After the first meeting he'd deemed Persi and her situation too complicated. He had complicated all his life from childhood through young adulthood. Nick was looking for comfort and ease. But Persi had stayed on his mind. After that first encounter, he'd returned to D.C. six months later and they'd driven out to his house on the Severn River. He'd kissed her and she let him know friendship was all she was offering. Since then Nick had been through one serious relationship with a dynamic judge in Florida, which could have led to an engagement, but, out of fairness to them both, he'd called it quits . . . she wasn't Persi. It'd been over a year and Persi was here in Paris—alone. The time had come for him to see if Persi was really what he wanted, or just an unattainable fantasy challenge he'd conjured up to spice up his life. Only time would tell the tale.

Persi stood there with the hum of the severed line in her hand. She hung up. Nick left no number or where he was staying or how he could be reached if she couldn't come. She had two days until she saw him. *How about maybe lunch or a dinner?* she wondered as she began shedding her clothes. *He was an unusual man*, Persi thought. He popped in and out of her life at the oddest times, but with Doxie and Drew gone and her social life nil, he would be a refreshing diversion. She liked his company and, if the club was as much of an icon as he said, she'd know about Bricktop's when Doxie returned. Meanwhile, *Mr. Nick Betancourt, it's just you, me, and Paris*, Persi thought as she changed into her house clothes and eyed her curves. "I wonder what this visit will bring?"

CHAPTER 12

The two days crawled by and finally a taxi deposited Persi in front of Bricktop's. The line wrapped down the quiet, skinny street before disappearing around the corner. An astounded Persi thought Nick had been kidding. She pushed the door open onto a one-story poster of him holding his sax with his name—*Now Playing Nick Betancourt*—emblazoned across its surface . . . *Now Playing.* It reminded her of the stories her grandparents told them about stars—Duke, Josephine Baker, Count, and Sarah having to go abroad to become famous before returning to the States and getting their proper due; "go where you are celebrated, not tolerated," her mother used to say. Maybe Nick could afford that house on the Severn River—not that it was any of her business.

"This way," the bosomy hostess said, leading her to a small table for two in front of the bandstand. The club was jamm-packed with black and white patrons, the low ceiling capturing the cloud of cigarette smoke, holding it hostage just above the customers' heads, while a thick smell of booze and good times snaked around, enveloping all; the club, lively and cracking with excitement even though the stage was empty except for a piano, set of drums, a bass, two mikes, and three chairs. A D.C. fire marshall would never have allowed the number of tables bunched upon themselves and lack of ventilation . . . but this was Paris and there were more outside who clamored to get into this dark, exotic tomb.

She let her raincoat drop and drape over her chair, reveal-

ing her animal-print sheath. She readjusted one of the spa-
ghetti straps back onto her bare shoulder, crossed her legs as
four-inch heels scraped along the aging wooden floor. Persi
ordered a drink and, upon her return the hostess refused payment with a "*compri.*"

"Hey, Persi. Glad you could make it," Nick said, threading
his way through the tables, offering perfunctory greetings to
folks elated to see him back in Paris.

"Hey." Persi's face broke into a wide grin at the sight of
him.

He bent to kiss her quickly on the lips, a gesture that surprised and titillated her.

"We're in Europe. That's allowed," he said, referring to their
first kiss when she reprimanded him for the European gesture.

"Yes, we are."

"You look great." He eyed her bare shoulders and the ruched
bodice of her dress that complemented her complexion perfectly. He couldn't wait to see her standing, knowing it hit
all her curves. "You let your hair grow," he added quickly,
redirecting his gaze.

"Had no choice. Haven't found a stylist yet."

"You're kiddin'? This is Paris."

He smiled and his dimple appeared. Persi hadn't realized
how she'd missed it.

"Gettin' ready to go on. Just wanted to make sure you were
all situated." He'd given her table an extra chair "just in case"—
thrilled she hadn't filled it. "See you after the set."

"I'll be here." She sipped her drink just as a pretty French
woman with auburn hair and a tight ass slid it on the vacant
chair next to her.

"*Bonsoir,*" she said to Persi.

"*Bonsoir,*" Persi replied, noticing that she wore Etienne parfum. *She's got taste and money,* Persi thought.

"I am Francoise," she introduced in a thick French accent, her red bow lips pouted seductively at the end of her name.

"Persi."

"Yes. I thought you were a man. Is Persi not a man's name in America?" She sucked on a long cigarette holder of Auntie Mame fame and puffed smoke, contributing her part to the cloudy atmosphere.

"Apparently not. I am not a man." Persi noted that her fine porcelain skin had not a blemish on it, her straight hair coiffured with the same precision as her eye makeup application. *A model, maybe?* Persi wondered.

"Nick and I are friends."

Ahh. Persi thought. *The plot thickens.*

"We were very close friends—intimate friends at one time. He's very good—exceptional, you know?"

Persi sipped her drink in response.

"But I was not ready to be serious and he went away. I want him back but he say no. I want to tell you—don't make my mistake. Or you will be sorry like me. Eh?" She shrugged her shoulders, took a long drag from the thin holder and left.

He's very good—exceptional, Persi mimicked in her mind. *I don't need you to tell me that, Francoise. Tell me something I don't know.* You can look at the brother and know that. . . well, a black woman can tell about a man's prowess and aptitude for the mattress mambo.

Persi pushed her drink away. *Okay, that's enough for you.* She stroked her hair. She'd missed her short, sassy cut but didn't trust many to cut it that short. French women loved their hair and she didn't want hers butchered, so a mid-length, blunt cut that she did herself and screwed into a fashionable Parisian chignon suited her. Nick noticed when she hadn't thought about it.

As the musicians took their places on the small stage, the crowd thundered in anticipation, straight through the introduction by the MC right up until the first note was struck. They played a nondescript, piano-lead in song that Persi did not know until Nick volleyed the trio into a sax-led "Betcha by Golly Wow." The crowd swayed with each note his firm, kissable lips blew from that cold, brass instrument. The crowd jumped to its feet at the last note. He grinned, bowed gracefully and winked at Persi before introducing a chanteuse. So captivated by Nick, Persi didn't catch her name, but paid close attention when Nick licked his reed and began an instrumental opening to "For All We Know." She was no Will Downing but her voice captured the essence of the lyrics and Nick's sax solo in the middle made Persi's body quiver and emit a thin film of pleasure. The piano, trumpet, and bass led on "Fever," another jazzy tune or two and then Nick played the one he'd played at Balzac's, "Nobody's Wanted More Than I Want You." It had been her favorite of that set back home and she looked at him, crossed her legs to keep pheromones from wafting toward him, and became totally spellbound by his presence. He commanded that sax and the crowd was bewitched by him note for soulful note. As the amber glow of the spotlight shone on his rock-hard jaw, he coaxed fluid, sensuous notes from the rigid brass and blanketed the audience with his magic. Like that scene in *West Side Story* between Tony and Maria at the dance, when everyone melted into prismatic darkness but the two of them—Persi felt that way; only she and Nick existed in this tiny club in Paris as he squeezed out notes just for her. Notes that she could feel wrap themselves around her like a loving embrace. She watched his lips perform oral aerobics on that mouthpiece and she wondered how they would perform on her . . . any part of her. Every part of her. His tapered fingers scaled syncopated rhythms along the sax, urging full, plump, sexy notes from its gold metal. His body swayed with bridled control and his eyes closed just as they would be if they made love, a tangle of long and luscious lashes cast a shadow on his cheekbones.

She came.

She shocked herself into a straight posture and almost cried out aloud.

ViVi with her timely G-spot shots and oversexed L.A. libido boasted of spontaneous orgasms while Doxie had told her about them when doing jumping jacks. Persi hadn't believed either of them . . . until now. Until Nick.

Wow, she thought, knowing hers were born of insouciant celibacy, horniness, and no male companion in the flesh for over nine months. She could have had a baby in the time she had not had sex. *Good to know my plumbing still works*, Persi dismissed, as she sprang to her feet with the audience at the song's end.

Persi stayed through the next three sets until four o'clock in the morning when she accompanied Nick to a jam session. The musicians played for two more hours before she and Nick decided to go to Chez Lautrec's for breakfast. Persi didn't want the night to end . . . well, the date to end. She enjoyed this jazzman's life although she knew it would not work for the Monday to Friday nine to five working girl, but she loved this Saturday night turned Sunday morning. Just as they were leaving the apartment, the sexy-voiced Francoise asked Nick, "Where are you staying, handsome?"

"Right now, the attic at the club."

"Eh!" Francoise pushed away the idea. "That is no place for you. You stay with me."

Persi could not believe the French woman's nerve. Right in front of her, asking Nick to come live with her? The bald-faced gall. Apparently, Francoise viewed Persi as no threat or consequence. Or maybe she didn't think Persi understood French. Persi paused . . . she was not Nick's girl; she was a casual friend.

"Thanks, but I'm checking into a hotel probably tonight."

"*Tres expensive*," a determined Francoise said. "My place— no charge."

"I have a spare bedroom," Persi offered in flawless French, wondering why her competitive streak reared its head right now.

Both Nick and Francoise turned to look at her.

"I have a two-bedroom flat. No one is using the second room now. You're welcome to it." Persi couldn't believe she invited such a move. "We Americans must stick together." Persi looked directly into Francoise's eyes. "No charge. No strings," Persi said, turning her gaze to Nick, who had a bemused smile playing about his lips.

"Why, thank you," Nick said. "I accept." He nodded agreeably.

"Great. Now you can buy me breakfast," Persi said turning to go. "I'm famished. Night, all!"

As the sober sunshine of a Sunday morning stung Persi's eyes on the way to Chez Lautrec's, she confessed, "I haven't been up this early on a Sunday since the Etienne children at the chateau."

They sat at a side table next to the window, ordered, ate, and spoke of the night they'd just shared. "You do that all the time?"

"I will for the first few weeks while I settle in with the guys. Jam sessions are thinly disguised rehearsals with tag-alongs."

"Is that what I am? A tag-along?"

"No. You're my landlady, right?" He tore off a piece of toast with perfect teeth as Persi watched his lips.

"No charge. Remember?" She smiled.

"You don't have to go through with it. I planned to get a hotel room tonight."

"Unnecessary. You need to save your money."

"For what?"

"For living. For your boys back home in Baltimore. So," she changed the subject, his finances or lack thereof were not her business. "After the first few weeks, what's your schedule?"

"Then, I just go for the sets. That kind of relentless night life can get old after a while."

"How long are you at Bricktop's?"

"Until Thanksgiving."

"Oh."

"Too long for a houseguest?"

"No. We'll figure it out when Doxie and Drew come back. Meanwhile, no jam sessions at my flat and no overnight female guests. Otherwise, you're as welcome as the rain in May to stay."

"Maybe I can repay your kindness with sightseeing jaunts to the countryside."

"That sounds good. I've got a few weeks to hunker down with the *Joie de Vivre* and then I get free time."

"I think you work too hard."

"You sound like Marius. He says I'm making them look bad. Americans have a different work ethic."

"Well, Europeans know how to balance and enjoy their lives. If you were in Spain you'd be taking a government, nationally sanctioned siesta everyday after lunch."

"Oh, really?"

"So what do you want to do today?"

"Honestly? Sleep. I don't know how you do it."

"Practice. Tell you what. You go get some sleep and I'll get my things, take care of a few errands and meet you at about four and we'll take it from there."

"Sounds perfect."

"I'm sure you'll be ready to eat again by then."

"You are getting to know me, aren't you, Nick Betancourt?"

Nick watched Persi write down the address and phone number on a piece of paper, trying not to be too excited about the prospect of seeing her every day for a few months. He observed how the morning sun caught in her sable-brunette hair, highlighted with a subtle golden copper he hadn't noticed before. He thought he'd memorized everything about her in her absence from him. The way her expressive, liquid brown eyes slanted above her cheekbones and lived under naturally arched eyebrows. Her slender features, painted with smooth cinnamon-ginger complexion, adorned here and there with a freckle. Her beautiful and interesting face bespoke of a full life outdoors in her tomboy days . . . surely the reason for her sturdy, well-proportioned body, honed by early athleticism or dance or both. Either she wore little make up or what she put on last night had vanished, but she wasn't the type who kept reapplying powder and blush, although she'd swiped a Chap Stick and lipstick across her mouth a few times. Natural beauty and a body—that body that wouldn't quit . . . the body where the thousand Nubian queens swayed her hips when she walked.

"Here you go." She tore off the piece of paper and handed it to him.

He just smiled at her.

"What?" she asked with a smile.

"Just happy we're going to be roomies. Give me a chance to get to know you better."

She looked at him quizzically.

He could see her mind working overtime . . . and that was her true appeal to him. In time, the face would fade and the body would sag, but her mind. Her brain would hold his interest for years to come . . . the way she thought. How and what she thought . . . and her confidence. That was why he just couldn't understand how she could be involved with the likes of Brad Shelton. Maybe his questions would be answered; maybe they wouldn't. Nick wasn't really concerned because Brad wasn't here with her now. Nick was—and he intended to make the most of it.

"Should I call first?" he asked, looking at the address.

"No. Just come by at four. You know where it is?"

"Exactly. High-rent district," he teased.

"You can thank the Etienne family for that."

She rose and he watched that shapely body, wrapped in animal-print chiffon, expose itself inch by inch; he helped her on with her coat.

"We'll get a key made for you while we're out."

"My very own key?"

"Well, you can't wake me up with your comings and goings at all hours of the night."

"I suppose not." His hands lingered as she shrugged on her raincoat.

She turned to him and said, "Well, see you at four."

"Four it is." He removed his hands and let them drop to his side.

"Bye." She kissed him quickly on the lips. "And thanks for a great Saturday night-Sunday morning."

"It ain't over yet."

Nick sat back down and waved at her as she passed the front window. *I volunteered to get him a key*, she thought. *What are you doing?* she asked herself as she ran across the street against the light. Despite his inquiries, in all those years she had never even hinted at giving Brad a key to her house. She rationalized that the two-bedroom Parisian flat wasn't her house; no mortgage and she herself was a temporary resident. It'd be nice to have company for a change, especially one who turned her on just by being. Tempted to call Doxie with the news that she now believed in spontaneous orgasms, she decided against it. She didn't want to define or explain the burgeoning relationship with Nick. She liked it being open and she was free to explore it without any comments from the peanut gallery. She was in Paris and whatever will be—will be.

She turned the corner and saw Collette and her young man standing in the street. *That was odd*, Persi noted. Sunday; maybe his business didn't operate on the seventh day. Persi scurried up her steps by twos, opened and shut her front door. She looked about the impressive room, then the dining room and went into the kitchen. All was well as she seldom used anything but the leather chair and table in the living room. She went into the spare bedroom and announced, "company's coming," as she surveyed the room. "Maybe if he's a good boy he can move into the mistress's room."

Once a week Magda cleaned the apartment; the maid took Persi's long body duvet for a regular pillow and put it across the top with the other pillows as she made her bed. Doxie called the body duvet Persi's substitute man. Maybe once Nick moved in and they explored their Parisian possibilities, Persi could store the duvet in the closet and cuddle up next to him instead.

She went into her bedroom, removed her clothes, washed her face, brushed her teeth, set her clock and climbed into bed, looking forward to this escapade. She deserved it and Lord knows needed it. She liked everything about him except his work ethic. No, that wasn't right, he had a good work ethic; it was his job. Persi couldn't see making a life with a man who played the saxophone for a living, put on karate tournaments, and had an ersatz construction firm. But she could surely play with him for as long as it fancied her—them both. In all her years, she'd never just gone for the animal magnetism of a guy. She'd been conditioned to always consider if he were her cerebral equal; would he be a good provider, was he of exceptional character, would he be able to engage her intellectually and emotionally—and maybe that was why she was alone. None of them measured up; Desi Fairchild came closest, but he did nothing for her sexually. She'd never had the liberty of going with a guy because she wanted to; because everything about him turned her on. She was always the Sinclairs' middle daughter; Diana's little sister and Athena's older sister; the smart black girl in chemistry at MIT, the ace researcher on stem cells at NIH . . . but now in Paris, she was on her own and . . . anonymous. Just a self-sufficient working woman with a hankering for a man she wouldn't date at home without a lot of questions on his pedigree, ambition, and goals. But here she could belly up to the smorgasbord that was sexy Nick Betancourt, strap on a bib, and eat to her fill. She rolled over on her side, looked at the empty space beside her, and let her hand glide across the pillow. *With any luck, he'll be sleeping here, beside me, in a few weeks,* was her last thought before she drifted off to sleep.

When her alarm sounded, Persi rose, showered, dressed in a pair of well-fitting, chocolate slacks and a casual silk blouse dipped in fall colors. Nick came on time. "Hi."

"Hi. Come on in." She watched him place his sax case on the floor, shrug off a shoulder strap, and drop a weathered, rich brown leather bag at his feet. "Is that it?"

"I'm a musician. I travel light. Me, my instrument, and my Gladstone have been all over the world. If I need more, I buy it. Like I think I might need a laptop soon."

"It's a ruggedly handsome piece of luggage," she said and thought, *Just like its owner.*

"Been everywhere with me." He took the two steps down. "May I?"

"Sure."

He roamed the flat and loved the apartment particularly his room: quiet, dark, and conducive to sleeping during the days. "Kitchen is small but I can make do."

"You cook?" She followed him in.

"Absolutely. I like this little rod-iron balcony."

"If you can call it that."

"Big enough for one. I can serenade the neighbors."

"The maid comes once a week on Wednesday unless directed otherwise."

"Maid service too?" he teased. "Only problem I see."

"What?"

"No shower in my bath. May I use yours?"

"Sure." Persi said, recalling that all her guests had.

He'd deposited his belongings in his room and they'd left the apartment, for a brisk walk to the Latin Quarter and one of Nick's favorite neighborhood restaurants off St. Germain De Pres on Rue L'Universite. With the nip of fall in the air, he had a taste for cassoulet. They sat at a small table for two in the window with the shimmer of a dim candle in their faces. They drank a robust cabernet, shared a salad, then an escargot appetizer, tore off pieces of crusty French bread eaten without *buerre* and used it to sop up the remnants of the baked meat-and-bean mixture. After three hours, they gathered their coats and strolled the winding, skinny streets characteristic of Paris. They browsed the bookshops, had a key made for him, and, unable to find Hershey's Kisses with Almonds for him, bought chocolate truffles and caramels from the confectioners and a few groceries to take back to the apartment. On the way home, they ambled across to Ile St. Louis, island home of Notre Dame, and got ice cream from Berthillon's. Persi had eaten the same dessert and flavor with Doxie and Drew. . . but it tasted very different with Nick.

As they sprinted toward the riverbank, Persi looped her arm through Nick's, like she'd done to Doxie. Thinking the gesture too much, once they reached the curb she attempted to withdraw it, but Nick held her close with his elbow, so she let her arm fall naturally with his as they walked along the Seine River home.

They climbed the steps and Nick said, "Let me try my key."

Even the way he slid the key into the hole turned Persi on.

The door whined open and Persi cut on the light as Nick

rounded the corner and put the milk and juice into the refrigerator, got a bowl for the fruit, and left the brioches and
croissants in their wrappings. "You don't have little critters,
do you?"

"Not that I know of."

"Well, I got to go. Ten o'clock. Showtime."

Persi had forgotten all about his working tonight. He'd seemed like he had all the time in the world.

"Sure you don't want to come?"

Oh, I want to come, but not to the club, she thought but said,
"I've got an early day tomorrow and for the next few weeks."

"You're always welcome. I guess we'll figure out our schedules as we go along."

"If you're quiet when you get home—that'll be enough for
me," she teased and pointed to her open fireplace that she
shared with the dining room.

"You'll probably be gone by the time I get home."

She chuckled and said, "If today was any indication—you're
right. I had a great time today."

"It's just the beginning. We'll have a lot to explore. You've
got quite a bit to learn about Paris and beyond." He stepped
in and kissed her lightly on the lips.

"Cassoulet," Persi identified playfully.

"Sweet dreams," he said as he grabbed his sax case, opened
the front door, and left.

She cut the light off and then thought better of it and left
it on for him. She walked into her room and glanced down
to the street and watched him walk away from her. "Humph,"
she said, and involuntarily thought of Brad; *men are always
walking away from me.* She watched Nick until he disappeared
around the corner. As she removed her blouse, her sight was
snagged by Colette across the street and her lover. *It was early,
only ten and he was leaving. Maybe I should stop trying to figure
them out,* Persi thought as she stripped, turned on the faucet,

and stepped into the water of her shower. *After all, I got a life in the making of my own.*

Over the next few weeks, Nick and Persi saw very little of each other. Their schedules did not jibe and they were more like ships passing in the night; the first weekend they were to drive to Versailles, Persi had gone to the chateau and ended up remaining until Sunday night, a cell phone apology Nick's only notice. During the days, he managed to make his presence known even if she did not see him—his evidence shone. Fresh flowers on the living room vase greeted her at the end of a long day with a Post-it note—*Sorry I missed you.* Or a cache of Granny Smith apples he'd picked up for her on the way home the night before. He'd bought a CD player and left his latest CD with a note—*Play me. Enjoy! Nick.* Or she'd come home after nine and smell something delicious greet her in the hallway and find that it was from her kitchen. Nick had cooked and left her a meal warming in the oven; the small kitchen table set with a note propped against a wine bottle. *Wish I was here. Enjoy! Nick.*

Persi put on his CD, ate, then showered and went to bed to his soothing, soulful sounds. Some nights she awoke and the light from the front room still burned, meaning Nick hadn't come home yet. Other nights it was out, meaning Nick was home—safe and sound—and when she rose in the morning his door was closed tightly against the stinging sunlight. So consumed with the final rollout for *Joie de Vivre* she hadn't time to consider or calibrate his comings and goings; he was always already gone for the evening when she arrived. Unlike any of her other guests, Persi was relieved that she didn't have to be responsible for Nick. He was no trouble. The Etiennes, on the other hand, were freaking out as the launch date grew closer. She'd spend much of her time mollifying and assuring them that the new venture would be successful and not compromise their name and stellar standing in the world of perfume. She'd even spent a few nights at the chateau missing Nick's essence—his jacket thrown over the back of a dining room chair, the window in the kitchen left slightly ajar—he liked fresh air; the nearly empty milk carton placed back in the refrigerator; a single hair he'd missed when cleaning the shower. Persi recalled the first time she saw the old-fashioned four-piece shave set, complete with badger brush, razor, matching stand, and bowl. She'd thought of her great-grandfather, who used to shave by frothing up his face with a generous lather from a brush, and then clean the shaving cream from his face with the razor, like a skiing elf slicing away icing from a cake. Great-grand used to clean his razor under running water between strokes, and Persi wondered if Nick did the same thing. She didn't know men still used these; over the years she'd only seen and heard the buzz of electric shavers.

One day, unable to stand the Etienne family when she arose the next morning, she'd driven all night to get home, arriving after midnight. She opened the door, staggered to her bed, and fallen asleep across the spread fully clothed. The next morning she'd gotten up, showered, washed her hair, and when she stepped out of the bathroom a bare-chested Nick stood before her. She screamed.

"Ooops," he said and left.

She gathered her robe and followed him out into the dining room area.

"I'll wait here for the cops," he teased, pulling on a robe. "Girl, you got pipes."

"I'm sorry," she chuckled. "You scared me to death. What are you doing—up?"

"It's a wrap until I return maybe next season."

"Oh, Nick. I meant to come and see you again but—"

"Hey, hey, it's okay. Don't sweat it."

"And I was going to ask you for a favor."

"Half my omelet?" he teased.

"You're in an awfully good mood for so early in the morning."

"Always am when I wow the crowd, leave them wanting more and know I don't have to go back and give it to them. . . until next time. Until I want to. What's the favor?" he asked.

"Will you escort me this weekend for the launch party at the Louvre?"

His face broke into a huge grin. "Do I need a tux?"

"I'm afraid so. But I can—"

"No sweat. I have to get a new one anyway."

"Oh, thank you. That's one less thing I have to worry about."

"Anything else I can get or do for you?" He looked at her, cinching the silk robe's belt around him.

"No, I got to get to gettin'." She glanced at her clock. "Do you need money for the tux or the name of a tailor?"

"I can handle it. Thanks." He watched her back into her room and close the door, surely forgetting that he could see her through the shared fireplace that ran from her room to the dining room. He watched her drop the robe and hoped that maybe she'd bend over and retrieve something from a drawer. She didn't.

"You have time for coffee or a brioche?"

"No thanks. I'll grab something on the way to the lab."

She reappeared in front of him in no time, dressed in a casually elegant, pinstriped suit over a gorgeous blouse with tiny polka dots and stylish, low-heeled shoes.

"That was fast." *The girl could rag,* he thought.

"I'm clean—that's all I'm going for now." She grabbed her briefcase and disappeared into the kitchen and plucked an apple from the bowl. "Thanks for the apples and the flowers and the CD and that cassoulet you fixed and—"

"You're welcome. One thing you have to do for me."

"What's that?" She stopped at the door.

"Now that my gig is over and once your weekend launch

party is a wrap—I want us to spend some time together." He walked up the steps and straightened the collar of her coat.

Momentarily, she lost herself in his soulful eyes and said, "You got a deal."

"Great." He kissed her quickly on the lips. "You look good. Have a great day." He opened the door for her.

"I'll try." She walked though and listened to it close behind her. *I'd have a better day if I could stay and play with what you're hiding under that silky robe,* she thought as she sauntered down the steps.

CHAPTER 13

The next two nights, Nick had been there when she returned from work but she was too exhausted to enjoy his company. The Saturday-night launch at the world-renowned Louvre
had arrived and, having to go early, she'd arranged to meet
him at the museum. She pulled her hair into a sleek chignon
at the base of her neck, slid the silky, Valentino gown she'd
splurged on from Evangeline's over her curves and donned
exquisite chandelier earrings of cut glass that dangled pro-
vocatively from her ears to collarbone. She slipped her legs,
as bare as her brown shoulders, in stiletto heels before she
checked her makeup for the last time. She gathered her purse
and opera cape, entered the limo, which deposited her at the
reception hall.

As intended, she appeared early enough to successfully calm
the Etienne family and present a visually stunning aura of
confidence and character. As she greeted society notables introduced by the Etiennes, seemingly everyone paused, the air
stilled and the room hushed. Persi looked in the direction that
drew all the attention. Her eyes converged with all others and
rested on the most gorgeous black man she'd ever seen in
her life. Tall, ruggedly handsome, regal, assured and, with his
mere presence, he took the breath of every woman in attendance.

"Damn! Who is that?" her assistant asked.

"My date," Persi said proudly. Unable to move, she witnessed his eyes casually comb the assemblage as they returned

the favor and, upon spotting her, she watched him walk toward her, a warm smile of recognition on his face. *Black Man Walking*, she thought. Is there anything more beautiful? More fundamentally cool? More sexy than a black man coming toward you with—whatever on his mind?

"Hi."

"Hi," she returned the greeting, their eyes locked into each others'.

He wrestled his gaze away, long enough to take in her form in that gown. "You look terrific." He spun her around once and the strapless, magenta-aubergine gown flared out dramatically before resting by her matching five-inch stilettos.

"You clean up pretty good yourself," she countered. They smiled and kissed hello before the curious crowd came closer.

"You've grown taller," he teased.

"I'm your height now."

"A perfect fit."

Both the perfume line and Nick Betancourt sensationalized the event. He paid just the right amount of attention to her without being cloying or underfoot. They sipped champagne retrieved from the trays of traveling, liveried waiters and danced to the music of the chamber orchestra discreetly nestled in the alcove.

"This is a ritzy, classy little affair," Nick whispered into her ear as they swayed.

"It's not Bricktop's, but regardless—you are still the hit."

A smile dimpled his cheeks.

How can a man this fine still blush when being paid a compliment, Persi wondered. Perhaps that was his sensual appeal. She knew every woman in here—old or young—wanted him, and Persi wanted them to think she had him.

As the launch drew to a close, Persi's face washed with relief.

"Excellent. You made it a smashing success," Nick told her.

"I'm glad it's over," Persi admitted, taking his hand.

"Did I tell you how stunning you look in that gown?" He ran his thumb under his bottom lip, turned her once, and the gown behaved as trained.

"Why, yes you did."

"No other woman could wear that color but you."

"I have to thank my natural melanin for being able to pull it off." She threw her bare shoulder at him and said, "I still think you are the most beautiful specimen here, sir. And I am not alone. You know what they are calling you? *Noire Prince. Chocolat Prince.*"

"I like that. It matches what they call you, *Noire Beaute.*"

"I thought it was *Noire Cygne.*"

"The Black Swan? Because you gracefully glide across a room."

"Why don't we get out of here?"

"I thought you'd never ask."

He kissed her hand and led her through the diminishing crowd, disappearing from the ball like Prince Charming with his Cinderella. "Let's go this way," he suggested, placing her opera cape around her and pulling her toward the Champs-Elysées.

Persi had successfully avoided the famous avenue since her first visit when she'd wished Brad here.

Nick walked backward, facing her. "C'mon," he urged her on and dismissed the limo.

She couldn't resist as she followed him. He held her hand tightly and she loved the feel of his warm skin in hers, the nearness and scent of him, the feel of walking in tandem with another human being—a man—a gorgeous man in a tux that fit him just right.

When they reached the center of the boulevard, Nick stopped. Persi followed suit. "Look. I wanted you to see this."

He stepped aside and Persi tore her gaze from his handsome face and, laid out before her, like a string of fallen stars from the sky, was the Champs-Elysées lit up for Christmas. Ablaze in a stream of silver lights from where they stood—all the way to the Arc de Triomphe.

Her heart sprang forth and her hands flew to her lips. "Oh, my, it's beautiful!"

She giggled, laughed and walked forward without him. The entire street, the trees, and the storefronts were all wrapped in silver lights; Disneyland and planetarium combined. She felt six years old again, when her mother and father had taken the family to downtown D.C. on the mall to see the Christmas tree lights by the White House, but this was spectacular!

He grinned and followed her steps, laughing because she was laughing; happy because she was happy. She ran back, took his hand, and urged him on up the boulevard. Something that didn't cost him a dime gave her immeasurable pleasure. "I had them do this just for you," he teased.

Joyful tears leaked from her eyes. "You know, I believe you." She felt embarrassed. Her heart filled like it never had.

"Hey. It's okay. It's Christmastime in Paris."

He took her face in his hands, wiped away the tears from her eyes with his thumbs and kissed her gently on the lips. Then their exploring tongues found one another's. Somewhere in the recesses of her mind, Persi realized that she had become one of those obnoxious couples she'd detested . . . with the public displays of affections in the middle of the street; kissing, hugging, cuddling, fondling; oblivious to everyone around them. She savored the taste of his tongue, which sent shivers down her spine, the feel of his body against hers, the touch of his hands under her coat, around her waist, next to her skin and she could give a flying fig about the anonymous folks in the street.

"C'mon, let's walk up to the Arc before we go home."

"I like the sound of that," she said to him.

They sauntered arm in arm up, the monochromatic silver lights serving as the spotlight to their destination. This was the Champs she'd avoided because of the painful, forlorn thoughts; of the never-made memoires with Brad. This was the honeymoon walk she and Brad should have taken. But Persi realized that this walk had been *her* dream and she reclaimed it. She could determine and cast whomever she wanted in her dream and she was gleeful to insert Nick's face, body, and being. He smiled back at her and set Persi's heart afire with joy and desire.

Arm in arm, they walked the winter wonderland of two thousand sycamore trees lit by tiny, fallen stars. When they reached the Arc de Triomphe, Persi turned into Nick and they kissed amid the magical lights, all traces of other folk peeled away, leaving just them in the midst of quiet cacophony. She felt little-girl happy; shoe-shopping happy; Obama-being-elected-the-forty-fourth-president-of-the-United–States-happy. She squeezed Nick's waist tighter and felt his nature rise.

When they pulled apart Persi smiled up at him and said, "I'm glad you're here with me."

"Me too." He grinned and his dimple agreed as well. "It's chilly. Let's get you home. You want a cab or can you still walk on those five-inch stilts?"

"With you beside me—I can glide home."

As he slid his key into the keyhole, she rested on his back and when the door sprang open they tumbled in. Laughingly, Nick flicked on the CD player as Persi shed her coat. Nick followed suit and asked, "Would you like some wine to warm your chilled bones?"

The voices of Donny Hathaway and Roberta Flack filled the dark room singing, "The Closer I Get To You."

"Actually, I think a dance will serve us just fine."

"May I?"

"Please."

Nick came to Persi and slid his hands around her waist
and she melted into him, relishing the feel of him against
her. She felt as nervous as a nineteen-year-old virgin, yet as
calm as a seasoned courtesan, loving that Nick could conjure
up this sweet chaos within her. His hands moved across her
bare back and she reciprocated under his cummerbund and
tux shirt as they danced, becoming one. He lifted her chin to
him and they kissed like old, experienced lovers who knew
one another's language. He pressed his lips firmly upon hers
and their tongues tangled deliciously, releasing scents and
sounds. As they swayed to the music, igniting themselves into
urgency, his hand unzipped the back of her gown. The expensive frock puddled around her "do me" heels, revealing pert
breasts tilted upward, offering themselves to his lips. His eyes
glistened with the sight of them and that dimple appeared as
he gathered her in his arms and carried her to the settee. He
gently placed her upon the elegant silk antique and she began
undressing him, removing the last barrier of cloth between
them. His exquisite muscular torso shone bare in the muted
pitch for her to see and appreciate. She watched him shed his
boxer briefs and his projectile stood at attention; ready, willing, and whittled against the semidarkness. He filled her senses; sight, sound, touch and it was time to taste again. They
inhaled one another in a kiss as he raised her body, grabbed
her magenta thong and, with one twist of his wrist, tore it
off. "I'll get you a new one," he whispered huskily in her ear
before he suckled her raisin-hard nipple, flicking, licking and
moaning, proceeding toward her apex of womanhood.

As she felt his taunt, satiny skin beneath her fingertips, he
seemed determined to pleasure her pulsating, swollen bud.
She thought she heard Phyllis Hyman from the CD, voicing
her sentiments, "Nobody's Wanted More Than I Want You,"
as the sweet melee of her mind, body, and soul transported

her into another realm, while she could still feel his expert use of both hands, lips, and tongue. Just before she let the shoreline of reality completely go, her checklist sanity reared its logical head as she murmured into his ear, "You have a condom."

"A condom?" He repeated. "Now, you are worried about a condom?" He panted and looked at her.

Not the response she expected or wanted. "Damn, Nick," came out on a rush of frustrated breath. She pushed him back and wrestled herself from beneath him, sat up on the couch, crossed her legs, and held her head. She couldn't believe his ill-preparedness as she tried to harness her desire for him, suppress months of deprivation and internally talk her body in from the ledge of ecstasy. She hadn't primed herself to just fool around, she wanted the whole megillah—a marathon with several innings; she wanted to feel him inside of her. He stroked her and she held up her hands resistantly, even his touch a tease for what she had in mind; all or nothing.

"I never said I didn't have one. I just said 'now you ask about a condom?'" He grinned and held the foil ticket to paradise in his hand.

"Oh, you got jokes? You think this is funny?"

He smiled mischievously and answered by planting little kisses on her lips, face, trailing down to her breasts and as he did, Persi forgot his little ruse in the middle of their lovemaking and thought, *This man has too much control,* as she began to sink beneath his skillful hands, lips, and tongue anew. In no time she was back where they'd started; overwhelmed by his sexual prowess and ability to satisfy her fully . . . all at once. When desire seized him and he could no longer play with her, he took her derriere adeptly in his palms and twisted her gently so that his latex-wrapped, mahogany manhood entered her fully, completely, expertly while massaging the outer and inner of her female being simultaneously. With each magnificent thrust, Persi thought she would dissolve into passion itself and never be heard from again. *What a way to go*, Persi thought as they climaxed together.

On this winter's night in a second-story flat in Paris, France, these two lovers, coated in their salty emissions, lay exhausted and sated. They panted until one could speak. "Well, Nick Betancourt," she breathed in jagged bursts. "You sure know how to show a girl a good time."

She felt his sweaty belly laugh against hers before he spoke. "Couldn't have done it without you."

Persi wondered if there was anything that Nick could not do well. After making love with him, she had a new respect for musicians. She'd never had any man show such agility in the use of both hands—working independently yet in concert as they extracted pure pleasure from every pore and synapse of her body. If Brad had been good and Rucker great, then Nick was *gifted*; he had gifted hands . . . gifted lips, body . . . gifted timing . . . and this was just their first foray into the land of lovin'.

As they lay waiting for the pulsating to subside, he had not left her yet. Persi savored the feel of him still lingering in her as Nick had no place else to go or be except with her. She stroked his back and smiled in the quasi-darkness as Donny Hathaway crooned "You Were Meant For Me."

"Penny for you thoughts," he said as he kissed the side of her face.

"I was thinking . . . what a perfect song."

"I did that, you know." He looked into her shining, liquid-brown eyes.

"I don't doubt that at all." She accepted his peck of a kiss on her lips. Like the first time she tasted chocolate ice cream and liked it, she wanted more. "Are you ready to go again?"

He looked at her and the most beguiling smile graced his lips followed by his dimple.

"This time . . . it's my turn. For me to pleasure you. You relax and enjoy. Let's freshen up and meet in the bedroom in fifteen minutes," she said.

"Don't have to tell me twice."

He was on time. Persi entered the bedroom and noticed three fresh condoms on the nightstand. She smiled and strattled him where he lay. This time, she gave as good as she got; this time it was less urgent and more playful; this time they enjoyed several positions before ending in the same rhythmic, juicy, orgasmic paradise. They fell into a deep sleep.

After a few hours, Persi stretched, pulled up the comforter against the chill and rolled over in the wee morning hours. "Ahh!' she gasped aloud.

She'd forgotten there was a man in her bed. He barely stirred as he turned toward her, his hand seeking the warm space between her legs. She let him, smiled with him as he found his target, moaned appreciatively and settled back down to sleep.

She looked at him as the light from the street lamp surrendered his shadowed image feature by feature. She absorbed his handsome face and those luscious lips that enchanted her beyond belief. She'd had overnight guests before, but she'd been ready for them to leave come morning light; Brad, she'd wanted to stay, but he couldn't. For the first time to remember, Persi had a man she wanted to stay and he could; a full-time man—a 24-7 man that she now knew could be addictive. He answered to no wife or children or entourage. He could stay as long as she chose and hold her . . . play with her, sample and explore all the love she had to offer. She listened to the rise and fall of his breath; slow, steady, and content—music to her ears. She eased out of bed to relieve herself, washed her hands and by habit, on the way back to bed, gazed out the window. From across the square, Collette was saying good-bye to her man and Persi couldn't help but think, *I got a man too.*

As she watched her neighbor separate from her man, Nick eased up behind her. He slid his hands around her waist and pulled her gently into his firm body and burgeoning third leg. Persi relaxed into him and smiled, reveling in the feel of his hardening manhood and knowing she would extract and deflate its essence in a matter of moments.

"Can't sleep?" he asked quietly, as his hands moved down to play with her swelling bud.

"Hum. Guess I'm just greedy." She turned into him. "It's been awhile."

"Help is here." He bent and kissed her as he cupped her derriere in his palms, squeezed her once, and lifted her to him. She wrapped her legs around his waist and he walked around the bed where they made love once again.

The next morning Persi woke up in bed alone and thought she'd dreamed all of yesterday until she heard the water running in the bathroom. She pulled on her discarded nightgown and entered the door in time to see Nick shaving.

"Morning, sunshine," he said.

His chest, bare and beautiful; a towel casually cinched below his navel. Persi touched his shoulders as she went and sat on the commode facing him. With her back against the wall she smiled at him.

"How you feeling this morning?"

"Right as rain," she said. "And you?"

"Never better." He dabbed the tip of her nose with shaving cream. "I was going to whip up breakfast but we're out of reinforcements. If we're going to have nights like last night—"

"We are."

"Then we need provisions."

He sliced away the white foam, revealing his brown face and rinsed the razor under the running water, just like her great-grand. He bent to rinse off his entire face and she grabbed her toothbrush, put paste on it, and began brushing. He splashed on aftershave and she bent over to spit.

"Mercy, girl," he looked at her backfield aptly presented to him. "You can't bend over like that and not expect me to react."

"Aren't you tired yet?" she teased with a grin, shrinking out of her nightgown top, displaying her breasts so she could bathe.

"I'd never get tried of that." His pools of darkness shone with desire.

She turned on the shower and stepped into the warm water.

"Mind if I join you?"

"Haven't you already showered?"

"But I'm about to need another one."

"Then. . . come in." She smiled and he laughed and they made wet, soapy love.

They finally managed to leave the house and walked to the outdoor flower market. "Every five days a lady needs fresh flowers," he proclaimed, paying the vendor for an armful of sunflowers and poppies.

"What are we going to do for Thanksgiving? They celebrate that over here?"

"Pilgrims and such? No. But we can find a turkey and cook."

"Okay." She picked up a tomato and then took three more.

"I do have a lot to be thankful for this year."

"Me too," she agreed with a quick kiss.

"Love those chocolate-toffee kisses."

When they returned home, his phone rang and so did hers. They laughed and answered their respective devices.

"Doxie girl, how you doing?" Persi said.

"So how did the launch go?"

Persi told her and they spoke of nothing in general and Drew in particular. "When are you all coming back? Before or after your ski trip?" Persi asked as she put the groceries away. Nick helped and tapped her on the derriere as he winked and left the small kitchen.

"You aren't terribly disappointed? I thought she'd like going to a European ski resort but her friends aren't there."

"She is an only child, Doxie."

"She doesn't realize how lucky she is. So what are you going to do for the holidays without us?"

"I'll manage."

"I feel just awful. I thought about letting her go and I'd come see you. You're all alone, far away from home for the first time at Christmas and—"

"I'll be fine," Persi reassured her friend.

"We didn't get to see you last Christmas or New Year's."

"That was awful." Persi thought of how horrible that "lost holiday" had been for her. "But this Christmas is going to be . . . awesome."

"Yeah? You gonna put on Donny Hathaway's 'This Christmas' and go for it, huh?"

"Maybe."

"Persi? You got a man!"

"Let's just say I am seeing someone, and I think you'd approve."

"Who? That fine Marius?"

"That man is married and I ain't touching him with a ten-foot pole."

"Who? Who? Who?"

"You sound like an owl." She eased open the kitchen door to see Nick still on his phone. Then she felt silly, like a teenager telling a girlfriend a deep, dark secret.

"Rucker Jackman? I knew that marriage wouldn't last. Oh, Desi Fairchild."

"What? No. Can you go any further back in time? Nick," she said.

"Nick who? Betancourt? Omygod! I *knew* you all were right for each other. I knew it. I told you so. Didn't I tell you so?"

"Yes, you did."

"This is fabulous! Girl, he is fine. ViVi will be so disappointed."

"Don't tell anyone, Doxie."

"Why? I'd shout it from the rooftops if he was my man."

"We're just friends. We'll see how it pans out."

"You not hittin' that?"

"Doxie-Fitz, how can you be so crass—"

"Only with you 'cause I know how prim and proper you are . . . but Persi, if you don't, somebody else will. Not me because of our pact and all, but ViVi would."

"The only reason I told you is because I didn't want you to feel bad about me being alone for the holidays. Now you know I won't."

"Shoot. I'm not sad, I'm jealous. Drew and I might never get back there again if he's there. And I wouldn't be mad at you either."

The old friends talked for another twenty minutes. When Persi hung up and reentered the living room, Nick was stoking the fire and talking about asphalt and construction stuff again. She went into the bedroom and changed her clothes.

Nick came in and swooped her up. She giggled. "You better watch your back, old man."

"Old man?" He tickled her. "We're going to have company for Thanksgiving."

"Really. Who?"

"My brother and his wife. Remember DeDe?"

"Great. They can have your old room 'cause it's you and me, babe, in here . . . all night long."

"They stay at their usual, Hotel Mimeaux."

She looked at how happy the news made him.

"They won't be staying long. They like to be home in Hawaii for Christmas with the kids. Maybe he's finally found out something about the Betancourt side of the family."

"Where you come from and who your people are, is important."

"Not to him. I'm the only one interested. He said he knew he and DeDe weren't related and their kids are normal. . . so he didn't need to know anything else."

"He sounds like a real character and I'm looking forward to meeting him."

"He wants to meet you too. I'm sure DeDe has filled him in. You know, how you mistook her for my girl."

"I did not—"

"Don't lie to me, woman. I can't abide by lying," he said playfully, but his eyes held a certain seriousness.

"I promise. I will never intentionally lie to you, Nick."

"I don't like unintentional lies either."

"I won't lie to you, period. Is that better?"

"Much."

They stayed in that night, cooked, ate in front of the living room fire, and fell asleep in each other's arms. Persi left Nick in bed as she went to work the next day. When she came home early, she could hear him playing "Nature Boy" out the balcony of the kitchen.

"Hey, sunshine, what are you doing home so early?" He put his sax down and went to kiss her on the lips.

Persi looked up at Madame Dumas's window, just as it closed. "Are you flirting with that old lady and her cat again?"

"She keeps me on the straight and narrow. You got flowers."

"Oh, really!" Persi wondered how she missed the cache of the glorious exotic floral arrangement. "From whom?"

"Don't know. The card wasn't addressed to me."

Persi felt a sinking feeling waft over her. It wouldn't be Brad. *Please don't be Brad,* she prayed as she opened the sealed envelope. "It's Jean-Luc, congratulating me on the successful launch and thanking me for making his family more money then he ever could. He is redeemed." She passed Nick the card as she went over and sniffed the fragrance. "That was nice. And you were right. I don't know about the work ethic of the aristocracy in France."

"What do you mean?"

"I went in and once they found out I was there, they sent me home. It seems that they don't expect me back until after the holidays and then only a few days a week until I've finalized the trajectory execution of my new ideas."

"The European way. It's about quality of output and not quantity in hours spent in the office. And you've served them up *beaucoup de bucks*."

"That's what they said. The presales on my new line is making millions for them and they haven't begun to explore the international market. Said I deserve a great break. To reconstitute my mind."

"Ah. Then bring your fertile mind with new ideas back to them after you take a great, creative break. I like the way they think. More productive. They're not changing your name to Etienne are they?" He gathered her in his arms. "That means we have to do something outlandish for the holidays. Want to go skiing?"

"Not much of a skier. But I can chalet with the best of them."

"I got it. Monte Carlo. We can train through Provence, stop at the various towns along the way and wind up at Monaco. There's never a bad time to visit that gem, although it suffocates under the huge crowd of tourists in July and August and when they have the race, but even in winter it can be nice and sunny as long as le mistral winds don't tunnel down from the mountains. What do you say?"

"That sounds like a fabulous idea," she agreed, happy that he hadn't suggested a Caribbean island like Brad would have. Anything would beat the meltdown she had last yuletide season.

"You know what I'd like to do? Sail the Greek islands while we're at it," he said.

"Okay, let's stay in the vicinity. South of France, even Italy, but Greece is too far. I'd like to keep my job, thank you," she said. "Your work ethic is so interesting."

"Do you work to live or live to work?"

"I work to eat and pay my bills."

"Okay. We'll do the Greek islands in the spring. There's plenty of inspiration in the Aegean Sea."

"You know where I get my inspiration?" she asked, sidling up to him. "Right now? Right here?"

"Where?" He played along, watching her undo the drawstring to his sweatpants.

Persi smiled as she witnessed his manhood rise to her touch.

"That's what I like. A man I can count on."

"I aim to please."

"Ooh la-la!"

CHAPTER 14

The Hawaii Betancourts landed and slept off the jet lag before meeting Nick and Persi for a late dinner at Chez Janou. DeDe remained as warm as Persi remembered and his brother, Brock, who DeDe called BB, was an older version of Nick; slimmer, with more character lines, amicable but more reserved. After the four spooned out the chocolate mousse portions they wanted, served in the same bowl in which it had been cooked, they decided to walk it off. Persi steered them to her favorite place, the magical, stunningly illuminated Champs-Elysées. Aptly shouldered against the frigid night air, they all began walking with their respective partners, but near the shops Persi walked arm in arm with DeDe and the guys settled in behind them.

"Even for this little bit of time here, my kids expect gifts from Paris," DeDe said. "They can't wear but so much in that tropical sun."

"Well, 'tis the season."

"You sure you don't want us to bring anything tomorrow?"

"Only your appetites."

They both looked back at the laughing brothers.

"'Tis the season for family," Persi said. "I've never seen Nick happier."

"I was about to say the same thing," DeDe said, "And it ain't about being with his big brother either." She eyed Persi knowingly. "I'm glad you all got together," DeDe continued. "I could tell my 'baby brother' was in to you when I met you back in D.C."

"Are you psychic?" Persi teased.

"No. I saw it plain."

"Well, he had a gig here at Bricktop's and he called me."

"Hmm. Who was here first? You or him?"

"I guess I was."

"I bet you the price of this trip that once he found that out he called Bricktop's."

"He plays all over the country . . . the world."

"Oh, make no mistake, he's good. I know they were glad to hear from him. But he picked Paris because of you."

"No."

"Why is that surprising?"

Persi looked back at him. He winked.

"No shame in his game," DeDe said. "I admire a man who knows what he wants and goes after it—whatever 'it' may be." DeDe grinned. "I'm happy for him, so is BB. Lawd, we sound like the Winans, don't we? DeDe and BB."

The women laughed.

"It beats what they used to call him, especially my parents . . . those 'bad Betancourt boys.' But I fell for mine when I was still going to an all-girl Catholic high school in Baltimore. My parents were outdone; they paid tuition for a private school so I wouldn't meet bad boys. He wasn't really; it took awhile for him and them to believe it. But I knew all along he was the one for me. Still is, though he drives me crazy at times. It's been a lot of years and I'm hoping for a lot more. Driving me crazy keeps my blood circulating."

"I can't conceive of Nick being 'bad.' He said he was angry."

"Not criminal bad . . . no records or reform school, but mischievous is a better description. Ms. Althea wasn't going to stand for having bad boys. They kept good grades and that set them apart from the real bad boys of the neighborhood. From time to time, my BB skipped school, but Nick went to school and kept himself busy afterward. But I've never described Nick as happy . . . until now." She squeezed Persi's arm.

"I'm sure there have been other women."

"Plenty. All sizes, shapes, ethnicities. But not one that made him happy like he is now. Not that BB and I can recall. Until you—with the guy's name," DeDe teased and said, "so much so that now BB thought it was as good a time to discuss a little family business."

"Oh, really. Nothing serious, I hope. Everyone is healthy and not broke."

"Nothing like that, but something that should be said sooner rather than later. I thought years sooner but you'll find these Betancourt boys have minds of their own."

"That's a good thing."

"If they listened to everybody else BB would never have gone into ATM machines or Nick into parking lots."

"True. They think outside the box," Persi said and realized that Nick wasn't in construction, but parking lots. Sax player, karate man, and parking lots. *A jack of all trades*, Persi thought. *I wonder what else I'll discover about him.*

The two couples reached the Arc de Triomphe and walked up the steps, bypassing the museum level, to the very top. They looked at the matrix of Paris laid out like spokes to a wheel, all lit up, but the Champs-Elysées beamed electric. Persi stood nestled in Nick's arms when DeDe and Brock approached.

"We're going to head on back to the hotel so we can be civil tomorrow," DeDe said.

"It was great meeting you, Persi," Brock said.

"You too."

"Hope you don't mind us opting for a hotel instead of staying with you but I like waking up with the Eiffel Tower between my legs. Metaphorically speaking," said DeDe.

"You could have me—"

"Hey, man! You just met her, let's keep it light," Nick

warned his older brother about being raunchy in front of Persi.

"Oh. Sorry," Brock apologized to Persi with that seductive Betancourt grin.

"I don't know why I put up with him," DeDe said. "Last chance—can we bring anything tomorrow?"

"Nope. And you have Nick to thank for scrounging up a turkey. We almost had a Thanksgiving goose."

"Thank you in advance Nick," DeDe said. "Night."

"*Bonsoir.*"

Cheek kisses circulated all around before a final wave. Persi and Nick turned back to the lights below. He surrounded her body with his, protecting her from the elements.

"Cold?"

"Not now."

"You and DeDe seemed to be having fun."

"So did you and your brother." She nuzzled against him and waved down at the couple who'd reached the street, watching them cross as they headed back to their hotel.

"He says he has never seen me happier."

"Really? That's what DeDe said. Think they talk to one another?" Persi ribbed. She then turned to Nick and looked into his face, reflecting the magical silver lights. "What do you say?"

"About what?"

"Have you been happier?"

"Hmm." He paused as if he were thinking the question over. "Maybe a time or two," he joked. "But not recently. Not so completely. Or effortlessly."

Persi looked up into his shining eyes. They were both still and quiet. As if on the verge of some revelation neither were ready to say or accept from the other. As if doing so would ruin the momentum of their perfect current existence. Bruised and battered hearts don't give freely. Persi thought of all the times, the years, Brad said he loved her. Told her they'd be married and honeymoon in Paris. But with this man who had never declared his love or promised her anything, Persi felt more unspoken affection from him than she ever had with Brad. Brad made her heart and soul lonely; Nick made them sing. "Actions speak louder than words," her mother used to say.

"Let's go home."

Persi and Nick made love that evening and again the next morning, sleeping late but rising in time to put the turkey in the oven. Nick went for bread and rolls at the famous Poilane's then to a *pasterrie*, hopefully, for a pear tart and profiteroles. Upon his return he opened the door on an absolutely perfectly decorated table. Ignoring the eight chairs around the table, Persi had set only the four nearest the kitchen and the second bedroom with an exquisite embroidered tablecloth, gold chargers with rustic plates, and wine and water goblets and gold silverware sat on matching cloth napkins. The centerpiece was the armful of sunflowers he'd bought; the table resplendent in golds, oranges and reds looking as if it were ready for a magazine shoot to grace the cover of some ritzy monthly publication. In all his days from childhood to now, Nick had never seen such a magnificently appointed, yet cozy and welcoming table . . . for him. For his family. Over the years, he'd looked from the outside in on such tables surrounded by happy families, but never for the Betancourts. Nick stood in awe.

"Hey," Persi said, coming in from the kitchen with a tray of foie gras and an assortment of cheeses. "What'd you get us for dessert?" She eyed the signature pistaschio-colored box. "Ooo. Laduree."

She placed the two plates on the living room table and took his packages from him.

"This is really nice," Nick finally managed, not trusting himself to say more.

"You like? I found all this stuff in that butler's closet over there. You'd be amazed at what the Etiennes have packed away." Persi left again and called, "could you open the wine?"

Nick came into the kitchen, got the corkscrew and the wine.

"Oooh, yummy," she said when she saw the goodies he'd purchased. "Good choices."

"I think the best choice I've made in a long time is right here," Nick said and grabbed Persi.

She squealed with laughter. Nick's semi-serious gaze calmed her. They kissed and the door knocker clanged. "Company's here," Persi said.

"Brother never did have timing worth a damn," Nick said, breaking his embrace.

"Be nice." She blew him a kiss.

DeDe and Brock came in with two bottles of wine and a pumpkin tart.

"My goodness, you didn't tell me you lived in a museum," DeDe said as she handed Nick her coat and descended the two steps, admiring the elegant surroundings. Persi gave DeDe the tour while the guys poured wine for everyone. "Look at this table!" DeDe exclaimed. "This is just beautiful, Persi."

They sat, ate hors d'oeuvres and sipped the wine until Persi announced dinner was ready.

"Nick, as host, you sit at the head. Everyone else just grab a seat," Persi directed.

"That bird looks great," Brock said. "My wife has attributes but cookin' ain't one of 'em." DeDe smacked him playfully with a napkin as Nick extended his hand to those next to him and all followed suit.

He bowed his head and said, "We are truly thankful for *this* day and all those to come. Please continue to bless and keep us in your good grace, whether we be near or far. Thank you for allowing me to share my life with my brother, his wife, and . . . Persi." His voice added her name just above a revered whisper.

Persi glanced up at him and their eyes met, each holding the other. "Amen."

She gave his hand a squeeze before letting go and going for the bread. Nick watched his brother and sister-in-law gleefully reach for the dishes. He wanted to just pause and take in the scene, but in classic Nick Betancourt, he clapped his hands, grabbed the carving tools and asked, "Now who wants what?"

Persi placed the hot rolls on the table and put a CD on the player.

"Who is that?" Brock teased. "I believe that is the best sax player I've ever heard!"

"You ain't never lied," Nick joked as he passed Brock a drumstick.

The four devoured the delicious American fare—scalloped potatoes, candied yams, brussel-sprouts sautéed in bacon in lieu of greens, and steamed cabbage with carrots, followed by French desserts, all accompanied by laughter and lies from childhood that rounded out this Thanksgiving celebration. "Oh man, I bought something," Brock said, going to the closet and pulling out a CD from his coat pocket. "Bam! I trust you will allow this to be played."

"The Drifters," Nick identified with a wide grin and put it on immediately.

"Your man has a sho'nuff Drifter jones," DeDe said to Persi, as they all watched, waiting for Nick to identify the first selection.

He grabbed Persi's hand and they began dancing. DeDe and Brock joined in as they did the old school cha-cha.

"'This Magic Moment,'" Brock said.

"*Everything I want I have*," Nick sang, "*as long as I'm holding you tight.*"

On "Save the Last Dance for Me," Nick twirled and spun Persi around the room like they were flamenco dancers. They laughed and finished the two bottles of wine brought, finished two more, followed by aperitifs, then coffee, strong and black. "Like I like my men," DeDe toasted and invited Persi souvenir shopping tomorrow. "While the guys do whatever."

Well after midnight, their company left with goody bags in tow and Persi and Nick set about cleaning up. He brought things in from the table while Persi wrapped and tried to figure out where to put the few leftovers. Nick began to wash the dishes, plunging his hands into the hot, soapy water.

"Well, Mr. Betancourt." Persi eased up behind him, enveloping her body with his. "I think our first dinner party was a success."

"Thanks to you." He couldn't vocalize how much it meant to him.

She lay her head on his back and let his movements ripple through her—like spoon-dancing. "Thanks to us both. We work well together."

He turned to her, wiped his hands on a nearby dish towel, and held her. "You look tired."

"I could sleep."

Persi managed to complete her nighttime regimen and climbed into bed, but Nick was too keyed-up to sleep. After almost four decades, he'd finally had the kind of Thanksgiving he'd dreamed of. All those years ago in his childhood, the fourth Thursday in November was just another day to eat alone . . . without your brother who ran in the streets . . . without your mother who was working so she could feed you hot dogs or pork chops the other 364 days . . . but you couldn't have both food *and* her. From the second-floor apartment on the back, he could see many a holiday feast but not one with his family. He'd shared a hot plate meal with Ulysses a few times but getting home before his mother did. In high school, he'd gone down to the mission a couple of years to volunteer to serve meals, and then during college he'd been invited to the homes of classmates with elaborate Thanksgiving productions—but they were not his family. As an adult professional, he'd spent many a fourth Thursday in November in exotic locales . . . where the food and the woman of the season were equally hot, but it wasn't a traditional Thanksgiving.

Nick went over to the bedroom window and looked back at Persi's sleeping form. But on this night—this Thanksgiving near his fortieth year on earth—he finally had a Thanksgiving he could call his own, with his people and his family, with stories and antics from his childhood and teen years. This woman had given that to him. She couldn't know how it touched his heart. She'd taken it for granted because her life experience growing up was different from his. But here she was . . . happy to have made him so. Oblivious as to how much he treasured it—how much he treasured her.

She stirred and turned over, her hand reaching for him in the night. He eased into bed and gathered her to him and she fell back into a deep sleep. Nick could not remember ever being this content. The thought of a future with her and their adding other little Betancourts warmed his heart and loins in a way no other women ever had. His brother and DeDe had been right. Nick Betancourt was happy—truly so, for the first time in his life. Nothing was going to rob him of this feeling ever.

The next morning, Persi dressed warmly for the nippy weather and waited on the platform for the train. She intentionally stood in the sun, basking in its rays and getting her daily dose of vitamin D. She was in good time for meeting DeDe at Galleries Lafayette's food court then onto Printemps, festively glowing in hot pink lights for Christmas. She looked at a woman she thought she knew. Persi smiled, the woman did not. When the train came, Persi boarded, sitting across from the unfriendly woman and watching the Parisian underground stops pass.

With a jolt, Persi realized why the woman looked familiar.

It was Collette, her neighbor from across the street with the husband who worked the early hours. Persi eyed the woman and noticed that up close she was older than Persi thought. She had a thin, fit body but her face had signs of age and sun damage . . . makeup lodged in the crow's-feet around her eyes and dark circles underneath. No work, no makeup, was Persi's rule. *Maybe Collette was meeting her husband for a little tête-à-tête,*" Persi thought.

Persi's stop came and she met DeDe, who greeted her with the double-cheek kisses and looped her arm though Persi's. Luckily for Persi, the French were into quality not quantity in Christmas gifts, so Persi had little to do now or later, but she accompanied DeDe on a mission for perfect treasures, which she'd ship to Hawaii. Persi perferred to discover perfect gifts for those she loved, like the hot-pink parka with a fur-trimmed hood and polka-dot lining for Drew she would have never found if she set out for it, and an English driving cap and matching leather gloves for Nick.

"Now if I could just find his beloved Hershey's Chocolate Kisses with Almonds. I'd truly be done," Persi lamented. "Best chocolate in the world here and he wants his imported from Pennsylvania," Persi teased. "That's my man."

DeDe chuckled and made the last purchase for her sister. "How about your sisters?"

"Every female on my list is getting something Etienne from the *Joie de Vivre* line."

"Oh. Can I get on that list? It smells divine."

"Sure. Know what I want in return for imported parfum?"

DeDe stopped and said, "I'm afraid to ask?"

"A shipment of Hershey's Chocolate Kisses. It'll make him happy."

"Is that all?"

They sat in a bistro by the window, storing their purchases against the glass pane. "Thanks for coming with me, Persi. If

I'd brought the kids I would have been ice-skating on the top of the Eiffel Tower and dragged into every decorated carousel line from here to Versailles."

The ladies ate and talked until DeDe had to get back to the hotel and pack since they were leaving early tomorrow morning. "We got a long way to go."

They exchanged double-cheek kisses, promised to keep in touch, and Persi was invited to Kaua'i with Nick's next visit. DeDe made Persi miss Doxie, so as she walked back to the subway she dialed her friend and got her voice mail.

"Hey, girl. I guess you and Drew are on the slopes. Hope you are having a ball. Miss you both. Talk to you next week."

There's just no substitute for your best girlfriend, Persi thought.

Since she'd dragged Drew's parka this far, Persi toyed with the idea of strolling the Champs to see the lights again. She bought and popped a chocolate truffle into her mouth for company and sauntered up the famed boulevard. Just ahead of her she saw a man with a familiar gait and when he turned to the side, she almost choked on the bonbon. Brad. Brad Shelton here, walking up the streets of Paris with another woman! Was that Trish or was it some other woman he'd brought? Without thinking she rushed up behind him. When he looked to the side, he saw Persi so close he swiveled to look at her.

"Oh. *Pardon moi.* I thought you were someone else." She apologized to him and his lady. *What the hell?* she asked herself as she backed away. *You crazy nut. What if it had been him? What were you going to do? Scream at him for coming to Paris without you? For bringing his wife or your replacement—wanting to face the woman who could get him to Paris when you could not. Either way, you shouldn't care. Why do you still care? You've got a man who treats you like no other. Why waste one nanosecond thinking about Brad Shelton? This is just crazy,* she thought.

"You have an odd, emotional, adolescent attachment to

that man," Doxie's words rushed back to her. She lived in Paris, France with a wonderful man. *What is wrong with me?* she wondered. She needed another script. A reset button. A heartbroken awareness and restless yearning tore at her flesh and she just wished she was thirty again and had never gotten involved with a married man. *Stupid and reckless behavior,* she self-admonished.

Persi decided to walk back home, let the cold weather clear her head, and get her thoughts together before she saw Nick. He knew how to love—where and for how long. Brad wasn't that talented in bed, but all the similarities they shared outside of bed made him a good catch; Brad, the reverse of the pure sexual enjoyment of Rucker Jackman. Brad epitomized her fantasy representation of what her life should be . . . could be. But Nick, with his gifted hands, was her current reality and hit all the marks . . . in, out, above, and below the bedroom. She was having the best time ever with him, even if there was no longevity to Nick . . . no "death do you part" permanence. Unfortunately, Nick Betancourt wouldn't play back in D.C.: who are his people, where are they from, from what university did they graduate? Who do they know? How are they connected? Persi questioned making a life with a saxophone playing, karate man who had parking lots . . . no matter how well he rocked her world. But she intended to enjoy every millisecond with him, for however long they piqued each other's interest. An uncomplicated, easy, and comfortable relationship with no professations or promises; no broken trusts. When it was over, she'd miss him but her heart would remember how amazing it was when they were together . . . and smile.

A car blew its horn, stopping Persi at the curb before she crossed the street. She'd put faith in Brad that he wouldn't hurt her—that he loved her and was truthful. But what riled Persi most, besides being dumped by her married lover, there was no vindication. As a scientist she dealt in formulas and proving theorems right or wrong. But she hadn't received her absoultion like Prince Charles and Camilla Parker Bowles or Mary Kay Letourneau, the teacher jailed for sleeping with her student and now husband as they'd ended up happily married, proving society wrong. Instead Persi had fallen on the seedy side of an affair where she'd been discarded by a man who said they'd get married; trusted a man who'd proven he could not be every time he laid with her. Brad performed true to form, but she'd had the unrealistic fairy tale ending—from honeymoon to heartbreak. Like Doxie said, "if he does it *with* you, he'll do it *to* you." Dump his wife for you; dump you for his wife. A lose-lose situation. In the end, they only shared stolen moments and made promises life wouldn't let them keep.

Persi's mind reeled.

She stopped at the corner, gathered her thoughts, and demanded that Brad be left here by the Pont Neuf Bridge. He'd snatched enough of her time and she determined not to give him another minute. She breathed in the crisp, chilled autumn air, hoisted Drew's parka over her shoulder, shifted her other bags, and began to walk.

"I'm going home to Nick," she said aloud and the sound of his name on her tongue, the recollection of his arms wrapped around her in bed, the touch of his lips on her skin, the sight of his love muscle at the ready to please her in unimaginable ways, put a satisfied smile on her face. By the time she reached her door, finagled the key into the slot and threw it open, she sang out, "Honey, I'm home!"

She dropped the packages, took off her coat, and hung it in the closet. "Nick?" she called out again, stepping out of her shoes. She peered into the dark bedrooms and rounded to the kitchen. The stove was cold. *He must still be with Brock,* she thought. She hung up Drew's parka and hid his cap and gloves in her bedroom closet. She took a shower, dressed in a tantalizing animal-print gown with matching robe, ate a piece of yuletide log with a glass of milk and dozed on the couch by the fire. She jerked awake. The fire had diminished to a flicker. The CD had stopped playing, all the lights were on and it was nearly midnight. Persi checked her cell phone. No messages. DeDe and Brock were flying out early tomorrow. Could the brothers still be out? Persi called the hotel. DeDe answered, "Hello?"

Persi became immediately alarmed as DeDe sounded fast asleep.

"Hey," Persi began. "I hate to call so late but is Brock there?"

"Yeah."

"When did he get there?"

"About four hours ago . . . why?"

"Nick isn't home, he hasn't called and that's very unusual. He'd call if he were going to stop off somewhere else. Did Nick say he was going to do something else? Does Brock have any idea where he could be? Was Nick all right when he left him?" All tumbled out in one sentence.

"Brock," DeDe said to her husband, nudging him awake. "Was Nick okay when you left him? Did he say where he was going?"

"Oh God, oh God, oh God," Persi prayed.

"Hey Persi," Brock's groggy voice came over the line. "He was fine. Maybe he went to get a drink."

"He has drinks here. It doesn't make sense. He's never done this before. He hasn't called."

"You want us to come over?"

"No. Why? Have a safe flight," she dismissed. The last thing she needed was a vigil and two people to entertain in the process. She looked out of the window. "Nick, where are you?" Why the silent treatment? Friends don't do this to one another. Should she call the police? The hospitals? Francoise?

Stop it, Persi. You trust Nick; he's never given you reason not to.

She threw more logs on the fire and as she stoked and re-vived the flames, wondered if Brock said something about her. Maybe Brock didn't like her. Could Brock know Brad? Could Nick have left her? Persi ran to the second bedroom and his sax case and Gladstone bag were still there. *He'd never leave his sax*, Persi thought. He would leave me . . . he wouldn't be the first—he'd be the second.

She heard the front open and ran toward the sound. There stood Nick. She rushed into his arms. "I was so worried. Are you all right?" Involuntary tears leaked from her eyes at the sheer relief of seeing him all in one piece.

"I'm sorry. Time just got away from me," he said quietly. He brushed the side of her face with tiny kisses.

"What happened? Brock said he left you four hours ago. Are you hungry?"

He smiled weakly and said, "One question at a time, sun-shine."

He went over to the fire and held out his hands as Persi slid his jacket from him. "You sure look good to me," he said as he sat in the big leather chair. Persi threw his jacket over the couch and crawled up into his arms.

"You sure feel good to me," she said. "Don't ever do that again! I'll be old before my time with worry."

Nick wasn't used to having someone worry about him. Or wait up for him without it feeling controlling or cloying; usu-ally signaling it was time for him to cut a relationship loose. But he welcomed it with Persi. It felt genuine and natural. "I promise."

"So tell me the where and why."

He supposed if he were to really have a chance with this woman, he'd have to open up; something he was not used to doing . . . but he'd never felt this way about a woman before. Opening up, sharing his thoughts might be the price he had to pay to keep her.

"My brother gave me some news today I hadn't expected. And I needed some time to deal with it. So I took a walk and sorted out my feelings about it."

Persi sat up and looked into his eyes. "Anything you want to discuss?"

He visibly winced and Persi restated her question. "Anything I can do to make it better?"

He smiled. "You already have. Just knowing you were here waiting for me gave me a reason to come home."

Hard as it was, Persi decided not to pry and then remembered something about "family business". . . but no one was ill or broke.

"It's about Ulysses Thigmont," he began slowly.

"The one the boys club is named after?"

"Yes. Seems he was more than just my mentor. Or a man in the neighborhood who took an interest in me."

Persi held his eyes in a soft, loving gaze as he gently pushed hair out of her face.

"Seems he was related," Nick said quietly. "My paternal uncle."

"What?"

"My paternal grandmother grew tired of life in Baltimore and when a fast-talking, slick-haired man from New Orleans came to town, she left a young Ulysses and her husband for greener pastures only to return twelve years later with Xavier Betancourt in tow."

Persi remained silent and non–judgmental.

"He and my father were half-brothers. Same mother. With over a decade's difference in age, Ulysses Thigmont became a father figure to my daddy, but by that time, Xavier's ways were set. All his young life he was itching to get back to Louisiana. A good-looking ladies man, he married my mother, Althea Brock, but once the responsibility of two sons—Brock and me—got to chaffing him around the collar, he headed back to New Orleans."

Persi gently laid her head on Nick's chest.

"That's why my mother was so dead against Ulysses having anything to do with me or Brock. Those two brothers couldn't have been more different, but my mother was taking no chances with her sons." He held Persi closely and stroked her bare arm while looking at the fire.

"She never knew how much that man saved me from myself and the neighborhood. He never laid a hand on me, but he would speak to me plain. 'I saw what you did to that machine. You think that was smart?' I'd reply 'no, sir,' and he'd ask, 'Then why did you do it? Must be tired of freedom and want to go to the reformatory 'cause that's where you headed less'n you mend your ways.' When I acted surprised he said, 'Don't do the crime if you can't do the time.'"

Nick chuckled, remembering. "'If'n I saw you, so did somebody else. Better watch it, boy. Your mama be tore up from the floor up if'n you get sent away.'"

Persi liked hearing Nick imitate the man who meant so much to him. She listened to Nick's words and felt his heart beating as she watched the fire dance before her.

"That's what a man is supposed to teach his son. Right from wrong. Which hand to shake and which hand to hold." He fell silent taking a trip, denying Persi access, but she understood.

"Boy, he loved the Drifters," Nick said, smiling. "Back in those days, older folks looked out for younger ones all the time. The ones with working parents." Nick thought of how intellectually he understood why breakfast might be the only time he saw his mother for the day unless he stayed up past midnight. He'd be with Ulysses or at the rec center—anywhere but to go home to an empty and cold house. No light left on, no warm meals in the kitchen. He'd begun with piano lessons but gravitated to the sax. . . the sax he could carry to bed with him and eventually warm its cold brass for company in the late hours when he heard gunshots or fights; men fighting men, men fighting women. Chaos, when he longed for quiet.

Intellectually, he knew that his mother volunteered to work holidays for time and a half plus bringing home fancy leftover food. Emotionally, he just missed her being there. When he came home here now, he relished pausing at the end of the street and looking up at the second floor-window where Persi had a light burning. Burning for him. As a kid, no one left a light on for him. Now somebody cared about his safe return home. He'd forgotten all about it, the way you do when you grow up and move on with your life. But that first night, when Persi had left the light on for him, it reminded him of what he'd missed—what he yearned for. He didn't fault his mother, who did her very best—better than best. But there were holes of childhood that couldn't be plugged up, so you just repress them and grow up . . . until that right person comes along . . . exposes and then fills your holes to overflowing.

Nick stroked Persi back.

"Seems my daddy came back when he became ill and none of his fancy ladies had time for an old, broke, sick man. Althea Brock Betancourt didn't have time for him either. She said she'd brought her sons this far without him and she was going to continue to do the same and his presence would only upset her household."

"Can you understand why?" Persi spoke for the first time.

"Unfortunately, I do. You reap what you sow. What goes around comes around. All the old clichés apply, but the intellectual and emotion always fought with me. My mother wasn't going to have a man come back into our house and, after ten years, try to be a father over two teenage boys. That had *disaster* written all over it."

He touched the top of her head with his lips. "Seems 'Uncle' Ulysses took Xavier in but his liver was shot from the fast life, no insurance and a quick death . . . but I remember . . ."

Nick sat up just a little. "I remember once going by Ulysses's apartment and seeing a guy Ulysses had given up his bed to. I asked who he was and Ulysses said, 'Nobody.'" Nick chuckled wryly. "'Nobody you have to worry about. You on your way to karate class?' He'd stood in my line of vision so I couldn't see past him. I'm sure that was my daddy."

Nick's eyes were dry but Persi's brightened with unfallen tears.

"I didn't know my own daddy. Never saw him to remember. Wouldn't recognize him."

Persi raised up and looked into his eyes and said, "He had to have some good qualities, Nick. Because you do."

"Well, the half-brothers with the wayward mother were both my role models; one on how to be, and the other one, how not." He sighed heavily. "I can't wait to be a father."

"You'll be excellent as you are with everything you do in spite of—not because of— and you're young yet." She grinned.

His handsome face dimpled with a smile. He almost said it. *I love you.* It was on the tip of his tongue but he couldn't. Wouldn't. He didn't want to tell her on the heels of such a negative conversation. His eyes glistened with love and he kissed her. That would have to do for now.

"What else would you have wanted? Would knowing who he was . . . who either of them were, have changed you?"

Nick ran his thumbnail across his bottom lip in his classic gesture. "I dunno know."

"Not so much your father, but Ulysses. You took care of him when he got sick, visited him. Paid his hospital bills. Got him a full military burial at Arlington Cemetery. Built and dedicated a boys club to him and put on a karate tournament in his honor. And—"

She loved summoning a smile from him.

"And you give out scholarships in his name for those who get accepted to a four-year college."

"Not as many as I'd like. I've got to work on getting those numbers up."

"Do you hear yourself?" Persi asked, hands perched on his hips. "What else could you have done for the man? I bet he is smiling down on you from up in heaven."

"Oh, he's the one—" He grabbed her so she tumbled upon him. "Who sent me you. Heaven-sent you are."

They laughed and kissed. "You know what else my brother said to me?"

"What?"

"He said that he's known this for over twenty years, but this was the first time he felt comfortable enough to tell me because I had you." He looked at her. "I think that thick-headed scoundrel is right for a change." He caressed her face in his hands. "I am glad that you are here with me when I found out. With you, I think I can take or do just about anything."

"You did pretty well before I came along."

"True," he teased and she pinch-twisted his side playfully. "Thank you, Persi," he said seriously.

"That's what friends are for. You are a very special man, Nick Betancourt."

"How about one of those chocolate kisses of yours," he said, puckering up.

"Are you hungry? Do you want to eat or are you ready for bed?" She stood before him.

"Where I come from they are one in the same," he joked. "I'll be in in a minute."

"Okay."

He followed the sight of a thousand Nubians in her hips sway beneath an animal-print gown and watched her disappear through the bedroom door. *That wasn't so bad*, he thought. *Sharing*. New, awkward, but he supposed he'd get better at it. He promised himself that he would never shut her out. All these years it had been mainly him and his thoughts.

He loved his mother and brother, but Nick was the stable, level-headed one in the family who always did the right thing, who maintained the positive attitude and never let the world around him get him down. During his melancholia, he preferred solitude, emerging only when his naturally jovial, self-confident self—the one his family knew, loved, expected, and relied on, reemerged. But now he had a woman with whom he could share his deepest feelings and she did not judge or think ill of him. Now he had a woman who looked on the bright side for him or with him. He had Persi Sinclair. And he loved her. *This is the one true thing I know for sure,* he thought as he rose, checked the front door, cut off the light, and followed her to bed . . . into the safety of her arms.

CHAPTER 15

Out of habit, Persi went to work again and even fewer people were there. She left her Christmas list, addresses, and fragrance assignments for her United States friends. In the old days Persi hadn't cared about other personnel and would have stayed on the job, savoring the quiet and busying herself with solitary formulas. But now she had a man. A man she'd left snug and warm in bed this morning. She decided to leave work and have lunch with him. She called him and asked, "Hey, handsome. What are you up to?"

"Six-two, one-ninety of prime, lean all male."

Persi laughed. "No argument from me. Want to meet me for lunch? My treat?"

"Love to. Lautrec's in an hour?"

"See you then."

"Can't wait."

She walked from the train and the harsh sunshine assaulted her eyes as the wind whipped her cheeks into a healthy red. She shrouded her coat collar around her neck and bent into the cold, breathing puffs of vapor. At Lautrec's, she passed the Parisians who preferred to sit outside in the sun regardless of the frigid temperatures, entered the nearly empty café, and took a secluded table for two around from the bar, next to the window so she could see Nick approach. She removed her coat and hung it on the rack, blew her hot breath into her freezing hands, and ordered coffee. When it came, she warmed her palms with the heat from the plain white cup and basked in the filtered sunshine streaking through the glass pane.

She was about to text Doxie when she spotted him. A lone, tall, gorgeous black man stopped by the light in a knot of white folks. He stood erect, patiently, as he waited for the signal to change and Persi smiled as her heart, recognizing he was near, began to do flips. She held her chin in her hand, knuckles against her mouth as she absorbed his essence from afar.

The light shone green and, like an athletic sprinter, he outdistanced the others in two strides. Long coat open, flapping in the wind like a superhero's cape, sunglasses set on regal cheekbones, jeans that fit in all the right places, boots, and those succulent lips. *BMW*, Persi thought. Black Man Walking; a sublime aphrodisiac, foreplay in and of itself. There are few things more distinguishable, more exciting than watching a black man move with the authority of a gunslinger in the Old West—half swagger, half sway, and all cool–suggesting a confidence and ease borne of experience in and out of the bedroom. From Denzel to President Obama and every smooth brother in-between, none had a thing on Nick Betancourt. He commanded attention by just being. She'd seen him do it at the perfume launch, she'd seen women on the street glower appreciatively at his form, seen women at the club take their own private trips with him as he blew into his sax . . . and now, as he came toward her, Persi remembered all the love they made. Seeing him freed all the chemicals in her body: dopamine, oxytocin, and adrenaline, internally collided in sweet chaos clamoring for release. She could feel him, inch by inch lower his weight *onto* her body, *into* her body as she lay bare, writhing, accepting all he had to offer her; placing pleasure with his measured lips and extracting every response of satisfaction from her. He brought out the need in her like no other, as they made love—on top of love. Her pulse quickened, her spine shivered, and her deep desire overruled her senses.

She came. Her body straightened at the surprise of it and then relaxed as she allowed the natural, rhythmic pulsating to ebb and flow.

When he spotted her sitting there, his face broke into a dimpled smile. He removed his sunglasses, pushed the door open, his eyelashes entering before he did. Persi caught the reflection of herself in his liquid eyes—she was glowingly blissful. Their unspoken love language beamed loudly.

Flushed and embarrassed, she accepted his firm, chilly lips on hers as she held his face in her hands and opened her mouth, flicking her tongue with his. He knew what she'd done. "You've started without me," he teased mischievously.

"I've finished," she confessed, her eyes glazed with contentment.

"That hardly seems fair, now does it?" He was still standing as he looked around and behind their table spotted a thick, green velvet curtain, doubling as a draped divider.

"What are you thinking?"

"I'm thinking I've got to play catch-up. C'mon." He winked, walked backward, and disappeared behind the heavy curtain into an adjacent closet.

"Nick!" Persi protested quietly. She looked around at the waiters, attending customers on the outside. She heard her chair scrape over the tiled floor and knew what she was going to do. She gave a quick look around and vanished behind the curtain and into the door left ajar.

In one swift motion, Nick closed the closet door, locked it, and proceeded to kiss her fervently. Kisses she was unable to resist. Long, languid, urgent kisses full of play and promise. Breasts sprung from silky confines, a skirt was raised, panties lowered, jeans unzipped, a condom donned, and nirvana sought and achieved in timeless ecstasy.

As the pulsating subsided they giggled like teenagers in the school cloakroom. "Now that's better. We're even now," he said.

"Not quite," she joked.

"Not finished? 'Cause I'm a full-service operation. I don't want to ever serve you half-stepping. You are such a bad influence on me," Nick teased as they laughed and rearranged themselves.

"I never did anything like this before you. I usually have a bed and privacy."

"See what you've missed? Wait until we take our trip. It may take us days to get there . . . on the road, off the road to make love, on the road, off the road." He helped her with her blouse. "Let's go home and finish this up right."

"We've got to stop and get some cream, coffee, bread—"

"Aw, woman. You are too practical for me. Let's get to goin' then." Nick eased the door open to see if the coast was clear. He then walked Persi out and laid fifty dollars in euros on the table for her cup of coffee. She looked at him quizzically and he said, "Hey, it was worth it."

The next day, Persi returned to work out of sheer habit and determination. There were fewer folks at the lab than before. She knew where to find Nick but decided not to call him first, but just go home for lunch; she didn't want to be banned from all the cafés in Paris. She trained home again, bought an armful of sunflowers at the market, and walked the few blocks to their apartment. She loved Paris even in the winter; regardless of the season, the city always had something delicious for the eyes, nose or ears around every corner. As she turned down her street she smelled something delectable, and thought maybe they'd go out for lunch if he promised to be good.

Persi climbed the steps and opened the door into the sight of warm embers blazing in the fireplace, a small, unadorned tree on the console by the window and the Whispers singing "Happy Holidays."

"*Déjà vu!* Lunch with you," she sang out, placing the flowers on the table, removing her coat, hanging it in the closet just as Nick rounded the corner from the kitchen. "Is this what you do when I'm slaving at work? Have a party?"

"'Tis the season," Nick said as he carefully enveloped her in his arms, a spoon poised in midair. "I knew you'd be home for lunch. It's Christmastime and no one is at work."

"Something smells good. Is that us?"

"Ummhumm."

"My not working is okay by me as long as the check keeps clearing," Persi said, kissing him on the lips. "You taste good. Do you know that I got a bonus from the Etiennes big enough to pay off my mortgage on my house at home? It's in euros so perhaps I shouldn't brag too soon."

"Hey, if you're good, you're good. Taste," he said, offering her a spoonful of lobster and corn chowder.

"Umm. Good! You made that?"

"From scratch. For our lunch. Thought we'd eat, maybe take in a little ice-skating on top of the Eiffel Tower or in front of the Hotel DeVille, whichever is less crowded, and then buy a few ornaments for our tree."

"Sounds great."

"Then we'll decorate and plan our holiday getaway."

"Still Monaco, right?"

"Well, I'll be doing a command performance on Christmas Eve at Bricktop's so I can pay for this getaway, but then we can go. By way of Provence?"

"I hear Provence is beautiful anytime of year."

"The eating is a gastronome's delight. Definitely Avignon, Marseille; maybe Cannes, St. Tropez, and Nice—"

"That's a lot of places."

"Usually you just go to one hotel and jump off to the surrounding towns that are only about an hour away, but we don't have that kind of time. We got to keep moving forward. We've got to be in Monaco by New Year's Eve."

"I hear they have spectacular fireworks. How much time do we have?"

"We'll do what we can and save the rest for springtime. I really want us to do a bike tour this summer," he mused.

Persi smiled at the prospect of longevity.

He put the spoon down and picked up his sax. "They wanted me for December thirty-first but we'll be in Monaco."

"You're good, can you be in two places at one time?" she teased, wrapping her arms around his neck as he cleaned his instrument.

"We can take the high-speed train to Avignon."

"Let's slow it down," she nuzzled him. "Quality instead of quantity. These places have been here for centuries, they're not going anywhere. Why don't we drive?"

His face split into a wide grin. "I got time. We can stop at Dijon and Lyon on the way to say, Marseilles, train it the rest of the way and rail back. Monaco's only a few hours back to Paris by train."

"Then that's it." She looked lovingly into his eyes. "Merry Christmas."

He stared back at her and answered, "Happy New Year."

Donny Hathaway's voice surrounded them with "This Christmas." Nick grabbed her hand and they began dancing. "Now. . . it is officially Christmas," she declared.

During the days leading up to Christmas Eve, Persi spent her time talking to and texting everyone from the States, while Nick spoke to his brother, DeDe, and their kids. He also talked to his mother, some of his friends, including KC, the Thigmont Scholarship Foundation reps, and his parking lot people. He'd hung up saying that after trudging down to the cyber café and having to wait almost twenty minutes, he was going to break down and get a laptop and make a visit home a couple of times early next year to get things situated.

"If D.C. is one of the stops, you can stay in my house," Persi offered as she hit the play button on the CD player.

"I got a place. Thanks. But I'd better check on your place for you."

Persi looked over at him. "You got a place in D.C.?"

"Um-hum," he said, checking the reed fit on his sax. "In Georgetown. That's where I was on my way to when . . . I met you at the restaurant."

"Okay, you have a house in Chicago—"

"That's a condo."

"A house in Georgetown and on the Severn River."

"A condo in L.A. and that's it. Regardless of the economy, real estate is always a viable commodity and I prefer to stay in familiar surroundings than a hotel when on business. You know I travel light, so I have everything I need at the respective addresses."

"So you have an address everywhere where you have a business?"

"Nothing extravagant, just functional. Like the Georgetown house is small. You've seen those tiny-tiny houses, but it is Georgetown—location, location, location. Good for re-sale."

She tried to comprehend it all as he blew into his sax and quickly added, "Did you know Georgetown used to be a black neighborhood back in the day?"

Persi looked at him with exasperation and said, "I know you aren't going to give a fourth- gen, native Washingtonian a history lesson on black Georgetown? It's where my people started and when folk realized its prized location, they pushed us to southwest, where my clan got off and went up to LeDroit Park, while the mainstream were herded on through northeast then southeast Washington into Maryland's Prince George's County, which has the most affluent black community in the nation."

Nick looked at her and said, "Thanks."

"But I digress. Back to the topic at hand—so what kind of car do your drive? A Ferrari?"

"No car. I take subways or cabs. Too much maintenance on a car and parking is always a hassle wherever I go."

"What else don't I know about you?" she wondered aloud.

"That I'm crazy about you," he said, wetting the reed with those lips and tongue before launching into his rendition of "Fever."

They joined friends of his for a Christmas Eve feast before Nick predictably blew them away at Bricktop's that evening with the dreamy, romantic "I Can Only Give You Love That Lasts Forever," and the bittersweet "What Kind of Fool Am I?"

The couple begged off early, went home, made love, and fell to sleep, arising early the next morning with all the excitement of two kids on Christmas Day. Hung in the socks over the fireplace, Nick discovered a huge box of condoms.

"For our trip," Persi teased.

"We'll need more than this!"

Matching cashmere socks for them both lay under the tree as well as a black terry robe, slippers, a travel shaving set, his classic driver's cap with matching leather gloves, and a pair of aviator glasses. The box of "imported" Hershey's Kisses with nuts thrilled him most. "These and the box of condoms. I'm ready to go!"

For her, a supply of chocolate, cocoa-wrapped truffles and three shortie, cami PJs and robe sets, and sexy lingerie. "Is this for you or me?"

For us both," he said, yo-yo'ing his eyebrows.

Bath salts and an exquisite gold-linked bracelet rounded out her yuletide booty. They both cooked breakfast, cleaned up, then set out on their three-hour adventure toward the warmth of southern France.

Nick donned his glasses and the cap and struck a manly pose. Persi swooned. The glasses set high on his cheekbones and formed perfect symmetry down the lines of his slim face, to his masculine, rock-hard, square jaw; all a prop for hall-marking those loving lips. "I dunno. Maybe I shouldn've given you those gifts."

"Why?"

"You are looking too fine, Mr. B."

As they headed south from Paris for Dijon, they ran into rain, pulled over, fogged up the windows as they made love and, once their passion had been satisfied and the sun returned, got back on the road. "Is it getting warm or is it just the company I'm keeping?" Persi said.

"Just so we outrun le mistral, we'll be fine."

"A little wind will never dampen our spirits."

They passed barren, winter-frozen fields that in a matter of months would be lit with purple lavender and splashed with huge, smiling sunflowers. The sky blazed clear, the sunshine strong and bright, and the smell earthy with the pregnant promise of unparalleled flora that can only been seen while driving through the French countryside. Undulating hills in the distance added to the romance that they were just two drifters off to see what the world had to offer. In their leisurely trek, they stopped and drank local wine at a roadside café run by a family, and dined on peasant food devoid of elegance but full of taste. Further along they stopped at an antique shop.

"This is gorgeous. Persi," Nick called as she looked at an antique amoire. "Wouldn't this billiard table look fantastic in the game room at the Severn house? I'd have it resurfaced and add new pockets."

"Look at that carving? Mahogany? I wonder how old it is?" Persi commented.

"It is sixteenth-century," the saleswoman said in French. "Used in the court of Louis the Fourteenth."

"How much?" Nick asked her.

When she answered, Persi noted, "That's somebody's yearly salary."

"If you send it to the United States for free, you have a sale."

Persi opened her mouth to object and then remembered she didn't have a nickel in that quarter and turned from them both, leaving Nick to his negotiations. Persi meandered around the shop noticing the ancient artifacts that in the States would be in the Smithsonian, but here, folks lived among them like treasured old friends. Nick and the saleswoman laughed so Persi rejoined them. Upon her approach, he opened his arms and placed one lovingly around her shoulder, while giving the saleswoman the Severn address.

"Who's going to be there to accept it?" Persi asked. "You don't want a million-dollar ancient artifact laying on the porch until you get there," she teased.

"Can I ship it to your house?"

"I wouldn't trust a bouquet of flowers to last on my stoop. Send it to Doxie's. I'll tell her it's coming. She can place it next to my car in her garage until you get there."

"Garage. Maybe she can put it in the house. No offense."

"None taken. It is worth more than my car."

Persi wondered about Nick's fiscal responsibility. He had multiple houses, no car, and splurged on things like this. She finally realized that it wasn't her business; they had no bills together and his credit didn't impact hers. Of course, he could just get a gig at Bricktop's or other clubs around the country and pay off any of his expensive but tasteful peccadilloes? She bet he didn't have credit-card debt but his method of budgeting would drive her absolutely nuts. Must be the musician in him—the freestyle flow of things. Or the yin-yang of martial arts. Or the freedom of having no chick, no child to be responsible for. Just him—loosey-goosey. It made for exciting, adventurous times, but wouldn't do for a stable lifestyle.

He put his classic cap on backward, so the bill was in the back and only his handsome face was aimed toward the windshield. With his own bebop spin on wearing the cap and his aviator glasses he looked like a model for an album cover Persi would like to own. He grinned over at her and winked as they pulled off. "Next stop, Dijon," he announced. "The ancient capital of Burgundy and home of . . .?"

"Mustard!" They laughed and she continued, "which refers to the method of mustard making and not the origin of the seeds."

"And the kir cocktail was invented here."

"Do tell. Black currants, crème de cassis. And Aligote red burgundy wine."

"That's what I like about you. More than a pretty face and a great body."

They arrived at dusk, checked into their hotel, and dined at a restaurant two doors down with signature regional dishes and wines; she ordered *boeuf bourguignon* with a pinot noir red wine and he, *oeufs en meurettes* with a chardonnay to comple-ment his poached eggs. They strolled off their meal walking through the lime and chestnut-lined paths of Cours du Parc, a park that dated back to 1671; they passed one of France's oldest museums, Museum Beaux-Arts, then the elegant Pal-ace of Dukes, and lastly, the opulent 1614 mansion that was now the Hotel de Vogue. Upon reaching their hotel, the couple went in, fell into bed and asleep. They rose the next morning, had breakfast, and went on a wine-tasting tour to one of the vineyards outside of town. They returned to Cen-tre Ville, the town center, and promenaded through the his-toric and scenic sights that escaped the bombing during the last two wars, and finished up with Porte Guillaume, and the Gothic-styled Cathedral of Saint Benigne, which dated from the fourteenth century—its abbey now converted into an ar-chaeology museum. That night they ate at another equally sat-isfying restaurant, walked and returned to their hotel to make love like the resident Dijonnais, slept, rose and ate before getting on the road again. With only a hundred and thirty-some miles to their next destination, they were in no hurry.

On the way to Lyon, Persi packed a picnic of burgundy wine, *jambon persillé*, crusty French bread, and Dijon mustard. They pulled off the beaten path and found a secluded alcove of chestnut trees near the Rhone River where they stretched a blanket under the heat of the day and placed the thin slices of ham on the bed of richly textured bread and grainy mustard and dined in one of nature's sanctuaries. They spent only one night in Lyon, the third largest city in France, before they were on their way to Avignon; stopping at Saint Etienne for a few hours out of sheer curiosity. As they sped down the road, the couple laughed, sang or fell into companionable silence, Persi reaching over and tenderly scratching the back of Nick's neck as they drove to their next destination.

When Nick pulled into Avignon, Persi took notice. An enchanting calliope of colors and textures titillated her senses and she knew she was nearing the presence of the masters, those painters who captured and ushered in the era called Impressionism. They pulled into 14 Place Crillon and their Hotel D'Europe, built in 1580 as the Marquis de Gravesons' palace, which was converted to a hotel in 1799.

As Nick checked in, Persi walked around this oasis of elegance and sophistication in the midst of the calm terrain. The décor was traditional and quintessentially French, and Persi thought she could just stay here forever. While Nick tipped the bellman in their room, she threw open the window-doors to the vista of the Rhone—breathtaking.

"To think this hotel is older than the United States of America!" Persi enthused.

"Kind of puts everything into perspective, doesn't it?" he asked, holding her as they looked out at their view for the night. "How we are all just a speck on the face of eternity." He let his lips brush the back of her neck. "Elizabeth Barrett and Robert Browning eloped here."

"I can see why."

"Also Napoleon, Victor Hugo, Chateaubriand, Charles Dickens, Tennessee Williams, Salvador Dalí and Picasso have stayed here, to name a few."

Persi turned into him. "And now Nick Betancourt and Persephone Sinclair have too."

They were contented to just walk the tranquil streets of the medieval town of Avignon with its imposing wall and famous fourteenth century Palais des Papes, the world's largest Gothic building, before crossing the medieval St. Benezet Bridge with its charming sites. They passed little art museums in historic homes, superb restaurants, and beautiful landscapes where Van Gogh, Gauguin, Matisse, and Cézanne all lived, played, and produced. These masters inhaled all the paradise Provence had to offer, before translating and exhaling it onto canvas with their oils and imaginations. Nick and Persi consumed all the culinary delights the town presented and their last meal consisted of risotto with asparagus, snails, and slices of pork belly and chocolate soup with gingerbread croutons.

After unsuccessfully persuading Nick to stay here instead of going on to Monaco, Persi reluctantly left the Hotel D' Europe and he drove the short distance to Aix-en-Provence just off A8 Highway and the Bastide Relais de la Magdeline. This twenty-four-room hotel, furnished with classic Provencal antiques, was a succession of stately salons with Gobelins tapestries and vermilion silk wallpaper, four poster beds with pastoral prints, curtains, and tile floors.

"Okay. I'm your captive. I trust that you know what you're doing. You can take me anywhere."

Nick laughed, pleased that she trusted him to know what pleased her. "You can make me happy in that four-poster bed later tonight. Right now let's go eat. We only have three days if we're going to make Monaco by New Year's Eve."

They supped on elegant country food including foie gras

with lentils, seared sea scallops, sea bass on a bed of mushrooms, and tender baby lamb chops flavored with rosemary.

As they lay in the four-poster bed after making love, Persi said, "It can't get any better than this."

"Is that a challenge?" His eyes glinted roguishly in the moonlight.

She allowed herself to be spooned by him.

Brad Shelton, the farthest thing from her mind.

CHAPTER 16

As the convertible spirited toward Marseille, Persi finished texting Doxie and Drew and looked up, inhaling the fresh air and offering her brown face to the sun's rays. A few miles later when they pulled into the seafaring town, Persi was immediately captivated by the picturesque port, vibrating with aliveness and rich with scenes plucked straight from the canvases of the museums' masterpieces. They checked into the Hotel Le Rhul Marseille on the Corniche with a private terrace that overlooked the charming port. "Chateau d'If is over there," he pointed.

"The real-life island prison of the fictional Count of Monte Cristo."

"My girl. Beauty and brains. I love it!" He kissed her. "You unpack and meet me downstairs in thirty minutes."

"Oh. Why do I have to unpack? Huh? 'Cause I'm the woman?" she challenged playfully.

"Unless you want to turn in the car."

"Okay. Unpacking is good. Thirty minutes it is."

"Wear pants."

A half an hour later, Persi went to the lobby, looked outside and saw Nick, curbside on a Vespa scooter, his hat on backward, his glasses covering beautiful soft eyes and his classic wide grin.

"I think I like the car better."

"Hop on. Ever been on a scooter before?"

"No."

"Yet another exposition compliments of yours truly. It's scooter and train from here on in."

Persi strattled the back behind Nick and held onto his waist.

"Umm. I like the feel of this already," he said as he sped away and off into the hillside, aiming for the limestone mountains that surrounded the sunny port.

The wind hit her face in staccato bursts as Nick zipped in and out of traffic, but then a partially petrified Persi . . . relaxed. She held on to the man with the great body and astounding mind, and a calm came over her as she realized that she trusted him with her heart, body, soul—her very life. She knew that he would not do anything to harm her; she released her death grip on his waist, let her chin rest on his shoulder, and delighted in seeing everything through his eyes. As cars whizzed at them, he dodged them with aplomb and they sped onward, upward, and out of the city proper. *This was the way Nick saw living—as an open book, full of adventure and promise.* That's how it'd been for him. Persi decided to enjoy this ride, figuratively and literally. Ever since he'd come into her world a few months ago, he'd done nothing but bring her joy and light into the dark corner of her nonexistent love life. This free and easy true citizen of the universe felt at home wherever he went and put no limitations on himself and refused to let others do so. Persi had never met a man like him before and never would again. He might be here for only a season, but there was a reason they'd had this time together. He'd already changed her life; nuturing, healing, and showing her possibilities. Spiriting away from Marseille on an unseasonably warm winter day, she giggled, truly enjoying the gift he was in her life. Too different for forever, but Persi'd treasure him while she had him . . . just the way they were.

She was entitled after being SOS—stuck on stupid— for so many years; she allowed herself to be manipulated and relegated by a man—but Brad did so with her consent. With Nick, her feelings were incomprehensible and brand new. She wasn't falling in love as much as he was awakening love deep within her. With every thoughtful gesture and loving embrace, he gave her a safe harbor whereby she could discover and reveal herself to him; he brought out the best in her and she wasn't afraid to share herself as she never had before.

As he whipped around a bend, Persi laughed with glee and basked in the luxury of having Nick with no expectations beyond a good time. No regrets. No restrictions. No impropriety. Like a rare moment that gets you by surprise and takes your breath away, being with him was intoxicatingly liberating. She'd look back on this period and know she'd already had the best days of her life.

"I love you," she said into his ear against the wind.

"What?" He inclined his head to hear her and keep his eye on the road.

"I'll tell you later," she yelled

Around a curve, they pulled into a bistro tucked off the main path he had to know was there to stop. They hopped off, grabbed hands, and sauntered to a small, terraced table with an unobstructed view of the Mediterranean Sea and part of the Marseille port. The fragrant, warm air swirled as the sun beamed upon them.

"This is lovely," Persi said as the waiter approached with menus. "This weather has brought everybody out."

"The French eat alfresco even in the winter. Just now they're not wearing sweaters." Nick grinned and tangled his legs with Persi's under the table. "Know what I want," Nick said before the waiter could leave. "Pastis, salads, and bouillabaisse." He handed his menu back to the waiter.

"Excellent choices," the impressed man answered.

"So what poison are you feeding me?"

"Would I do anything to hurt you?" He smiled, reached for her hand, and kissed it.

The waiter returned with two glasses partially filled with liquid and a beaded carafe of water. When he poured the water into the drink, it turned a milky yellowish white.

"Pastis. The national drink of Provence; although in Greece they call it *ouzo*, in Turkey *raki*, and Syria *arrak*. To us!" Nick toasted and sipped with Persi following suit.

"Ahh. It's like drinking liquid black licorice."

"It's star anise, black and white peppercorns, cardamom, sage, nutmeg, and cloves."

"Interesting. Is this like the absinthe that was declared illegal in 1915 and drove Van Gogh insane?"

"No. Absinthe has wormwood, which is a hallucinogenic. Pastis is licorice and legal." He rubbed her back. "Don't like it?" She screwed up her face and he called the waiter over and ordered a *diabolo menthe* for her.

She sipped it and said, "Now this is more like it. *Qu'est que ce?*"

He smiled and confessed, "Green mint syrup and lemonade. A popular soft drink for French children."

"It's delicious . . . refreshing."

"So what were you saying to me on the way up?"

"Oh—" She looked at his handsome face; the way the solar rays played hide-and-go-seek with his masculine features. She rubbed her hand in his and said, "That I'm glad you thought of this trip and how much I am enjoying it."

He eyed her skeptically. "That's too many words."

"How do you know if you couldn't hear me?"

The waiter brought the salads and the croutons for the bouillabaisse.

"So what's on our agenda for the rest of the day?" she asked as she ate a forkful of greens sprinkled with the herbs of Provence. Nick revealed their plans and Persi longed to ask how he knew of all these places. Had he been here before and, if so, with whom, but she wasn't ready to reciprocate. If she were with any other guy she would have. But she didn't want Nick asking questions about her love life—specifically Brad. So she didn't open the line of questioning and could call him intrusive if he were to. She didn't want to discuss the biggest mistake of her life. This trip, this time with Nick, was to erase all memory of her former indiscretion, and Nick was doing a terrific job. He was 180° from Brad Shelton . . . 180° from D.C. and everything Persi knew and believed. This entire experience was a dream, and Nick Betancourt was her dream weaver.

The waiter came bearing an assortment of grilled fresh fish for them to select. Placing the hearty pieces in the bowl, another waiter came up to ladle the saffron-infused broth over the fish.

"Now this is bouillabaisse, not that goopy fish stew they try to pass off," Nick said, waiting for Persi's reaction.

"Oh my God! This is nectar of the heavens."

"Huh? Worth the trip?"

They sat in the heat, breathing the fresh salt air, drinking pastis and *diabolo menthe* and enjoying one another's company. No rush. No place more important than where they were—like all the other lovers who stared at the Mediterranean below as if it were television, watching the sun amusing itself on the shimmering sea.

"*L'arte fa niente.*"

"The art of doing nothing," he translated the Italian phrase.

"Must be the key to life. The reason Europeans have a longer life expectancy."

"The U.S. prides itself on multitasking and checking items off a to-do list. We can't relax to save our lives—cell phones, texting, working long hours, trying to get ahead and, once there, trying to stay."

"We're on sleep medications and antidepressants." Persi looked out over at the calm sea. "If they could just get a whiff of this."

"Europeans also walk or bike everywhere, take naps, eat incredibly fresh food that hasn't been picked and shipped three thousands miles, no preservatives, and they savor every meal with family and friends."

"It's a good lifestyle, huh?" She bent forward and he met her halfway and they exchanged licorice kisses.

"I think that's the key right there." He kissed her again, tasting her lips. "Good lovin'."

"Doesn't hurt."

"Ready for dessert?"

"What I want is back at the hotel." She smiled and smirked.

"I heard that." He raised his arm for the check.

They headed back to town and walked the Panier, the two-thousand-six-hundred-year-old section that had seen Marseille through the Greeks, Corsicans, Napoleon, and even Hitler. In the seventeenth century the middle class moved out and the section became a working-class enclave for seafarers and immigrants; their color-washed façades and fine yellow stone houses dotted the neighborhood full of churches, bridges, a prison, and the finest chocolatiere where Cassanova had paid a visit. Here Persi and Nick stopped to sample various concoctions. Persi decided on a delectable fig and rum bar, while Nick liked the subtle uniqueness of chocolate with fennel and onion. They strolled past the Rue de Lorette to the hotel, changed, had dinner, and headed for Cours Julien, an eighteenth century section known for its bohemian *flanerie*.

"Hanging out," Nick translated for Persi as they passed a French hip-hop club.

"Well, who would have thunk?" Persi wondered out loud.

"I bet they even have reggae, soca, and ska somewhere here if we had time to explore."

They turned into the Blue Nile jazz club and got a small table near the stage. The musicians played a set and then recognized, in impeccable French, "Nick Betancourt."

Persi clapped her hands with the rest of the patrons and shook her head at how her boyfriend was as famous as he was unassuming. They wouldn't let him sit down without sitting in on a set. Nick acted like he was asking Persi for permission.

"Oh, Negro, please," Persi said, fanning him off with a smile as Nick went into his front jacket pocket and pulled out his own reed.

The original Boy Scout, Persi mused. *Always prepared.*

Persi thought how wonderful was his passion for his music. He loved his job and to play that sax, anytime, anyplace, anywhere. Again Persi silently admitted that she loved this man who was dedicating a song to her.

"This is for my lady right here," Nick said in flawless French.

Remaining seated, she waved to the crowd, blew him a kiss, and wondered how many languages he spoke. She rested her chin in her hand and listened to the opening notes.

Nick played a haunting rendition of "Song for You."

Along with Donny Hathaway's "You Were Meant For Me" and Phyllis Hyman's "Nobody's Wanted More," it was one of the three songs he routinely played for her after they made love; it brought tears to her eyes. Although instrumental, Persi knew the lyrics fit Nick perfectly, of how he'd been so many places in his life and time. . . but they were alone and he was playing this song for her. This would be one of the nights Persi would remember when they were no longer. Now, his eyes were closed and there was no one but the two of them in this club. He loved playing the sax as much as making love— she recognized the same passionate expression.

At four in the morning they left the club and went back to the hotel and made exquisite, familiar love before rising to catch the high-speed train. With time of the essence, they only waved toward St. Tropez, Cannes, and Nice. "We'll do that some other time," Nick promised.

Persi looked at her text messages and enthused, "Oooh. Drew got her period!"

"Okay. Too much information," Nick said.

I was hoping to be home for that, Persi thought. The three of them planned to celebrate with a Woman's Day to commemorate this special passage.

"Wow," she said to Nick. "Seems like she was born just yesterday and now—in some cultures she's a woman."

"She could be some man's wife. Have children."

"Okay. Not ready for that."

"Time waits for no man or woman. We have such a short time on this earth."

Persi sighed and then looked at Nick. "I'm glad some of my time here coincides with some of yours."

A smile dimpled his cheek and his eyes danced. "Me too."

Persi thought Marseille her favorite place, but upon their arrival in Monaco, the old port city was merely a distant recollection. She wondered how much more perfection she could handle; she'd have to return to Paris to get a rest from all the adventure.

In Monaco, a fairy tale city perched high atop the Mediterranean Sea, Persi envisioned Grace Kelly reigning over the principality. They honored the reservations of a five-star hotel overlooking the splendid coastline where the city spilled down the hill to the sea. Plush, elegant, marble and—Persi swung the balcony French doors opened into the sunshine. "Breathtaking . . . just as I imagined."

"Little more crowded than it should be, but it's the weather drawing like-minded folks."

"It's warm just for us. Not just fifty but nearly seventy degrees." She turned into him.

"Thank you, Nick. We got here with two entire days to spare."

"I am a man on a mission." He smiled at her.

"Which is what?" She tiptoed to kiss him.

"To give you a New Year's Eve you'll never forget."

Last year's one I'd like to forget, Persi thought. It was as if Nick knew and wanted to redeem last year's catastrophic negative with an unbelievable positive. "You are well on your way," she said as he lifted her into his arms. She threw her head back and laughed with bliss.

"Well, what do you want to do first?" he asked.

"I'd like to mess up that perfectly made bed over there with the most handsome man in Monaco."

"I do like the way you think."

"I like the way you make love to me. Especially in the afternoon—and then at twilight and at night . . . oh my God. And when you wake me in the wee hours of the morning."

"Who wakes whom?"

"Details. It doesn't matter . . ."

They made love, slept in, and emerged early the next morning. Nick arranged with the concierge to visit the legendary Casino de Monte Carlo for that night after dinner at the Bollito Misto at the Hotel Hermitage. When told about the formal dress code for New Year's Eve, through the concierge, the couple visited the designer dress shop in the Hotel de Paris, where they pranced and paraded and finally selected a white dinner jacket for him, and an ecru satin gown for her with a high front and plunging back to the waist. In a money-is-no-object fashion, they arranged to have the clothes altered to fit their frames to precision. That night they donned after-five attire and played in the Salon Europe, a lesser casino, cashing in at European roulette and blackjack tables, saving the Salon Prives for tomorrow night.

"You are really quite good," Persi said and thought, *Maybe he augments his income as a highroller gambler.*

"I'm good at a lot of things," he teased with a wink.

"And modest too," she shot back and noticed a Saudi prince in full regalia staring at her.

"Blow here for good luck," the prince commanded, flanked by bodyguards.

Persi bent over and blew on the prince's dice; her eyes never left Nick's.

The prince won. The table exploded. "You are my good luck charm," the prince declared.

"Here, please take this chip."

Persi refused.

"Please, it is customary. You offend me if you do not. Not good international relations."

"Thank you."

"Your skin is a wonder. Bathed in a thousand rays of the sun. Toasted a deep, golden brown and so smooth. Come and drink with me."

"I don't think so, Ahmed," Nick interrupted, taking Persi's hand. "The lady is with me."

"Thanks anyway," Persi said to the prince, delighted with Nick's reaction.

"Where are we going?"

"It's time for us to get back to the hotel."

"Why? I was having a good time and I have this chip." She held it up amusingly.

Nick cut his eyes and fought the impulse to snatch if from her hand and throw it away.

"Nick? You aren't really mad, are you?"

"Dogs get mad." He did not trust himself to speak any further as he busied himself with the valet who hailed one of the hotel cars.

"Nick." She sidled up behind him and slipped her hands around his waist. She pressed herself against his solid back, rubbing her front against his athletic butt.

The car pulled up to a stop. Nick opened the door for her—his jaw flexing and releasing. She sat in the back and slid her derriere across the white leather and looked longingly, suggestively, into his eyes as he climbed in behind her. She scooted closer to him, crossing her legs and pressing her breasts against his arm, wondering how to stop his pouting about another man's interest in her. She ran her hands up his thigh, felt his nature rise, and squeezed gently. "What can I do? What did I do?" She kissed the side of his face. "You can't help it if you have a good-looking woman on your arm. You should expect it." She kissed his cheek again. "Unless you're used to dating dogs."

Under her lips, she felt Nick's face flex to squelch a laugh.

"Gone home at two with a ten and woke up the next day at ten with a two, huh?"

He side-glanced her playfully but didn't speak.

"Ah. Now the secret's out," she teased. "I'm the best you ever had."

Whew, she thought. *Joking worked. Thank God the man has a sense of humor.* She couldn't endure another horrible New Year's Eve under her belt.

"Would you kindly not feel me up in the backseat of a car," he counter-teased. "I am not that kind of man."

"Oh." She backed away and sat demurely on the other side. "So sorry."

They rode in silence for half a block before Nick humorously tackled her and she laughed. They were still laughing when they entered the expansive lobby.

"Mr. Betancourt. I've taken the liberty of placing the formal attire in your room."

"Thank you," Nick said. "Everything else all set?"

"Yes."

"Good." Nick pressed a healthy tip into his hand.

Persi began to notice how solicitous the staff had become to them. "Who do they think we are?" she asked Nick.

"I don't know. But they're doing a damn good job mistaking us for somebody."

"Somebody black and rich."

"For once it's working *for* us."

Nick made purposeful love that night, proving to Persi that prince or not, she was with the best man to make her body sing, her soul shout, heart soar, and her toes crack. She was deliciously exhausted when New Year's Eve day dawned. They completely missed the morning hours and, rising at one, the remainder of the day sped by with manicures and pedicures, and in-suite spa treatments. They lounged in the hotel's signature fluffy robes and contemplated when they'd get dressed and give the folks a show.

"Mr. and Mrs. Denzel Washington?"

"We don't look like them."

"Will and Jada?"

"You are too tall and built to be Jada." He sipped champagne. "Maybe I'm just a retired basketball player and you're my woman." He gestured, making a three-point shot. "Swish."

"Well, you're half right. I am your woman." She crawled into his arms. "Or maybe I'm the famous one; a Tina Turner with my young boy toy."

"What?" He kissed her nose. "You hungry?"

"Yes."

"Then it's showtime. We're going to be a beautiful couple out for a great New Year's Eve."

"Sounds good. I'm going to get dressed."

Forty-five minutes later, Persi opened the door from her bathroom. In front of her was the *prince noire*, a gorgeous black man in a white dinner jacket. His clean-shaven, smooth chocolate skin set off by the light starkness of his attire turned to greet her. He was model-perfect. Persi let out a long wolf whistle. "Wow. You are one good-looking Prince Chocolat."

"Betancourt. Nick Betancourt," he introduced ala James

Bond as he fiddled with his cuff link. His classic smile dimpled his cheeks and then he swiveled, facing Persi. It was his turn to be mesmerized.

Her shapely body had been poured into that off-white satin gown, form-fitting but not vulgar. The shiny fabric scanned her body before collapsing dramatically into a fishtail around the ankles, which flared when she walked, reminiscent of the old Hollywood stars. The visual collision of her cinnamon-ginger skin against the ecru fabric was stunningly spectacular. Only he knew that the hue of her complexion—the color that the women in the south of France spent hours burning in the sun or lying in a tanning bed trying to emulate—was natural, supple, silky, and easy to touch.

She threw her shoulder up to her chin in a classic vamp stance and her chandelier earring dangled at her collarbone.

"Ready to stroll like Harlow though Monte Carlo?" Nick asked as he crooked his arm.

"I dunno. You think the world is ready for us?"

"Let's give them a go."

Persi gathered her purse and strutted in front of him as he was treated to the bare back he'd first fallen in love with, punctuated by the hips moving seductively beneath the thin, satin material. The tantalizing dip to the waist invited attention, but denied access . . . except by him.

"Mercy, girl. You are fine! *Beaute noire.*"

"Takes one to know one."

The comely black couple garnered second looks as they passed, oblivious to the attention they stirred in their wake. They took their seats in the posh, Belle Époque restaurant and dined on succulent lobster. Deciding to role-play and become their own and everyone else's New Year's Eve fantasy, Persi produced a long, black cigarette holder and the maître'd practically broke his neck lighting it for her. After dinner they nixed the Rolls-Royce and walked to the Monte Carlo Casino. They literally stopped traffic; the dapper, handsome man and the alluring black enchantress, as they strode into the ornate, Baroque environs with the history and marble floors. They entered Salon Prives and assumed seats at the blackjack table.

Nick placed bets, lost some but then won big, seemingly an invitation for the curious crowd to come closer. European roulette was next.

"I guess you can add gambling to your list of accomplishments," Persi said. "Why not English roulette or *punto banco?*"

"English and American roulette is just an easier, faster version of the French. *Punto banco* is the South American version of baccarat. Now, *chemin de fer* is baccarat for the wealthy and experienced—too rich for my blood."

"My head is about to explode from all this. I can do craps."

He smiled and winked at her as he placed his chip on thirty six black; her age and complexion. "This is the last time I can bet your age; the numbers only go to thirty-six."

"Well, old man. Your age isn't even on there."

"Ouch."

It won.

He let it ride.

Again—it hit.

Persi scarcely thought that this time last year she'd been miserable, in the midst of a toxic brew of emotions; love, hate, disappointment, depression, and deep, Mississippi Delta misery; her own private nervous breakdown that no one knew about. But this New Year's . . . she was having the time of her life. An unimaginable time, a complete fantasy that she could not have dreamed; having neither the previous experience nor capacity to conjure up an evening like this. At eleven-thirty, hordes of people who'd flown or sailed to Monaco, were drawn outside by the legendary fireworks. As they rung and perched on the casino terrace, the kaleidoscopic spectrum of lights seemed choreographed with the bombastic concert of classical music.

Nick cashed in his chips and placed his hand at the small of Persi's bare back. "Ready to join the fun on the terrace?"

"I am." They strolled out on the upper patio of the casino overlooking the harbor with tranquil yachts that'd transported the revelers here to ring in the New Year.

"Thank you, Nick."

"For what?"

"For this unbelievable new year." As she looked into his eyes, folks around them started chanting the countdown.

"You are most welcome." He gathered Persi in his arms and they kissed. Deep, languorous, heartfelt and soul-stirring.

"Happy New Year!" the crowd yelled around them and fireworks exploded against the serene, black-velvet sky.

Persi stood in front of Nick, wrapped in his arms and they watched the colors blaze in intricate patterns above them. Persi laughed from sheer joy of being here with this man in Monaco; shoe-shopping, Obama-winning-the-election-happy all over again. Nick had the capacity to make her blissful . . . nothing could go wrong or be spoiled as long as she was in his presence. He had out-redeemed last year in the most beguiling way.

Nick bent over, bushed his lips over her ear, and whispered, "Marry me."

CHAPTER 17

"What?" Persi turned to face him, her eyes sparkling with the vibrant reflections of the night.

"Marry me," he repeated, a smile dimpling his cheeks.

Persi stared at him. She'd waited all her life for this moment to arrive. For a man she loved completely to love her back enough to ask. A man who knew her inside out—warts and all. A man who excited her, challenged her, titillated her, and made her laugh. A man she could see "forever after" with. A man she didn't have to lie to because he knew it all and loved her enough not to care. A good man, a honest man, an imperfect man, a man who wanted to comfort, protect, and support her. A man in whose eyes she could see forever. This man stared down at her now waiting for an answer.

"Are you drunk?" Persi tested, her heart beating wildly, wondering why she hesitated.

"With love for you."

He never mentioned love; she never mentioned love—never said it aloud to each other, but like oxygen, they breathed it all around them.

"You love me and I love you," he said, as if reading her mind.

Persi swallowed, her eyes never leaving his.

"Some people say it all the time and it doesn't mean a thing. We've never said it, but I feel it. You feel it?"

She put her hands to her chest as if trying to quiet her raging heart; her emotions lurched forward and leaked from her eyes. "I do love you, Nick," she admitted with such relief. . . of truth spoken, recognized and returned. "I didn't think I could or would . . . but I do."

"So what do you say? Do we start this new year off right? Together. Persi, you're everything I need and more."

He wiped tears from her eyes.

"You're crazy. We can't get married now."

"Why not?"

She began to chuckle nervously. "We're in a foreign country. We don't have—"

"There you go with that logical mind of yours. We have everything we need. You, me, and our love. Money is the universal language that can make anything happen." He tapped his pocketful of euros. "How about this? We get married now and when we get back to the States, you can have any kind of wedding reception you want. We can have it at the Severn house if you like; a combination celebration of our marriage and open house."

Persi giggled and shook her head. This was a fairy-tale fantasy. She tried to breath in this rarefied air—air she'd never sniffed before because she couldn't remember ever being this joyful before. Never in all her thirty-six years. "You're after my money, aren't you?" she teased.

"I swear I've paid off my student loans and I will never ask you for money. All the money you make is yours."

"Oh, Nick," she laughed. "You don't know anything about me. I might be after that money in your pocket."

"Won't have it after we plan this wedding. Won't it be a great thing to tell our children and grandchildren?"

Persi stopped laughing. In the intellectual faraway, she thought she'd have children . . . one day; but now she raced toward that eventuality with a man who tickled all her senses. Could this really be happening? Was he really serious? "But you don't know anything about me, really."

"I know you're healthy. I know that between your scholarships and your parents, you didn't have any student loans."

"How do you know that?"

"I ran a credit check on you like you were one of my employees."

"You have employees? Your parking lot people," she joked.

He hunched his shoulders and said, "Pretty much," and then became serious. "Besides, I've been listening to you, Persi. What you say and what you don't. I know you love your father but felt betrayed by him because he married Sylvia too soon. I know you love your sisters and friends. I know you're a good person with a big heart and a fearless spirit. I know you demand honesty and integrity from your man and have no respect for a man who has a fear of success or rests on his past laurels; you get bored with a man who doesn't keep striving or becoming. I know that we don't know what tomorrow or the next day or year holds, but we can get though it—whatever it may be—together. I know there are no guarantees in life. I know you riled me up the very first moment I saw you. I know you have no credit-card debt and your teeth are sound."

She laughed at him as purple rivers from the fireworks streaked in his face.

"I know I can make you laugh. And I get up every morning wondering 'How can I make Persi happy today?'"

He moved in to hold her nearer. "I know no one gets out alive and we all have a finite time here on earth. I want to share the last fifty years of mine with you. So what do you say?" He scooched down a few inches to look levelly into her eyes. "If we don't, the only thing we have to lose is each other."

She put her hands to her mouth and closed her eyes to his imagine. She tried running logical "why not" reasons through her mind, but none would come. Pure emotion screamed at her, "Take it. Take the gold ring, Persephone." She was exhausted from always being the cautious and sane one. Of do-

ing what was expected and good for her as deemed by someone else; not only educationally and with career choices, but
dating the right men, networking and cultivating the right
relationships. Only once had she stepped out on her own—
with Brad. But that negative turned into a positive because
despite that personal catastrophe and the toll it took, if it
weren't for that misstep she would never have come to Paris.
Would never have met, been courted by, and now proposed
to by Nick Betancourt. Was he her redemption? Should she
chance loving again? Could the man whose company she treasured and rationalized she'd only have for a moment be her
forever after? Should she ignore her mind and follow her
heart and soul? For once she wasn't going to over think it,
analyze or run a tally of the pros and cons. *Do it, Persi!* her
heart yelled. *You deserve him.*

Nick was quiet.

Persi opened her eyes just as the final explosion of colors
blasted noisily in the air over the Mediterranean harbor. "Yes.
Yes. I'd love to become your wife." She threw her arms around
his neck.

He laughed uproariously and picked her up from the ground
and twirled her around as folks dodged the five-inch heels and
the gossamer flare from the bottom of her gown.

"I have a confession to make."

"Uh-oh," Persi said.

"I met briefly with the hotel's wedding planner for a 'just in
case' I had the nerve to ask and you said 'yes' scenario."

"You did?"

"Before all this, the original plan was that I'd ask your father for your hand in marriage when I went to the States in
January and then come back and ask you. I thought Valentine's Day would have been good."

"You're just an old-fashioned, traditional guy."

"Well, I want some man to ask me for our daughter's hand

one day. All proper-like. When your father was a rolling stone like mine . . . you want to look the father of your future wife in the eyes and hope to see a resemblance. That means you aren't marrying your half-sister."

Persi laughed with him. "So what do we do now?"

"Blood tests and a choice of venue. Since January is not the height of wedding season, we have carte blanche except the garden wedding in full bloom."

"I don't care." She kissed him. "I don't like the blood test but that's a small price to pay for happily ever after."

"After the blood test and we're married, we won't have to use condoms ever again. I'm looking forward to running into you like a river strong."

"Oooh. That sounds lusciously sinful." They kissed again and snuggled nose to nose. "I've never had sex without a condom," she said.

"Glad to hear it."

The next day they met with the excited wedding planner, signed documents, had blood drawn, selected the music and venue; the final decision—the terrace on which Nick proposed with topiaries and a trellis of imported flowers overlooking the Monaco Harbor. Persi discussed wedding-dress preferences with the planner before the couple went in search of rings. They breezed in and out of the famous jewelry designer boutiques at the Hotel de Paris; Cartier, Van Cleef and Arpels, Chopard, where the diamonds dazzled large and glitzy.

"I am a career woman and have to be practical. I need to wear the puppy to work," she said, inspecting the rows of offered possibilities.

As Persi circumvented the showroom once more, from her peripheral vision, a splash of gold caught her eye. A thick, twenty-four-karat solid-gold cigar band gleamed up at her; its center, a large, red heart-shaped stone. "A ruby?" she inquired of the salesman.

"Yes. But we can change it to a diamond."

"No. This is it. I've found mine."

"You sure? A diamond would be—"

"No." She slipped it on her finger. "Fits perfectly. Goes right up the knuckle but I can still bend my finger." She hugged him. "Now what about you?" She thought of Doxie and how her three-karat diamond ring proved no assurance of a happy marital life.

"A solid-gold band," he said to the salesman, "to match my fiancée's."

Fiancée, she thought. *I am a fiancée.*

Once Nick selected his, the salesman asked, "An inscription?"

"Yes," Nick said.

While Nick made arrangements with the photographer and musicians, Persi selected a dress from three possibilities presented by the wedding planner . . . an ecru strapless sheath with a chiffon overlay of little delicately, embroidered pink and green flowers and a short veil. The couple dined and returned to the hotel and made love for the last time as an unmarried couple. "You can donate the condoms to charity," she suggested jokingly.

"Gladly."

"We shouldn't see each other the day of our wedding."

"That doesn't apply to us. We're different. We're special."

"We're magic," she said.

"I love you, Persi," he said quietly. "I love you with all I am and all I have."

Persi smiled in the darkness as she snuggled against his chest. "Then that's all I need. You're all I need. Now and forever."

He contently gathered her to him. He thought he'd never find her. She represented every woman, everything he ever wanted in his life for himself and his unborn children. He reveled in the ease, stability, and love they shared. There was nothing he liked better than to reach for her in the middle of the night and feel her scoot next to him, warm and tender. He savored the boring normalcy of two committed people in a room by a fire—one reading, the other doing a crossword puzzle. He knew what she did not, they both shared issues with abandonment; for her, her mother's death, and then her father's shutting her out. For him, his mother's working and how he awoke at midnight and watched his mother drag herself in and, having given the one bedroom up to her sons, fall asleep on the couch. His wife and mother of his children would never have to do that. Nick clamored for an ordinary life and with Persi he felt he could have it and enough energy to give her whatever excitement she craved. Nick listened to Persi's contented breathing change into a register of deep sleep. He smiled into the night, closed his eyes, and joined her.

A few hours later, Nick awakened with a jerk. Persi was not beside him. He looked over and she was standing in the window, looking out at the sleeping harbor with its twinkling lights. He immediately relaxed and thought, *There is my future wife; it is our wedding day.* He got up from the bed and approached her at the window. Bathed in the early-morning light of a brand new year, the view was awe-inspiring. "Not having second thoughts, are you?" He slid his arms around her waist and she placed hers over his.

"It's not you I'm worried about. You're nearly perfect—"

"You say that because you're in love." He chuckled. "You ought to know I'm stubborn and quick to anger if I don't practice the five tenets." He kissed the side of her temple.

Like a nightmare stealing her happiness, the subject of morality awakened Persi. She thought she'd buried it deep but it snatched her peace at about three AM. She didn't know how to broach the subject of Brad. It seemed to stick in her craw like a piece of decaying meat. If she could just clean it out, rinse, and get on with her life. She wanted nothing between her and her husband. Certainly Nick knew about Brad. Maybe not the hideous details but surely Nick knew about her dalliance with a *married man*. How could Nick trust her knowing that she was capable of taking somebody else's husband to her bed over and over again? Her indiscretion showed no regard for the institution of marriage, how could he expect her to honor what she'd dishonored for five years?

"Shame. A shame," Nick offered quietly, as if reading her mind.

"What?" she whispered, thinking it was spooky the way he kept doing that.

"Shame and its cousins, guilt and regret." He gently brushed hair from her face with the side of his hand. He smiled at her. "Personally, a life without regret is not worth living. You never learn anything by doing things right; you only learn from mistakes. Some lessons are harder and more expensive than others; some take chunks of your soul and leave your heart beaten and battered, but if you learn from them . . . you're not apt to repeat them."

Persi shivered and Nick held onto her gently but firmly.

"Moral irresponsibility. At our age, we all have some." He began rubbing her arm in soothing strokes. "I was fourteen when I got my girlfriend of the same age pregnant. We'd have been fifteen-year-old parents. All I thought was, I'm not ready to be a father or have a wife and baby. I had dreams and goals—college, a good job, a house, car, and then wife and children and a dog. Instead, by having unprotected sex, I became just another statistic—an at-risk, inner-city, teenage father working somewhere at minimum wage to support myself and my family. I'd never leave my child like I was left. But I was so disappointed in myself. I let myself down . . . my future down. My potential down. It was my fault. My horny, selfish, immature mistake. The very life I sought to avoid, I'd stepped right into."

Nick backed up and sat in the big chair by the window.

Persi climbed into his lap and rubbed the back of his neck.

"I was more happy and relieved when her period came then she was. But that was the longest, most depressing two weeks of my life—ever. I learned from that one mistake. I learned moral responsibility and have never had sex without a condom no matter how fine the woman." He kissed her lips. "So I know something about lapses in morality. If you're lucky, they aren't lasting."

"But you were a teenager. I wasn't. There is no excuse for what I did."

"What can you do about it?" he asked simply. "You're too hard on yourself. Too judgmental. Striving for perfection, which is humanly impossible to achieve, can make you miserable. All you can do is be the best you there is. " He stroked her bare thigh. "There's no reverse button in life, but I think you've learned what's important. Who's important. Like me, I think a lot of it was tangled up in your teenage years, but we're both grown-folk now."

"Yes, we are." She smiled at him in the darkness.

"Besides, if he were to come back here right now—free and clear—what would you do? You wouldn't go with him, would you?" His eyes implored.

Persi's breath stuck in her throat. Her heart began to race. "What?"

"If he said, 'Persi, I made a mistake. Trish and I couldn't work it out because it was you I loved all along.'"

"How could you bring him up right now? Right before we get married? Do you really want to hurt me?"

"That really wasn't my intent. I didn't mean to upset you."

"There is simply no comparison between the two of you and I can't think of you in the same—"

"Okay, Persi."

She tried to regulate her breathing, knowing she was overreacting, but couldn't stop herself.

"I supposed we should just discuss him once and for all,"

Nick said. "Get it all out in the open and be over and be done with him. Never, ever mention him again."

"Fine. You never did like him, did you?"

Nick stopped and contemplatively rubbed his thumb across his bottom lip in thought like she hadn't seen him do in quite awhile.

"It wasn't so much a question of like or dislike," he finally said. "*Disappointed* is the word I'd use. Here's a guy who had everything—two parents, one a famous doctor. Lived in a big house, got a new car for his college graduation, never had to worry about food, shelter, clothing, tuition, books or ever being alone. He was different from me. I didn't even know black people like him existed. I bet Brad only read about time-and-an-half. I lived it and no child of mine will ever know it. Later, I had to get—then keep—my scholarship and still take out small side loans for other incidentals." He chuckled wryly. "Hell, Brad was at Columbia when I came and there when I left . . . he could afford to stay and play in college a few extra years." Nick clicked his teeth and said, "All he had to do in life was to decide what kind of man he wanted to be."

Nick scratched his chin. "And that's who he came up with. A grown-up version of a privileged, arrogant, spoiled brat. A disappointment. Starting out ahead of the pack the way he did, he should have done so much more with his life. To whom much is given, much is expected."

"I'd like to think my kids—our kids, will begin with a head start in life. But they'll grow into responsible men and women we can be proud of. Besides lots of love, they'll have chores, allowances, and values. So B.S. is my role model of how not to raise a kid."

"B.S." Persi repeated. She'd never thought of his initials before.

"Bullshit Shelton," Nick said absently, "his line name when he pledged. He was full of it. Lame and no game."

And I fell for it hook, line, and sinker, Persi thought. P.S., her initials—postscript—which she'd been in Brad's life all those years. Nick Betancourt—N.B. *Note bene*—note well. The universe was trying to tell her something.

"There are some things I know for sure, Persephone Sinclair," Nick began. "If it weren't for Brad Shelton I would never have met you. For that I am grateful. From the first time I saw you in that restaurant, I wanted to get to know you better, but I had to bide my time while you tried to set me up with Doxie."

Persi gasped with surprise and smiled.

"You're not the only smart one in this couple." He returned her smile. "It's our wedding day. And I intend to make everyday we are together happy for us both. I know that I will love you when you are old, gray, sprout chin hairs, your bones are too brittle to make love, and our teeth are side-by-side in a cup on the sink."

Persi chuckled and said, "Your oral aerobics are stellar. Just so those gums still work."

They both laughed and he held her. "Like I said before, we don't know what's coming our way, Persi. But whatever it is . . . we'll handle it together. Fair enough?"

"More than . . ." She held him. "I love you, Nick Betancourt. I'm glad we had this little talk."

"Just so we keep the lines of communication open. Everybody wants to go to heaven but nobody wants to die."

"Meaning?"

"Everybody wants a great relationship—"

"But they don't want to do the work it takes to get and keep one."

"And it takes work. Marriages run amok because one of the two gave up, took the easy way out, turned his back on the vows and decided to freelance."

Persi thought of Doxie.

"After the five year-honeymoon phase," Nick continued.

"We're gonna hit some rough spots. Because we're us—two intelligent, strong-minded folks who think our way is right. We'll have differences of opinions, but just so we can always talk it out and keep our level of love and respect for one another, we'll be fine."

As they walked back to bed together, it had not gone unnoticed that she didn't answer her action if Brad were to come back. Nick figured as long as they stayed abroad, they were safe, and he'd worry about the States when they went home for good. By that time, they'd be so in love and maybe have a couple of babies that she would say "Brad who?"

CHAPTER 18

Nick awoke and looked at Persi sleeping comfortably in his arms, as the sun escaped the billowing sheers and caressed her face. This was how he'd begin each new day, with his wife beside him. He'd been relieved that they'd had a talk before their nuptials. His feelings for Persi soared beyond respect and admiration, beyond love, beyond cherishing . . . he was blissful. He thought bliss was reserved for the movies and in songs and though he'd aspired to bliss, he figured if he failed at achieving that state, at least he'd find love. He'd settle for love. After the pregnancy scare of his teens, he'd practiced safe sex, stopped smoking, and wholeheartedly embraced the discipline of karate, judo, jujitsu, aikido, and its tenets beyond the machismo of being able to defend himself on the streets. He'd decided to date a different kind of girl; not the fast, flashy and free, but maybe a girl of substance, like Persi had surely been in high school. Only would a Persi-type have dated him. So he determined to be someone beyond the rank and file in which he'd been placed by the accident of birth. He began applying himself as his mother, teachers, and Ulysses Thigmont advised.

"Hi," Persi said to him.

"Good morning." He smiled down at her. "Sleep well?"

"What do you think?"

Their gaze locked into one another; he looking at her, looking at him, looking at her—avoiding the word that now seemed inadequate to identify what they felt. Love. He'd accept love from her. But he felt bliss.

"You are my bliss, Persi."

She loved the romance of this man, smiled up at him and kissed his lips tenderly in response. *This is the man in whose arms I will awake for the rest of my life,* she thought. *Lucky.*

"How's that for our daughter's name? Bliss Betancourt."

"Sounds like a stripper. You know what Chris Rock says about that," she said. "The main duty of a father is to keep his daughter off the pole."

They laughed.

"What do you want to do today?" she teased.

"For starters . . . love you.

"Sounds good to me."

At noon, the couple dressed in their respective wedding attire, he at the hotel and she in the chapel near the garden terrace. Another brilliant, warm winter's day embraced them as the official stood under an arbor of imported demi-orchids to echo the delicately embroidered flowers in Persi's exquisite wedding gown. The small orchestra began playing "You Were Meant For Me" and Persi superimposed Donny Hathaway's voice as she walked slowly toward her husband-to-be, resplendent in the white dinner jacket. The photographer snapped pictures as she wound her way on the slate walkway, stopping when Nick took her hand and they stood on a raised platform with the harbor as a dramatic backdrop.

"This is beautiful."

"Not as beautiful as you are," Nick said quietly, folding his hand over hers.

He did not like the short tulle veil concealing her from him, so he lifted it from her face. She beamed at him.

They shared a private, intimate look enjoyed by couples in love who need no words to convey what they felt—to do so would trivialize the emotion.

The official asked for the rings, and said, "Nicolas, repeat after me."

Persi laughed. "Nicolas." *His name is Nicolas Betancourt,* she thought.

Nick took Persi's ruby-heart embedded in the gleaming gold and poised it above her left hand third finger as he repeated the vows. He then turned it so she could read the inscription.

Bliss.

Persi's heart filled and joyful tears spilled from her eyes.

He slid the ring onto her finger and then wiped her tears away.

Her heart thumped as she repeated the wedding vows and slid his ring onto his finger.

The orchestra played "A Song for You" and they were caught up in a magic of their own making. At the end, the official pronounced them "man and wife." Mr. and Mrs. Nicolas Betancourt. Persephone Sinclair Betancourt.

Persi remembered so little from the cacophony of activity: the bouquet of the same flowers lodged in the trellis, the champagne toast, the cake cutting, the photographer snapping, and the orchestra playing—all she wanted was her husband to herself.

I have a husband, she thought. A wonderful husband.

They ate leisurely on the terrace overlooking the harbor full of stately yachts. Smiling, laughing, talking, accepting well-wishes of passersbys until they were alone.

"Well, Mrs. Betancourt. Are you ready for our honeymoon?" He rose and extended his hand.

"I am." She took it and they sauntered in the solar rays down from the terrace's perch through the colonnade toward the harbor. She gathered up the train of her wedding dress and walked with him onto the wooden planks of the pier before she asked, "Where are we going?"

"To the *Sea Goddess.* Our honeymoon destination. We don't have time for a cruise, we'll save that for our six month-anniversary this summer." He swooped her up and she squealed. "Right now, we'll settle for rockin' this boat."

Nick walked Persi up the plank to the deck and into the parlor. The captain greeted them with champagne and Nick gave him the sign to launch. She returned to the outer deck and watched as the yacht pulled away from the dock and Monaco, which tumbled down toward the sea to wave and wish them well.

"Oh, Nick. You're going to have to play a lot of sax to pay for this."

"If you're happy . . . then it's all worth it."

He kissed her as her veil rippled in the breeze.

"Despite the weather it's still winter, so we're just going to dock in the middle of the harbor away from everyone. Spend a few days, then you have to get back to work."

"Yes, I do. Just in case I have to chip in for this . . . wonderful wedding."

"Happy?"

"Blissful."

The couple changed into their clothes, dined on deck before they retired to make their first love as man and wife. Their first love without a condom—him since he was fifteen and she . . . first time ever.

Foreplay started on a starlit deck with a champagne toast and ended in the master stateroom with their usual urgency and craving to consummate their love. They proceeded naturally, each pleasuring one another in proven ways, but when he rose above her in his nude majesty, the silhouette of his hard manhood poised for entry into her soft center, Persi waited for his unencumbered penetration. He eased into her, relishing each inch, each moment before he melted into her quivering being. They became one, in a rhythmically, sensuous crescendo of desire, want, and need. A smile graced her lips at the feel of his skin on her skin, as tremors replaced the pulsating. He called out her name, she griped his thrusting haunches, and she felt his liquid love flow and fill every pore of her body. The contract and release of all he had to give was the most astonishing love she'd ever made. Persi wondered, *Does every lover in the world, make each other feel the way Nick makes me feel? Have mercy.*

The next afternoon, they went to shore where Persi sent Doxie and Drew an old-fashioned telegram:

Married in Monaco. Details at 11!

Love ya!

Mrs. Persi Betancourt. Nick says hi!

They trained back to Paris, watching the countryside fly by and looked at their wedding album. The photographer had done an outstanding job of capturing the essence of them, the striking couple. Was it just the look of love shared by all newlyweds?

When they reached home, Nick picked her up and carried her across that threshold. "The real world. Ugh. Our honeymoon is over."

He snuggled. "I'm going to make sure our honeymoon never ends."

"Just think when we left . . . I had no idea I'd return a married lady."

He shot her a devilish smile and winked.

"Slick Nick, huh?"

The rest of the weekend they spent reclaiming their normal life, taking down the Christmas tree, restocking the kitchen, and telling their friends about their union. That Sunday night Persi prepared for her return to work and they'd gone to bed early. On her way back from her nocturnal bathroom visit, she admired how her ruby caught the sparkle from the streetlight. She went to the window to watch it glisten and saw Collette and her man across the courtyard. *I have a man too,* Persi thought. Then Persi heard screeches and pleading and she noted that there was a parked car with a woman and three children. Persi only caught snatches of words as the man threw up his hands and got into the car. Collette draped herself on the rod-iron gate. Persi then realized that Collette was the other woman, and the man was going back with his wife and children.

The car drove away and a crying Collette sobbed on the steps. Persi'd had the scenario all wrong; Collette was the older, other woman, not the young woman with the devoted lover. He'd been someone else's husband. The unfolding drama seized Persi's heart, as she was intimately familiar with this pathetic tale and needed no further tutelage. Persi offered no judgment but thought, *There but for the grace of God*. Persi had successfully escaped a similar ending and, despite the initial pain, deemed herself lucky to have severed her ties when she did. In a few years, Persi could have become an older woman still saddled with love for a married man she'd never have. Nick stirred and turned over. Persi looked at him sleeping peacefully in bed and smiled. She was "Sadie. The married lady."

She climbed into bed, next to her husband. She snuggled up against him and he opened his arms to enfold her without waking. She wondered what she would do if another woman dared insinuate herself into their happy home; she wouldn't go after the woman, but Nick might not live. Persi took no vows with any woman but she had with Nick and it was he and she who'd deal with any breaches. In the great karma of the world, she hopped that having another woman invade her heaven would not be her cosmic payback for what she'd done to Brad and Trish. She hoped the powers-that-be knew she was young, stupid, and sorry and not punish her.

"Bliss," Nick murmured and kissed her forehead absently.

Somehow, Persi wasn't really worried. Nick's unparalled honesty guaranteed—demanded— fidelity from them both. Besides his strong moral center, he seemed to be lit from within with a genuine reverence of life, while being at complete peace with himself—who he was, where he'd come from, and where he was going. Blessed was what she was, and intended to stay.

The next evening when Persi came in from work, Nick was on his laptop making arrangements for his visit to the States and talking with his brother. He kissed his wife hello and handed her a message.

"Brock says hi," Nick said.

"Hey, Brock and DeDe."

She slipped out of her shoes and changed her clothes, returning to the room with "Something smells good."

"It's me," Nick teased. "And shrimp and grits."

Persi laughed.

"I wanted a chili half smoke from Ben's Chili Bowl but they don't deliver." He stood up from the computer and gave her a full-frontal hug.

"Hmm. You feel so good to me." Persi grabbed him.

"So who's this Desi character? Anyone I have to worry about?"

"What?"

"The message I gave you. He called and is coming to Paris and wants to visit."

"Really?" Persi went to the bedroom to retrieve the message and laughed.

"I haven't seen Desi for ages. What fun! You'll like him."

Persi called him and found out the particulars. They talked for thirty-five minutes before hanging up just as Nick served dinner.

"You know, every working woman needs a wife," she teased.

He grabbed and kissed her. "Like every good *wife*, I expect my payment in the bedroom."

"No. That's my payment in the bedroom."

"Hey, we all get paid in the bedroom." They sat and said grace before diving in to the vittles.

"Oh, this is good, Nicolas."

"Tell me about Desi."

Persi relished sharing stories about her old friend with her new husband.

"Jamaica, huh? So which one was he interested in? You or Doxie? Never mind . . . stupid question."

"It could have been Doxie but it wasn't," Persi toyed with a smile. "You know how you have those great friendships with guys that you don't want to ruin with sex?"

"No, I don't."

Peris chuckled. "We did make a pact that if we weren't married by the time we were thirty-five we'd marry each other."

"Well, you just made it," Nick teased. "He's welcomed to stay here."

"He's staying at the Ritz—"

"We'll have him over for dinner a few times. Got to get the four-one-one on a high school Persi."

"He's partial to the food and women of New Orleans so we can have jambalaya—"

"And I'll do sazeracs.The first cocktail in the United States circa, 1800s. First made of cognac and Peychaud bitters, then in the 1870s rye whiskey."

"Yuck. I'll stick to my *diabolo menthe*," she sassed.

"If he's a true connoisseur of N'awlins, he'll know and appreciate the drink and I'll do dessert as well."

"Great. We work well together."

"Yes we do." He leaned in for a kiss. "I would have loved going to Jamaica when I was in high school. Me and my buddies were lucky to make it to the beach." They chuckled and Nick continued, "From what you've said about your dad I'm surprised he let you go."

"It was my mother; the wanderlust-adventurer of the pair

who believed that well-rounded women should travel. So whenever one of her daughters had the opportunity to leave D.C. and widen their horizons, she was all for it."

"Sorry I never met her."

"She was a heck of a woman. Schoolteacher and acting principal on her way when she got pregnant with Diana. At my father's insistence, she came home to care for her, then me and Athena and never got back to her career." She smiled at Nick. "She would have loved you. You are her kind of man."

"Yeah?"

"She would have loved your *joie de vivre* . . . and the way you love her daughter."

"That is my pleasure," Nick said with a wink.

Persi came in from work and sang out, "Honey, I'm home."

No answer.

"Something smells good as usual!"

She went into the kitchen and Nick wasn't there but she lifted the lid to the pot and tasted.

"That man can burn."

There was a note:

Don't eat it all. Went to get a baguette and dessert.

Love,

N

Persi put the surprise cache of Hershey's Kisses by his spoon and went to change from her work clothes into drawstring lounging pants, a T, and cashmere socks. The doorbell rang. "Nicolas Betancourt."

"I'm Mrs. Nicolas Betancourt," Persi said, and accepted his tickets for his trip home.

She put them by his laptop and began to set the table.

With the laptop there and waiting, Persi thought of trying to find *filé*, a sassafras spice, for her gumbo and jambalaya. She sat down and decided to Google Nicolas Betancourt for curiosity and fun. Upon Doxie's suggestion, Persi had Googled Nick Betancourt and found out about his sax playing notoriety. "Let's see about Nicolas," she said with a mischievous smile. Persi typed in his name. While searching, she poured a glass of wine, took a sip, and went back to the screen. She looked at a page with his name emblazoned across it and she clicked the first entry.

Nicolas Betancourt: Parking-Lot Magnate and Philanthropist.

Persi blinked, as if waiting for the words to vanish or explain themselves. She scooted her chair closer and double-clicked again. Information appeared on the mogul who owned and operated airport parking lots at D.C.'s Reagan National, Dulles, Thurgood Marshall–BWI, O'Hare in Chicago, and LAX in Los Angles as well as Dallas, Atlanta and Houston. She clicked on another entry and learned of Park and Fly, the seven-year-old company that owned eight off-airport parking lots and garages, noted for their brilliant crimson-and-cream shuttle buses that provided transport from terminal to cars. Persi continued reading, her eyes fixed to the screen, her mouth agape and reading aloud. "In the last year, revenue jumped from 11.1 to 31.3 percent. A change of 182 percent since its inception. The multimillion-dollar management corporation began with sixteen employees and now boasted of three hundred from reservationists, the courteous drivers, shuttle-bus mechanics to the vendors who provided newspapers and bottled water to customers. The young mogul was contemplating adding on Orlando before taking his concept internationally."

"What?" Persi said. This must be another Nick. She needed a picture. She searched the next two entries and came upon a bio.

Born in Baltimore, Maryland, graduate of Columbia University with MBA-JD . . .

Suppose she was married to an imposter who'd lifted this

man's identity? *Oh, no,* she thought. *Was she in love with a fraud? She loved him. She was staying with him. Should he risk going back to the United Sates? Would he be arrested? I need a picture.*

She was on the second of forty pages of entries.

"In 2009 he sponsored an inaugural ball at the JW Marriott in Washington, D.C. for disadvantaged people who probably would not be invited to any other balls. He put up five-hundred thousand dollars of his own money and recruited over a million from corporate sponsors for ball gowns and tuxedos, limo rides, and plush hotel suites. President Obama and First Lady Michelle stopped by and shared one dance. . . ."

She could see her Nick doing something like that and his folks in Baltimore would get the first invites and limo rides to and from. Persi needed a picture to verify that her Nick was this Nicolas—"a reclusive man who shuns the media." Persi searched a few more entries for a picture. She finally clicked on one and there an image materialized.

"Oh! What the—"

Nicolas Betancourt, the handsome likeness of her husband, an image old enough to be from his college days, stared back at her.

Her eyes were still riveted to the screen when Nick entered.

"Hey, Bliss. How was work today?" He bounded in with a bag and a quick kiss for her before disappearing into the kitchen.

"You're rich?" she asked him.

"In the only way that counts." He returned for a real kiss and saw his picture on the laptop screen. "Oh. That? I'm comfortable. Got to pay those employees." He grinned.

Persi's mouth hung open, her eyes searching for an explanation.

"My money won't be a problem, will it? I hope not."

"You could have told me."

"Never seemed like a good time and I would have sounded

like every other black man you ever met. Braggin' about my
job and how much money I made. There was no easy way to
say, I got a few dollars. We'll never go hungry." He winked.
"Did you taste the coq au vin?"

"What else do I not know about you?"

"Nothing bad." He shrugged his shoulders. "My brother
has ATM machines in Hawaii; we bought my mother the
house in Annapolis and a car." He tried to think of things
that really weren't that important to him. They were things—a
way to keep score but if he lost them all, he wouldn't care.
He'd just amass stuff all over again. "Oh, I own Bricktop's;
her niece manages it. I have an apartment on the top floor of
the building, but I wouldn't pass up the chance to stay with
you." He grinned. "It all turned out okay. Don't you think?"

She stared at him, processing what he'd just said, relieved
that he wasn't wanted in the States for identity theft.

He went to her and said, "It's just material things, Persi.
None of it has anything to do with you and the love I have for
you. I'd give it all up tomorrow. Will it come to that?"

"But you could have told me. I should have known." She
didn't know how or when but she should have been informed.

"Would you love me anyway?"

"Of course."

"The good thing about it is you loved me when you thought
I was broke. Excuse me, 'A sax-playing karate man.'"

Persi cut her eyes. *It's better than him saying he was in deep
debt*, she thought.

"Want me to give it up?"

"No. You worked hard for your money. I just don't like us
having secrets."

"I don't consider it a secret. It's right there on the Internet.
Honestly, I don't think about it a lot beyond my responsi-
bilities. Money—it's a means to an end, not the end in and of
itself."

She smiled at him, patiently. "Spoken like someone who has goo-gobs."

"Not always."

"I guess that's why I'm so proud of you. You've done good. Where you've come from and where you are now. That's pretty remarkable."

"Only in America," he said, gathering her into his arms, "could I end up with a remarkable woman like you."

"You know exactly what to say, Nicolas Betancourt. What's your middle name?"

"Don't have one. Too poor."

They laughed.

"Ready to eat?"

"Oh, yes. We have a lot to discuss over dinner tonight."

"Oh, no. No. No." Persi held her head as she counted the days on the calendar again. "I cannot be pregnant. Not now. It's all wrong."

"Hey, Bliss," he called from the front door and found her in the bedroom. "What's the matter?"

"I think I'm pregnant." She collapsed on the side of the bed.

His face split into a jubilant smile. But seeing his wife's dour expression, he decided to temper his joy.

"Why so glum, Persi?" He knelt before her. "That's great news. You are a married woman with a husband who loves you."

"Oh, Nick. It's all wrong. It's too soon."

"Who says?"

"I'm not ready. We're not ready."

"We aren't?"

"No. Not by a long shot. Jeez. How could this happen? My birth control is fool proof."

Nick watched his wife mope around the house for two days and, if he hadn't loved her so much, he would have taken offense. They loved each other and were financially set; there was no reason why they shouldn't be shouting their news from the Arc de Triomphe and calling all their family and friends Stateside with the expected date of the blessed event. In trying to make sense of her melancholia, Nick surmised that perhaps she wanted to avoid an argument on child care once the baby was born. Persi enjoyed her career and didn't want to be a stay-at-home with her children like her mother had, and Nick wished his mother could have. It was something they could discuss. On the third day, her period came and Nick witnessed Persi become herself again. Ecstatic, relaxed and in love, the way the news of their having a baby should have made her feel. Although relieved that the Persi he loved was back, it marked the second time in their short marriage that her reaction gave him pause. That she wasn't ready and could not or would not articulate why, gave Nick the same sinking feeling as when he'd asked her about Brad's coming back. It meant that she wasn't sure they were ready; Nick preferred not to think about Brad and if Persi still had feelings for him—the smoke from a distant fire. Bringing any of it up now would insure an argument and give more credence to something that eventually, would work itself out. Maybe she needed more time and distance.

She hugged him with wild abandon and said, "It's nice to know when we're both ready that we shouldn't have trouble getting pregnant." She looked expectantly up into his eyes. "Isn't it?"

"Yeah. I'm still a little disappointed—"

"We'll be fine. I'll cook today. How's that for a celebration?"

CHAPTER 19

When Desi arrived on a trail of cold air and surrendered his coat, he and Nick immediately bonded over the famed cocktail.

"You live in New Orleans, man?" Desi asked.

"Off and on. Played there a heck of a lot."

"Persi said you were a sax-man. You make sazerac like a native. Lethal and good. It's easy to make but hard to master, and you got it. No absinthe, right?" Desi teased with a lilting West Indian accent.

"I use pastis to coat the glass," Nick said.

"But it still has that reddish-orange color. You got to show me, man."

Persi watched two important men in her life get to know one another; one past and one future. They sat for dinner and after saying grace, Nick asked, "So tell me about Persi in high school?"

"Be kind," Persi warned Desi Fairchild. For their friendship and Nick's enjoyment they revisited the old days right on up to the present.

"I had to meet the man who could win Persi's heart," Desi concluded. "We were supposed to get married if we hadn't found anyone by, what was it? Thirty or thirty-five?"

"How's that going for you?" Persi joked.

"Ahh! So cruel." Desi clutched his heart and they all laughed.

"Seriously, you must be ready, Desi. An unmarried, childless fertility doctor."

"A very successful fertility doc," he clarified and continued, "I am ready and, since you are out of the picture, I do have a lady in mind."

"Details."

"It's complicated," Desi hedged. "But I intend for it to come to fruition shortly. There are certain considerations that I must respect." He looked at Nick and said, "I must say, I have not been this in love since your wife."

"She's taken," Nick said with a smile.

"Yes she is. I've never seen her so radiantly happy," Desi said.

"My husband's chocolate rice pudding makes me radiantly happy. Ready?"

"Absolutely, Persi-girl. Bring it on."

The trio talked into the night and Persi met Desi the next afternoon on Rue Faubourg Saint Honore for shopping as Nick finalized meetings to maximize his time while in the States. Within the next three days, Persi took her husband to the airport and offered a teary good-bye. "It's our first separation," she said. "I don't think I'm going to like this."

"Next time you'll go with me."

"You're only staying a week," she verified.

"That's the plan," Nick said and kissed her gingerly on the lips as the final call blasted from the airwaves.

"I miss you already," she said.

"I'll call you every night and text you all day long."

"Promise?"

"Promise. Love you."

"Love you too."

The next day while at work, Persi received a text message from Nick: *I'm eating breakfast at Roscoe's Chicken and Waffles in L.A. What are you doing?*

Missing you like I never believed possible, Persi texted back, knowing with the time difference it would be hours before she'd get a response. She'd taken one of their wedding pictures to be reproduced, bought a frame that had *Amour* etched in its glass, and wound her way down Saint Germain de Pres, her Chinese food smelling delectable. She briskly walked across the bridge by Notre Dame heading for home, trying to outrun the cold, happy her husband hadn't mentioned the California temperature this time.

She climbed the steps and opened the door into her chilly, dark apartment. "*Ugh!*" she thought as she peeled her winter coat from her body and set the food on the table. She flipped the switch to the CD player and listened to Luther Vandross's voice envelope her, but instead of comforting her it made her miss Nick even more. She changed out of her French-couture frocks into sweats, put a match to waiting kindling in the fireplace, and went into the kitchen to get a dish and silverware . . . for one.

After eating, she washed her dish, spoon, and fork, and pulled out her fragrance sheets to review them before tomorrow's meeting. She took out the frame that would house their wedding picture before the week and placed it on the coffee table so it would be the first thing Nick saw when he entered the apartment, her welcome home surprise for him. He was moving fast through the States; he'd been to Chicago before the weather turned, was in L.A. now, and on his way to the metro D.C. area, which would include National, Dulles, and Marshall Airports . . . and a visit to his scholarship foundation. He was busy and she was bored and slightly homesick, promising to accompany him on the next trip and get a face-to-face dose of her family and friends. The texting, the emails, and the phone calls were a nice substitute but nothing took the place of hugging and eyeballin' those you love. Persi worked and one evening had Jean-Luc and Claudia to dinner since they had not come to France for the holidays.

She lit the bedroom fireplace and looked at their wedding

album before deciding what she was wearing to work tomorrow: the Chanel suit like the one Doxie wanted. She eyed the images of her and Nick and marveled how the photographer had been a true artist in his ability to catch the mood, tone, and the love in their eyes with a camera. He'd not only made every frame count but made it appear as if their wedding had been attended by a cast of thousands . . . neither of whom were Doxie and Drew.

"Aw . . . next time," she said closing the album and double-locking the door—usually Nick's job.

Nick bristled against the cold and rang the bell again, anxiously waiting for Doxie to answer. He'd called ahead to make sure this was a good time to pick up the antique pool table that he'd had shipped from France. Doxie had said that her friend would be here to help load the truck so maybe the couple was engaged in an activity that took some time. *Okay, I'm horny and missing his wife,* he admitted as he rang the doorbell again. He thought of walking around the side of the house to the garage for a peek but a black man dressed as he was with a moving truck could get shot or at least the cops called in this neighborhood, so he waited patiently. Finally he heard movement on the other side of the door. It whined open.

"Hey, Doxie," Nick greeted.

"Hi Nick. Sorry it took so long, I was indisposed," Doxie replied.

"No problem." Nick stepped in and looked at her. She looked different. Slimmer. "This is nice." He looked around the foyer so as not to stare at her.

"This is your first time here, isn't it?"

"Yes." The wedding picture of him and Persi on her mantle snagged his attention. He beamed as he went over and picked it up.

"Miss her, huh?" Doxie said from behind.

"You have no idea." He returned it gently to its place. "Is Drew here?"

"No. Not yet. Would you like something to eat or drink?"

"Oh, no. Thanks. Just want to pick up the table and get it to the house before dark."

"Sure."

Nick noticed that she seemed relieved. "Thanks for keeping it for me."

"No problem." She began walking toward a side office.

"Oh. Wow. It's surely packed well. I thought you'd put it in the garage."

"Not after Persi told me it was a historic piece." She picked up the phone, hit the speed dial and said, "He's ready."

"I really owe you."

"Just treat my girl well and continue to make her happy."

The doorbell rang and Doxie slowly moved to answer it. "This is my neighbor's boy who'll help you get it into the truck."

After Nick and the boy moved and secured the table onto the truck, Nick tipped him twenty dollars and went back to thank Doxie again.

"Thanks again. Persi's waiting for you and Drew to visit."

"We'll be there. Do you have someone on the other end to help you unload it?"

"Yeah, they're workmen there. I'll get one of them."

"Good," was all she said and made no motion to be more hospitable.

"Well, take care."

"You too. Kiss Persi-Sin-Bet for me."

As Nick drove toward the Severn River he couldn't make sense of the peculiar visit. True, if Persi had been with him it would have been altogether different, but the house was dark and quiet and Doxie didn't seem herself. Not that Nick knew what "herself" was. He didn't really know her and the few times he'd seen her he could count on one hand. . . maybe two, but she hadn't been the object of his interest. Maybe she was pissed at him for keeping her girlfriend away. Maybe she was pissed that he'd married her in France and denied her that girlfriend thing. Maybe it was just a bad day; she'd been sleeping and he'd interrupted. It wasn't for him to figure out or comment on something for somebody he knew nothing about. He'd take his pool table, set it against the wall in the billiard room, check on the flooring the men were refurbishing, fire up the geothermal heating system, spend the night there and he was on his way back to his woman—his wife—his life in France. He missed her like crazy.

"Nick!" Persi squealed when he walked into the apartment, jumped into his arms, and smothered him in kisses.

"Miss me?" He returned the kisses, dropped his Gladstone bag, and held onto her.

They made love on the couch in front of the blazing fire. "You hussy. Right in front of the windows. We didn't even pull the drapes."

"They're just jealous."

They looked dreamily into each other's silent eyes, saying those things that only they could say to one another without uttering a word.

"Oh! Look at this," Nick said, seeing their wedding picture for the first time.

"Surprise."

"What a great day that was."

"What a great trip that was," Persi said, rubbing his bare back.

"I think Doxie's a little miffed that we got married over here and she wasn't included."

"What? Nooo."

"How does she seem when you talk to her?"

"Fine. Of course, I've been doing most of the talking because I have all the news. She knows how happy you make me."

"And vice versa."

"Why?"

"No reason." He held her tighter. "She looks different. Slimmer."

"She's probably dieting to loose a few pounds before spring."

"You should see the house, Persi." He decided to change the subject and not get his wife needlessly upset, but he wanted to get her back there soon, just in case. "The floors are gleaming to their former glory. I'm probably going back in a few weeks."

"And I'm going with you."

"No argument there." *Then you can look in on Doxie yourself,* he thought. "I'll even spring for first-class."

"Oooh, you do love me. Mr. All-Seats-Arrive-at-the-Same Time.'"

"No need to waste money."

"Oh, cry me a river."

"What's for dinner?"

"Reservations. Chez Janou?"

"Then back here for dessert," he said, yo-yoing his eyebrows.

"Yummy."

"Look at you with a red nose," Persi teased Nick. "Where'd you get these sniffles?" She cuddled him and felt his head. "You are warm. Why not stay in bed all day?"

"Are you kidding me?" Nick protested weakly. "I've got no time to be sick."

"Well, you need to take the time and honor the cold or

it'll get worse. There's nothing you have to do today that can't wait."

Nick pulled the cover up over his head as Persi headed for the kitchen and returned with a big glass of orange juice. She sat on the side of the bed and that motion caused him to peer up at her from behind the blanket.

"Even sick. Look how adorable you are. Take these and drink."

Nick obeyed and Persi gave him a quick kiss. "When I come home, I'll make you old-fashioned homemade chicken soup. That'll kick this cold's butt."

Nick awoke midday to the sound of children getting out of school. He couldn't believe he'd slept that long. He'd never had a cold or the flu to remember. The Betancourt boys had come from hardy stock. That DNA, coupled with a mother who couldn't afford to take off and get paid, was motivation enough to stay healthy—besides, they didn't want to miss the free school breakfast and lunch programs. Nick could never remember homemade chicken soup; salty Campbell's chicken mushy-noodle the extent of all soups chicken he could recall.

Later that evening, he vaguely recalled a kiss, a woman changing clothes, another kiss, a hand to the forehead, and a feeling of sublime tranquility. The fragrance of soup simmering on the stove roused him from a contented sleep.

The motion of the mattress depressing beside him and the weight of a body caused his eyes to open.

"Hey handsome," Persi said with a smile. "I hate to wake you but you do need nourishment. The elixir for all that ails you."

"Smells good."

"You're not the only cook in this family. Maybe the best, but not the only. How do you feel?"

"Better."

"Any nausea?"

"No."

"Just some twenty-four hour bug probably incubating from that flying Petri dish they call an airplane. Feel like eating?"

"Absolutely."

"Want me to feed you?"

"No. But stay with me."

"I can do that."

"I've never been sick before."

"You waited for me," Persi teased. "The tickets came so we have to get you in tip-top shape for another flight in a week."

"I'll be cured by tomorrow."

"Okay, Superman."

"I like the way you take care of me."

"Ditto," Persi said with a smile.

Nick reemerged fully himself in two days and they made love thrice to prove it. The following week, as the airplane banked, Persi looked out of the window and saw a sight that unexpectedly overwhelmed her with emotion. The monument majestically speared the sky, the Jefferson Memorial rounded its shoulders while the Lincoln Memorial remained flat-topped and Kennedy Center tilted to welcome her back. "Home," she said quietly as her eyes brimmed with tears. Until now, she hadn't realized how much she'd missed her hometown; capital of the free world.

"So what do you want to do first?" Nick asked, as they stood in a queue for a cab. "Go see Doxie?"

"I'd like to see my house, then your houses—on the Severn and in Georgetown—and get Mrs. Fitzhugh a birthday gift at Mazza Gallerie. Neiman Marcus is her store."

"Okay. The houses are now ours, not yours and mine, and how is Doxie's mama gonna feel about you coming from Paris and buying her something at Neiman's?"

"She'll never know."

In Neiman's, Nick stood before an elaborate display, blocking it from Persi's sight and when she came to him, moved with a "tah-dah!"

Persi laughed. All things Etienne, including her new *Joie deVivre* line, bloomed before her. "Wow," she said as a spray lady approached her with a sample whiff. "No, thank you."

"Look what you did," Nick said, beaming at Persi. "You did that."

"Yes, I did," Persi agreed and laughed with delight. Besides Nick, another dream come true.

"How are the sales?" he asked the woman behind the counter.

"We cannot keep it. It flies off the shelf."

When they completed the impromptu shopping spree, which included gifts for Drew and Doxie as well, a cab dropped them off at her house on Logan Circle.

"Home," Persi said as she opened the door, only then remembering that her car was in Doxie's garage. She turned up the thermostat and walked around the house she missed.

"I get to see the upstairs now?" Nick teased.

"Mi *casa es su casa*."

He held out his hand and said, "Show me."

They made love until twilight.

"Guess Doxie will have to wait until tomorrow."

"First thing?" Nick prompted.

"Any time after noon'll be good."

"Does she know you're coming?"

"It's a surprise. I cannot wait to see them!"

"I'm going out to the Severn house and will get groceries on my way back."

"Oooh. I thought we'd go together."

"I think your girls will want to see just you. We'll catch up later. They're no beds or furniture to speak of 'cause you'll be decorating it anyway you like . . . except for my rooms."

"Oh, really? You know what kind of bed we want. Any from our trip to Provence."

"Okey-dokey. But right now, we need sustenance. You know what I want on this Saturday night in D.C.?"

"A chili half smoke from Ben's Chili Bowl."

"You get points for knowing your man."

That night they picked up the food and brought it back with the television a backdrop for their conversation. They decided to take advantage of being home with a notorious sound system and plenty of bass, and danced to Sly and the Family Stone, James Brown, Prince, and Graham Central Station, ending with Mandrill. They emerged from the top-floor recreation room funky, sweaty, and hot, took a shower, and managed a little Saturday-night loving before falling asleep.

Persi awoke in the wee hours, slightly disoriented at first. With a gasp she looked over and saw a face she didn't recognize—a face not Brad's. *Oh, God,* she thought with guilt as she slid from bed to the bathroom. Okay, she self-soothed, exorcizing her thoughts from Brad and this house. It'd been that way for five years, besides Rucker Jackman, no other man or loving occurred here. With her low defenses and sleepiness, the natural default was to her last—Brad. She wondered if being here in this house, being in D.C. would invoke unwanted memories, Brad Shelton being the first of them. She and Brad could never have a sleepover unless his wife and kiddies were out of town. She and Brad never had the luxury of time to eat, dance and do as she and her husband, Nick, had. Nick replaced Brad while in France. Did coming here mean that Brad would take over again? The Brad who hurt her? The Brad who discarded her? By tomorrow night, her husband Nick would supersede Brad here in D.C. as he had in Paris. *Just relax and go back to bed with Nick,* she cajoled herself.

She slid back beside him and he automatically enveloped her in his arms as he did in their Paris flat. She smiled contentedly. She loved Nick as a woman and did not have an odd, unnatural adolescent attachment to him.

"You okay?" he whispered.

"Fine."

The next afternoon, Persi called Doxie and they chatted briefly without her friend knowing she was standing on her porch. Verifying Doxie was home, Persi rang the bell and waited for her to appear. Drew opened the door and they both burst into tears.

"Auntie Persi!"

"Hey baby." They clung to each other before Persi backed her up. "Look at you! How you've grown since I saw you last!"

"You came." Drew couldn't stop crying. "I knew you'd come!"

"Oh!" Persi drew her to her. "I have some things for you. Where's your mama?"

The doorbell rang again and Persi opened it.

"Mrs. Fitzhugh!"

"Persi! Thank God you're here."

"Happy birthday, I have a gift for you in the car." Mrs. Fitzhugh, usually not a demonstrative woman, grabbed and hugged Persi. "I guess I should go away more often," Persi said, looking at the teary pair.

"Well, look what the cat dragged in," Doxie said from behind. "*Bonjour.*"

Persi turned toward the sound of her friend's voice. Then she saw her. The sight of Doxie stole her breath. Her mouth opened but nothing came out.

"You two better get a move on it," Doxie said above a whisper.

"Yes. Drew and I are going to the Kennedy Center to see the Alvin Ailey Dancers, then she and her friends are having a sleepover," Mrs. Fitzhugh said.

"Mom, do I have to go? Auntie Persi's here." She began crying again. "I don't want to go. I want to stay here with you and Auntie Persi."

"No. It's all planned. Drew, you have to go with your grandmother."

What bizarre world have I entered? Persi thought, but said, "Drew, I'll be here all week. We'll catch up. You can come spend the night with me or vice versa. Okay?"

"But—"

"You don't want to disappoint your Grandma on her birthday, do you?" Persi asked eye-level with the child. "It'll give your mom and me time to catch up before we all get together. Okay?"

Reluctantly, Drew got her coat and kissed her mother and Persi good-bye.

"Have fun," Persi said, as Mrs. Fitzhugh's eyes pled with her daughter's best friend.

When the door closed, Persi turned to Doxie and asked, "What the hell is going on?"

CHAPTER 20

"What do you mean?" Doxie asked as she slowly walked to a nearby chair.

"You're not fooling me and you're not fooling that little girl. You may be fooling your mother because she wants to be fooled—"

"Such drama on a Sunday afternoon, Persi," Doxie said, as she eased herself down.

"You look like death standing on a corner eating crackers on a rainy day."

Doxie chuckled at that old saying of her grandfather's they never could figure out the meaning of. But it brought a smile to her friend's slender face.

"Seriously, what's going on?"

"I'm taking supplements and herbs—"

"A diet, Doxie? You can stop now 'cause you've passed your target weight. You are rail- thin."

"Jeez, you're like a dog with a bone."

"Your coloring is ashy—not just in need of petroleum jelly in a D.C. winter ashy. I mean ashen. Your eyes are dull and vacant and you're moving slow."

Doxie didn't have the energy to fend off Persi.

"So what is it? What's making my friend disappear? Tell me Doxie. Say it out loud!"

"Okay. Okay, jeez, I found a lump in my breast—"

"What?" The news took the wind from her lungs. "When?"

"It's only been a month or so."

"What did your father say?"

"He doesn't know. No one knows."

"What?"

"Cmon, Persi. I know the drill. Chemo. Radiation, mastect—

"Suppose it isn't?"

"I have a feeling. A woman knows."

"If it is . . . you've got to save your life."

"What kind of life would that be . . . no hair, no breast."

"Are you kiddin' me?!" Persi hadn't meant to scream. "You selfish bitch. What about your daughter? You'd leave her alone at almost twelve because of vanity?"

"Damn you, Persi."

"I was seventeen when my mother died and I still haven't gotten over it. I wish my mother had radiation or dogshit, whatever it took to save her life. I would tote that ball-headed, one-breasted, old woman wherever she'd like to go and be proud of it."

Doxie was quiet.

"If you don't do it for yourself, do it for Drew."

"She'll be fine. She'll have you and my parents."

"Oh, God, Doxie, there is no substitute for a mother. None." Persi's eyes brightened with tears. "Even after all these years and all my supposed accomplishments," she choked on her words and stopped speaking. She swallowed and began again just above a whisper. "My mother gave up. I always felt that she didn't love me enough to fight. To fight to stay here with us." She gritted her teeth to squelch all the feelings being summoned, then closed her lips tightly around them.

"What kind of life would it be with no breast?"

"Well, there it is." Persi hit her exasperation limit. "Isn't that the worst-case scenario these days? You have another one. They can make you another one. Look at that actress who had two cut off and she's wearing strapless dresses."

"Spoken like a woman with two healthy breasts."

"For the time being," Persi snapped. "My mama had it. The likelihood that I and my sisters might get it is high. And if I have to give up a breast to live? So be it. Take it! Take 'em both. Breast be gone!"

Doxie fell silent again and Persi knew that she was scared. Persi couldn't believe that she was going through this damn disease yet again . . . first her mother, now her best friend, but it wasn't about her this time. Medicine and science and treatments had come so far. But fear. Fear will be the death of us women. Bright, intelligent, accomplished women fear a disease and its implications. How do we make such stupid decisions? Doing nothing, being the first one. *How do I replace fear with hope?* Persi wondered. "I think you have an odd, unnatural, emotional adolescent attachment to those breasts," Persi said.

Doxie heard the words she'd thrown at Persi regarding dating Brad hurled back in her face. "You have a good memory."

"Among other things," Persi said. "Some things are profound and worth remembering."

In the quiet stillness Doxie created, Persi wondered if that adolescent infatuation with Brad had turned to stone. It made no sense how she held on to the thought of that man; not so much the man as the *idea* of him and what he represented to her. Safe, sound, solidly secure, and ensconced in the upper middle class so that, if she died at forty-four like her mother, she would never have to worry about her children. The way Doxie wouldn't have to worry about Drew. Persi could not have that security with Rucker Jackman or Desi, who'd move them to L.A. or take them to Jamaica; she wouldn't even have that security with Nick. Money yes, but not that connective, supportive, nurturing life of generational protection.

"I'm taking extra vitamin E, selenium, gogi berry and—"

Doxie stopped her litany of anti-cancer supplements. "It's only been a couple of months."

"It could be IBC, Doxie. Inflammatory Breast Cancer, aggressively running rampant through your body to other organs."

"It's not. I have a lump. No bug bites or an inverted nipple; no IBC symptoms."

"So you've thought about it."

"I'm not an idiot."

"Oh, really?"

Good, she's defensive, Persi thought and said, "Your father is the number-one oncologist in the country. How would it look if his daughter were to die of cancer? Talk about embarrassing. All over a mound of flesh called a breast?"

"What man is going to want me? With only one breast?"

"A *man* will want you with one or none. It's the emotional little boys who can't handle it. A great tool for weeding them out, don't you think?" Persi asked with a smirk-smile.

"You are sick."

"No, you may be, but once we see your father tomorrow, you'll be on the road to recovery. Whatever they say to do, we'll do. You know they are doing tremendous things with plastic surgery and silicone these days. I might even get a boob job if yours turns out looking better than mine."

"Those little things?" Doxie scoffed.

"Nick likes them." She stuck out her tongue.

"Tell him thank you," Doxie said. "He told you without telling you and I appreciate that. He let me own my disease. Even if you won't."

"Yeah. He got me here in two weeks and didn't let me freak out. He's a keeper." She smiled. "So let's call your father now before you change your mind. Do I tell him or you?" She looked squarely at Doxie. "All I'll say is that Doxie found a lump in her breast and wants you to check it out.'" Persi went and got the phone.

"I'll dial," Doxie said, and did. As the phone rang, she added "thank you" to Persi and then a "Hello, Daddy—"

Persi left the room, singing, "That's what friends are for."

The next day Persi went with Doxie for the examination, then the biopsy. The following day was the lumpectomy and Persi escorted her friend to the first round of chemotherapy. Having received extended leave from her position with the Etiennes, Persi tended to Doxie and Drew while Nick worked between the Logan Circle address and the house on the Severn; finalizing the installation of the solar panels and all the structural maintenance, so that only the task of decorating remained.

"I miss you," Persi said to Nick from Doxie's house.

"Miss you too. I need a conjugal visit," Nick teased and Persi laughed.

"We both do."

"How's she doing?"

"She had another chemo treatment today and that drains her so she's sleeping now. Drew and I just finished up math homework and she's getting ready for bed."

"You're a good friend."

"You're an excellent and understanding husband."

"I aim to please."

"You do. How are things going with you?"

They chatted for more than a half hour until Drew came to kiss Persi good night. "I'll call you back in a few minutes," she told Nick.

"You sound tired. Why don't you turn in too. I'll talk to you tomorrow morning."

"I'll be home tomorrow afternoon and we can see about that visit."

"You know where to find me. Love you."

"Love you too."

Nick hung up the phone and went to the kitchen for a cup

of tea. While he still needed his morning cups of joe, Persi had gotten him into the habit of herbal tea at night. As he prioritized the recipients of the Thigmont Scholarships at the computer in the small office off the kitchen, he heard a tap at the back door. He pushed back the curtain covering the window and looked directly into the eyes of Brad Shelton.

Nick inhaled deeply and swung open the door. "What do you want, man?"

"May I come in?"

"Why?"

"I don't like standing out here on the back-porch stoop under this motion light."

Nick barely stepped back so Brad could enter and asked, "Why are you here?"

"I saw movement so I thought the woman of the house was here."

"Mrs. Persi Betancourt?"

"Ah, yes. I heard about that."

"Still. You're here."

"Well, we go back a long ways. I thought since she was in town—"

"Let me say this. She is not and will never be available to talk with you in this house again."

"I don't believe that's your call. This is *her* house."

Nick fought to control his temper, running the five tenets through his mind. "As a man who doesn't respect his own marriage, I suggest that you respect and honor ours."

"You should leave my marriage out—"

"And you leave mine," Nick snapped.

Brad looked at him and said, "We never did get on, did we?"

"No, we didn't."

"So when you saw my chick on the side you decided to go after her—"

"You arrogant bastard—"

"You won't find any bastards in the Shelton family." He raised his eyebrow disdainfully.

"Persi and I have nothing more to do with you."

"So you say, but you wouldn't even know her if it wasn't for me. If I hadn't sent you to the restaurant to break our rendezvous that night—"

"That was then; this is now."

"Shall we ask the lady?"

In a millisecond, and before he realized it, with one hand Nick had grabbed Brad in a chokehold by the neck and thrown him against the nearby wall. Brad was turning reddish blue as he struggled for air before Nick released his grip. Brad coughed and gasped for oxygen.

"You're crazy," he finally managed. "I ought to call the cops."

Nick took the phone and slammed it on the granite counter. "Do it," he ordered, stepping back and crossing his arms over his chest. "You can explain what you're doing here."

Brad rubbed his neck and could feel welts rising. "I say we let her choose between us."

"I say you leave here before I do something where the coroner, not the cops, are needed."

"Just a Baltimore thug," Brad whispered under his breath.

"Come again?" Nick stepped toward Brad, as he stepped back.

Inching along the wall, Brad moved slowly for the door.

"I'm going out on a limb here, Shelton, and asking you, for once in your pathetic, excuse for a life, to do the decent thing. Persi deserves to be the first and only lady in her man's life. If you ever cared about her, let her move on."

"That's some advice coming from her husband." Brad grinned wickedly. "If I have you brought up on charges, she'll know just who she is dealing with."

"Do that." Nick realized there was no appealing to a non-existent, unselfish Brad. "You know where to find me."

Brad stood smugly at the door, his hand on the knob. "Just because she's in love with you, doesn't mean she's over me. Her heart belongs to me." He opened the door hurriedly and exited quickly.

Nick slammed the door behind Brad. After all these tranquil years, he was furious with himself for losing control; embarrassed and angry at his deportment. An adolescent reaction like Brad had said something about his mama, talking about his woman . . . his wife, casting aspersions on her character. He banged one fist into the other; he wanted to strike out but calmed himself with his controlled breathing. He knew Persi loved him; he knew she was in love with him, but the discussion they'd had right before they were married gnawed at him. *If Brad came back you wouldn't go with him . . . would you?* She'd gotten upset, as she had when she thought she was pregnant; both times should have been joyous times for them but she'd hesitated and seemed conflicted. She'd held back as if waiting. Waiting for what? Nick didn't want his fears realized. He loved her so unequivocally, like he'd never loved before or could ever love again, but could she love two men at the same time? She'd made her choice so Brad's suggestion of letting her chose was absurdly preposterous. *Who would she choose?* Nick wondered. He never wanted it to come to that.

Drew, Persi, and Doxie sucked on orange popsicles as the last drips of chemotherapy entered her veins, killing the possibility of reoccurrence.

"And she didn't loose a hair on her head," Persi said to Drew.

"All the chapeaus I could have gotten you to send me from Paris," Doxie said.

"That's a heck of way to get free hats," Persi said.

"When are you going back to Paris, Auntie Persi?" Drew asked.

"Trying to get rid of me?"

"Lord knows I can't afford to keep you, so you better go back to your j-o-b," Doxie said.

"You have to come and see the Severn house before we leave. All we have now is bedroom and den furniture and an almost fully equipped kitchen, but you'll get the gist of it."

"Can I help you decorate when you come back, Auntie Persi?"

"Absolutely. In fact, one of the bedrooms is yours to do with what you like."

"Goodie."

"Oh Lord. You spoil that child so," Doxie said.

"That's what aunties are for."

"Until you have your own."

"I'm working on keeping my built-in babysitter happy," Persi teased. "Umm, that was good. Drew," she said, savoring the orange taste on her tongue. "Could you get me a purple one this time?"

"Sure." Drew left the two women in the treatment room.

"So, how's work going?" Persi asked.

"I'm glad to be back and have something to do besides think about the next treatment. Now, all I have to do is get microwaved and then I'm through."

"I think the correct term is radiation."

"I like microwave. Makes me think of food."

"We do like to eat."

"Persi . . ."

"Yeah?"

"Thank you."

"You would have done the same thing for me. In fact, you have."

"When?"

"It wasn't cancer, but it was Brad . . . the odd, unnatural adolescent attachment."

"Hardly the same. A man . . . a disease." Doxie thought. "Okay, maybe close, but Brad wouldn't have killed you. I would never have gone for testing if you hadn't been your usual irritating, bossy, control freak, interfering, relentless, pain-in-the ass self."

"Okay . . . is this supposed to be a compliment?"

"Thank you, Persi. I'll never be able to—"

"You have. Your friendship has been pretty special to me for a lot of years, Doxie-Fitz. I just don't have the time or inclination to break-in another friend. The years I spent honing you . . ."

"Negro, puleeze."

"Did I tell you about Desi-Fair coming to see me?"

"In Paris? How could you forget to tell me that?"

"We did have other things on our minds. Like kicking cancer's ass."

They laughed and slapped five.

"Really, Persi.You look happy."

"I am." Persi smiled. "The love of a good man? Too cliché'?"

"Not if it's true."

"I think I finally know what love really is. Not what I contrived it to be. Brad wasn't the man I thought he was—I wasn't who I wanted to be with him. It wasn't going to turn out like I wanted." She hunched her shoulders.

"Stubborn."

"Those five years I lost . . . time. Myself," Persi lamented quietly. "Obsessively romanticizing a life with Brad that couldn't exist anywhere but in my mind. Auditioning for a part that was already cast."

"I should have had you committed to St. Elizabeth's," Doxie said. "But now . . . the way you and Nick look at each other. All Obama-esque."

"I love who I am when I'm with Nick. I'm more 'me' with him than I've ever been. I'm not calculated or analyzing the end results. I just am. He allows me that freedom . . . to be me. And he has that unspoken, unconditional acceptance and trust that no matter what I do or say, he doesn't judge me; he doesn't withhold or shut me out or resent anything I do or say." Persi stopped gushing and smiled. "He heals me with every heartbeat. He knows the real me, my secrets, and accepts and loves me as I am. So, finally I can exhale, relax, breath, and keep discovering things about myself, knowing he'll be there. And he still looks at me like I'm a marvel." Persi laughed. "We're having a good time." She blushed.

Nick and Persi lay in the stream of warm, winter sunshine with the clear blue sky above and the river below.

"The geothermal-zoned heating really works," Persi said. "It is hot in here."

"The furnaces have nothing to do with it." He snuggled closer and she giggled.

"I love this house, Nick. I love that we can lay here *au naturel* and not have to pull a shade and no one can see us."

"Unless they're in an airplane."

They laughed.

The remnants of their belated Valentine's Day celebration were strewn about the room. The crystals had been scattered in the fireplace and sent off sparkles during the night. The brush that accompanied the chocolate paint still open but hardened—the dark confection long ago licked from parts of their bodies before they made love. Rose petals stuck on their skin and embedded in the thousand-count Egyptian cotton sheets. A bracelet to match her wedding ring—a train of ruby hearts encircled Persi's wrist. She'd given him an oil-painted portrait of their wedding picture, the artist capturing the love they shared perfectly.

"Our brunch guests will be here shortly. We'd better get to stepping."

Doxie, Drew, Dr. and Mrs. Fitz, Jean-Luc and Claudia, and Doxie's Mr. Sparkless, whose name was Harold Mitchum, had formed the core of the expected company. But when Mrs. Althea Betancourt wanted to meet her new daughter-in-law and see the house, Persi decided to invite her father and Sylvia, and her sister Athena and her brood. Then Nick invited his best buddy, KC, and his wife, who had only spoken to Persi by phone but wanted to meet the woman who "tumbled the great Nick Betancourt." Then Drew asked if her two best friends could come and so the small soiree had grown.

"Just wait until our next trip back," Nick said, fastening the back button of her ruffled halter top. "There will be a houseful."

"Before we do this again, we must get some furniture. I do love the bed you selected."

"We could do it now, if you had time before you had to get back to Paris."

She went to him and encircled him in her embrace. "I want to build this house slowly, piece by piece. Not go out and buy whole rooms of already staged suites."

He bent and kissed her. "I like the sound of that. Built to last. No trends."

"Only our own. I don't know when we'll get back. This spring I want us to take the same trip through Provence."

She then turned to him. "But when will we get to do the Cracker Barrel tour? There are five hundred and fifty-one of them in forty-one states. You know how I love Cracker Barrel."

"You're crazy." He came and gathered her in his arms and kissed her.

"Crazy about you," she admitted.

"For the Greek isles, we can charter a yacht and invite a few couples."

"I do have a job, Nick."

"Only because you enjoy it," he teased with a wink.

"Well." She went over to put on her earrings and stepped into her palazzo pants. "I'll be back in the spring to do the Walk for the Cure and the Multiple Sclerosis Walk, get my yearly physical . . . the dentist, mammy, Pap smear—"

"Okay . . . too much info."

"You want me healthy, don't you?" She brushed her body against his.

"You already are." He responded in the only way he knew how.

The doorbell rang.

"Showtime!"

"Ma, this is Persi," Nick introduced his bride proudly. His two favorite women in the entire world finally face-to-face.

"It's a pleasure to meet you," the attractive, older woman steeped with Nick's features said.

"I'd like to thank you for raising the most perfect man," Persi said.

"I like you," Mrs. Betancourt said with a smile. "Call me Althea." She looped her hands through her daughter-in-law's and son's elbows and said, "Show me this fortress you call home."

Everyone explored, "ooh-ed" and "ahh-ed" over the impressive house with the preteens wishing for the summer when they could swim in the pool. They jaunted down to the pier, sat in the empty boat garage, and watched the frigid Severn drift by.

Persi began putting dishes in the washer and her father came in.

"Your mother would be very proud, Persi."

"Hi, Dad. You startled me."

"Sorry. Didn't mean to."

"I could see her here. Hosting sorority, the PC's or The Society meetings."

"She'd manage to get in here some kind of way and bring her friends."

"I really can't take any credit for it. Nick picked out this house before I was part of his life."

"But you'll bring the heart to it. That's what men want from their women. Heart and soul."

Persi poured more hot chocolate into the tureen without responding.

"I had a nice conversation with your husband. He apologized for not asking me for your hand before you all got married in Monaco."

"That's Nick."

"I haven't seen you this relaxed and happy in quite some time." He leaned against the granite island in the middle of the kitchen. "Since you were a little girl . . . a teenager."

"Since Mom was alive."

He chuckled. "Always straight to the point."

"Saves a lot of time."

"I guess I'd do some things differently if given half the chance."

"Wouldn't we all. Can't un-ring a bell. You do what you have to do." She began slicing the cheesecake. "We all do."

"I was lonely and scared and I had Athena—"

"Dad, please. That's all said and done and there's nothing we can do about it now. Except move past it."

"You were always so strong and self-sufficient."

"Ha," Persi had to laugh at how her father saw her. "Not always, Dad. I had to learn how after . . . Mom passed, and you shut down and when you opened up again, you did so for Sylvia. I understand now. But I didn't then. You and I took care of Mom. Diana was away at college and we shielded Athena as much as possible and then—*poof*— I was on my own."

Her father stood and began to walk toward her.

"It's okay, really. It made me who I am today and I'm grateful. I had to postpone a few of my dreams and wants, but that's made them all the sweeter now that I have them." She heard Nick's voice from the dining room and smiled. "I am happy for me and for you, Dad."

"I think you are both very lucky."

"I agree with you one hundred percent."

"We're okay, then?"

"We have no baggage, Dad. I have another porter now." She grinned. "As long as I don't mess it up."

"I don't think you could do that. That man loves you."

"Nice to know." She smiled and handed him the tureen. "Would you take this into the butler's pantry for me?"

"Okay. I'm sure the kids will need this once they come back in."

Four hours later the lasts of their guests were gone, the bags packed for tomorrow's flight, and Persi and Nick prepared for bed.

"You heard Doxie say I should have done a better job of setting you two up? She loves this house and said she could see herself here."

"She wants this house, not me." Nick stoked the fire and closed the screen.

Persi stepped into her gown. "I like Harold."

"Yeah. He was funny. Why'd you all call him Mr. Sparkless?"

"At the time, Doxie didn't feel he was the man for her. Let's say she's changed her mind."

"I'll say. As he told those jokes, she looked at him like she could eat him with a spoon."

"Funny how a man you didn't think much about can morph into someone you can't live without." She climbed into the covers Nick held open for her.

"Like me and you? It was hardly love at first sight."

"Good, that stuff doesn't last. It's that slow-building, foundation-laying love that works."

She snuggled against him as the fireplace flames danced across their faces. This is what Persi loved best, the lounging quiet couples did after a dinner party or on the drive home, second only to pillow talk after the lovemaking, it was all golden and special and as intimate as the lovin' itself.

"How do you feel about going back to Paris tomorrow?" Nick asked, rubbing her thigh.

"A little sad. I don't want to leave those I love and I'm glad we're leaving from BWI Marshall and not National. That way I won't have to see the monuments. But I miss Paris; our life there, the city, the pace, the food, lifestyle, our flat, and my job."

He laughed. "I'm glad you said your job last. That's progress."

"After a few years we'll come back here permanently. So I intend to enjoy Paris now."

"We can live or go anyplace in the world you like. So don't limit yourself."

"Oh, that's right. I keep forgetting you are filthy, funky rich."

"And if I lose my fortune tomorrow?"

"I guess I'll just have to take care of you."

"A kept man?" He snuggled against her. "No way."

"I'd have to pay you for your services?"

"I'd gladly do those for free." He spooned her tightly. "Wanna sample my work?"

The Betancourts retuned to their Parisian life. They put new CDs in their rotation, cooked and ate and spent the weekend snuggled together waiting for the warm weather. Nick's routine consisted of getting up and going through his karate paces as he brewed the morning's coffee. On this particular morning, she heard "Happy Birthday" being played in the distance before Nick and his sax appeared over her head as she lounged in bed. The personal concert was followed by breakfast in bed, good loving, and going to Shakespeare and Company, the oldest English- language bookstore in Paris, for a copy of *The Hunchback of Notre Dame* for Drew's English assignment. Nick bought a disposable camera and took a picture of Persi holding the book up in front of the real Notre Dame for Drew to use as a bookmark.

"She's more apt to enjoy the required reading if it comes from Paris," Persi said.

"Add the fact that her Aunt Persi gave it to her," Nick said.

They took the book to FedEx and used up the rest of the film taking pictures of themselves on her thirty-seventh birthday. That evening, the Betancourts checked into the Ritz and enjoyed a candlelit bubble bath in the deep tub before room service brought them nourishment. "I love you, Nick."

"Happy Birthday, old lady."

The following week Persi went to work and Nick tended his business via his laptop, fax and cell phone. He occasionally sat in at Bricktop's but with winter still grasping the Paris landscape, the Betancourts stayed close to home, laying in front of a fire roasting marshmallows, dreaming of a time when they'd venture out for more than a brisk walk or a run to the store.

On this Saturday morning, Nick rose early to snag the best foods the open-air markets for their dinner. "What are we having?" she asked.

"Dunno until I see it. Europeans plan meals by fresh ingredients, not recipes."

"I know whatever it is, it'll be delicious." Persi opted to sleep, preferring Nick's cooking to eating out. She pulled on a robe, washed up, combed her hair, and padded to the kitchen for a cup of coffee that scented the flat. She sat at Nick's laptop to answer a few e-mails, her body still revved from the early-morning love they'd made.

The doorbell rang.

Nick must have forgotten his keys, she thought as she pushed send on an e-mail and answered the bell.

Persi swung open the door.

"*Bonjour, Bruce!*" said Brad Shelton with an irresistibly familiar smile gracing perfect lips.

CHAPTER 21

Persi stared at him without blinking. Her heart beat erratically, slamming against her chest, her pulse screaming in her ear at the sight of him. Tall, handsome, and here in Paris. How long had it been since she'd seen him?

His eyes swept her body, remembering, savoring. "Paris agrees with you, Bruce."

Persi quickly closed her robe and cinched it at the waist. "What are you doing here?"

"I've come for you, Bruce." He smiled. "It's you and me. You are the one for me."

Madame Dumas from upstairs started down the steps and Persi pulled Brad into the apartment and closed the door quickly before he could be seen.

"Glad to see you too." He reached for her and she backed away.

"Don't touch me."

"Why not?"

"I'm a married woman."

"I'm a married man, but we'll both rectify that soon, won't we?"

"You cannot be serious."

"As a heart attack, Bruce."

Persi stared at him, unable to wrap her mind around Brad Shelton being here in Paris, standing in her living room.

"Seriously, Bruce. I've tried with Trish, it's not working. Know why? Because it is you. It's always been you. I love you and I want to marry you so we can have the life, the children, we've always wanted. You do still love me, don't you, Bruce?"

His eyes pled, his body called, and she was simultaneously disgusted and enticed. She felt her mind and heart fight among themselves. Her head split open and she thought she'd either vomit or pass out.

When the gods want to drive you crazy, they answer your prayers. She thought of that old movie line and whispered, "this cannot be happening. This is a bad joke. I've moved on."

"Have you really, Bruce? It hasn't even been a year yet—"

"It's been over a year."

"Not by much. We were together for five years. Are you sure you weren't just using Nick to get over me?"

"Of course not. He's a wonderful man—"

"Sure he's just not a seat-saver for me?"

Persi opened her mouth to protest, but Brad pressed on. "The novelty of your marriage will work another year or so, then the differences will drive you crazy." He stepped toward her and she did not move. "But I'm back, Bruce. I've come to save your from all that and take you home where you belong with me; the wedding and marriage you always dreamed of can be ours."

Persi began to sweat, to hyperventilate. A pain stabbed at her right eye.

"I've told Trish I'm leaving. She knows everything, just like you wanted. That's how committed I am to you and me." He took her trembling hand as his piercing honey-sage eyes held hers.

"I know you can't leave right now, you'll have to tell Nick. If you like I'll stay with you and we can tell him together. Whatever it takes. You're the one, Bruce."

"Get your hands off my wife," Nick said lethally, slow and low from behind.

Neither Persi nor Brad had heard him come in.

Persi jerked her hand away from Brad's.

"Look, man," Brad began. "I don't want any trouble."

"You come here, to my home, and tell me you don't want any trouble?" Nick seethed but did not raise his voice. He let the bags drop on the hardwood floor.

"Listen, you probably knew this was going to happen eventually," Brad continued.

Nick's breath was fierce and shallow, his nostrils flared and his fists balled by his side.

"Nick," Persi spoke up. "Nick, don't do anything you'll be sorry for."

"What?" Nick head's jerked at the sound of his wife speaking unfathomable, absurd words.

"I don't want anyone to get hurt," Persi added.

In a nanosecond, Brad evaporated from his purview and Nick was in the room staring at his wife. In that moment, he looked at her and all the hurt he fought to conceal brightened his eyes.

"What?" he managed to repeat just above a whisper. All the love they had, all the love they shared, all the love he intended . . . destroyed by Brad's mere appearance. Or had Nick been the thief? Had he stolen a few months from Persi and Brad? Were they the ones meant to be together for all eternity? The notion made Nick ill.

Against all hopes, dreams and positive thinking, deep down, Nick dreaded this day, but thought it may come. In his mind's eye, he thought he would surely kill Brad. But now, here Nick stood, facing the love of his life, and he felt impotent, weak, and beaten—he'd given his all. He closed his eyes against the image of her. He did not know this woman—his wife. This was not his Persi. This was a possessed woman he didn't recognize or want. What was he to do? Make her stay? He couldn't force her to love him. *Change the things you can, accept the things you can't, and the wisdom to know the difference,* reverberated in his mind. It was Brad's doing, but her choice. If she wanted to go . . . he had to let her.

"Let me just go and talk with Brad, Nick. I'll be right back. Then we'll talk."

This woman wanted to go and talk with Brad. His Persi would be standing by his side, incensed, and together they'd call the police if Brad refused to leave. Nick's heart had told him if this happened, he and Persi would turn *toward* each other, not *on* each other. He didn't know, like or love this woman who faced him.

"Brad. I think you should wait downstairs for me. I'll be right down," Persi said.

"Are you sure?" Brad asked, taking Nick's quiet for defeat, as he slid past "the husband" for the door.

Nick closed his eyes again, and breathed deeply before opening them. Unseeing anyone he knew in the room. "If you go with him, Persi," he said quietly. "Don't bother coming back."

"I have to go, Nick. Just to talk to him."

Nick stood shaking his head without saying anything. *There's nothing for Brad to say to you, Persi. What are you doing? Throwing us away?*

Persi disappeared into the bedroom and hurriedly put on jeans and a blouse, grabbed a coat and said, "I'm just going—"

"I will not be here when you come back," Nick promised.

She hunched her shoulders and made nervous, indistinguishable gestures in answer as she vanished out the door.

Nick stood there not believing what had just happened: a nightmare he never truly thought would happen. But it just did. He thought he'd loved her enough for the both of them, but he'd been wrong. She hadn't answered him the day of their wedding; she didn't want to be pregnant because she was waiting for Brad to come and get her. How could he have been so stupid? Nick was on the rebound, any guy would have served her purposes.

He struck the wall with his fist. The sixteenth century plaster did not give.

"Brad—" Persi began as she approached him.

"Come to the train station with me, Bruce. I have to get to the airport." He hailed a cab and they got in. He tried to kiss her; she turned so he only got her cheek. "Okay, I understand, Bruce. We've got nothing but time. We're going to be so happy, Bruce. Our dreams are coming true."

Persi remained dumbfounded and, she hated to admit, perversely flattered. Habit forced her to automatically revert; a ninth-grader and the captain of the football team. They had history.

I was married—I am married, she thought. What was this imperceptible force pulling her toward him? Her rose-colored glasses fogged up as she began seeing him as a whiny, self-centered man-child who wanted what he wanted when he wanted it. Brad the cad.

Abruptly, the odd, unnatural, adolescent immature force released its grip on her like a spring-loaded vise, and freed her mind to think clearly. For the very first time, she looked at Brad Shelton objectively. He was a married man she used to date who was now free. *So fricking what?*

Persi looked at him; his mouth was going a mile a minute but she was not interested in anything he was saying.

He is no prize, her mind said. *What he did* with you he will do to *you,* her heart added.

She admitted that she loved Nick, but not with her whole heart as she should have. Was she fearful of ever loving again or had she kept some love in reserve for Brad . . . for revenge? *Well, here he is. Do you feel any love for him now? Brad is what you wanted all these years? Are you crazed, Persi? Have you lost your mind?*

"You're quiet, Bruce," Brad remarked with a smug, triumphant smile.

She looked at him like he'd sprung two other heads and a tail.

"I'll go back to the States now and you'll follow in a few days."

"Brad, I have a job—"

"It's time for you to come home so we can start our new life . . . together."

Persi looked over at Brad. The Paris landscape sped behind him just beyond his ear. Then . . . the bubble burst. Poof!

Magic gone. *What a colossal fool I've been twice!* Persi laughed and thought, *This is the man I pined for?* There was a time when she would have killed to have him spew this . . . nonsense. But that was long ago and far away.

"I'll work out something until you come home." He was almost talking to himself. "I guess we can live in your house until we find one befitting us somewhere."

"I like my house and where it is."

He looked at her for a moment, as if allowing for her outspoken behavior and then continued, "But if I get my house in settlement we can stay there."

"The hell you say. I don't want to live in your hand-me-down house?"

"But Bruce—"

"Wait a minute. Trish—" She paused, it felt strange to speak her name out loud. "Won't Trish and the girls want to keep the house?"

"They're supposed to be moving," he said sarcastically.

"You're putting them out?"

"More like they're putting me out. They're moving to California."

"What?"

"We can thank that 'ex-husband' of yours for strangling me

the night I came to see you. Trish took the welts around my neck for passion marks."

"What? When did this happen?"

"I saw the lights on in your house and he took exception to my coming to visit his wife."

As Brad explained, the term ex-husband stung her ears and gutted her heart. Nick defended her honor and hadn't told her because that's what husbands do; not run around or cheat on you—they defend you. Clearly, Nick loved her more than she did him; he gave too much and expected too little in return and Persi hated her part in it. She'd flown off the handle when asked what she'd do if Brad came back . . . and he had. And what had she done but run off with him? She'd panicked when she thought she was pregnant with Nick's baby; the first time he'd been fourteen and sad, this time he was ready but she was not . . . and now this. She'd hurt Nick in so many ways, when all he did was love her. Love her to death— and now. What was she doing in a cab with this fool? Even his wife, Trish, was uprooting her girls and moving to the coast to get rid of him.

"California."

"It's where her future husband lives."

Persi looked at him. "That was fast. A future husband." *Who's making love to your old lady, while you were out making love?* Persi thought. This situation grew unbelievably obtuse.

"Some fertility doctor from Jamaica of all places."

Persi's mind clicked with recognition. Could it be her old pal Desi to the rescue? She didn't need rescuing, Trish did, but Persi could use a good laugh. "Dr. Desmond Fairchild?"

"I think so, you know him?"

"It's complicated," she'd recalled Desi saying. A married woman with three children certainly was, but if anyone could make it work, it was Desi-Fair.

"He's a wonderful man. Trish and the girls are very lucky."

And suddenly, Trish's stock soared in Persi's mind. If Desi loved her, she must be a courageous, outstanding woman who'd been trying to make her marriage to this asinine man work. *Truth is stranger than fiction,* Persi thought as the cab halted to a stop and she began laughing at the sheer ridiculousness of it all. White folks may have six degrees of separation, but black folks have two and a phone call.

"You'll have to share the joke, Bruce," Brad said as he paid the cabbie and climbed out. Persi closed the door between them.

"What are you doing?"

"Brad, listen to me. It's over. It's too late for you and your white horse to ride in and take me away. But I want to thank you for this final closure. I no longer have to hope or wonder what'd happen if you came back. I know. You have nothing I want or respect. I have at least I hope—I still have a wonderful, perfect-for-me man at home."

"He's a no-class, Baltimore thug."

"Which beats a ball-less, bourgie brat any day. Nick Betancourt has more integrity and class in his little toenail than you have in your entire six-foot-frame. And whatever my man is . . . I am his."

"You two deserve each other," he spat.

"I hope you're right. But this is our last good-bye." She looked at him and wondered what she ever saw in him—the true litmus test that it's over. In flawless French, Persi gave the cabbie instructions to return her to where she'd been picked up.

"Bruce! Wait. Bruce!" Brad screamed at the car as it left the curb.

"The name is Mrs. Persi Sinclair Betancourt," she said as the taxi eased into traffic.

Please be there, she prayed as the cab moved slowly through the traffic. She was in a hurry to get to Nick, yet afraid he'd be gone. Fear had dominated her life so long. Fear that her mother would die; fear that she wouldn't live up to her legacy; fear that she would never find true love; fear that Brad would never leave his wife; fear that if he did they wouldn't really make it; fear to love Nick completely without reservation the way he loved her; fear that Doxie would die; fear that Nick wouldn't be there when she got there; fear that he wouldn't take her back; fear that she'd hurt him so deeply he could not forgive or forget the pain. Weary of fear, Persi conscientiously chose to replace all her fears with hope; To dwell in possibility the way Nick did.

Please, please be there, she repeated her mantra in her mind as she twirled her wedding ring nervously around her finger; the big ruby red heart with *Bliss* engraved inside. She cackled aloud at the sheer emotional release of no longer caring about Brad. Even if Nick rejected her, she would in no way, shape or form consider Bradford Myles Shelton. So completely over him, Persi finally saw him for the pitiable excuse of a man he'd always been. The rose-colored glasses permanently removed and smashed to smithereens.

"Please be there," Persi said aloud and realized that they were stuck in traffic. "What's happening?"

"A demonstration or accident," the cabdriver answered nonchalantly.

Persi couldn't stand sitting here, she'd rather move toward Nick. "I'll get out here."

She paid the man, flung open the door on Saint Germain de Pres, and began running. She ran from the left bank across the bridge past Notre Dame to the right bank, thinking, if Nick wasn't there he'd probably be at Bricktop's. As she cut through the side street, the top of their apartment building became visible. *Suppose he's not here either.* With his resources he could go to the airport and take the first plane going anywhere he chose and divorce papers would be the next word she heard from him. *I just won't give him a divorce,* she thought as she ran down the street to the front door and up the steps. She flung open the apartment door with a bang. She couldn't catch her breath. Their wedding picture dead ahead on the coffee table with his ring flung in front of it.

Oh no! she thought as she looked to the right and there were his things—a Gladstone bag, laptop, and his sax case—just like when he moved in. So much had happened in such a little time. She panted for her breath as she ran into the bedroom and then the second bedroom . . . *Where is he?*

She went back out front to where his bags sat. He'd leave her, but never his sax. She closed the front door and when she turned around, he came out from the kitchen.

She smiled with relief.

He looked at her coldly. Through her, like she was a stranger who'd invaded his privacy.

His hand wrapped in an iced towel.

"You're hurt," she said, stepping toward him. His frozen gaze stopped her.

"Plaster walls don't give. What did you forget?" Shards of arctic ice punctuated each word.

"You. I forgot you and what we have—"

"Don't. Let me keep a little of what I thought we had—"

"We *have,*" she said stubbornly, changing the verb to present tense.

"You showed me that it was all an illusion. My illusion," he said quietly.

Persi knew her husband. She knew his determination and resignation and she knew the look in his eyes. Hurt—high, wide, deep, and all-encompassing. Her heart filled to overflowing and her eyes brimmed with tears that she'd done this to him. "Nick—"

"I'd planned to be long gone by the time you came back. I didn't intend to see you again."

Tears spilled down her cheeks. "Can't we talk about this?" she asked above a whisper.

"I heard you. Your actions speak louder than words. You made your choice."

"I made a mistake."

"Yet again. With the same person."

"I don't love him. I'm not sure I ever did, but I know I don't now."

"Look, we gave it a shot. It didn't work out. I'm as optimistic as the next guy—I pray to God and still row toward the shore, but this boat has docked. This is where I get off."

"Nick—"

"Persi, I'm no man's backup. I don't want to hurt this way ever again." He bent to get his bags. She touched his arm and wiped her tears away, wishing them gone.

"Nick, don't push me away. I love you and only you. You are the man I want in my life."

He stood tall but did not trust himself to speak. The pain behind his eyes penetrated her gaze. He finally said, "You were supposed to be my last dance."

"I know. Can we start over with no secrets? No reservations, no threats or ghosts hanging over our heads. It's all over. He's come, gone, and I'm still here. With you. Where I chose to be because you are the one, Nick. It's you I love and want to build a home with. I cannot see my life without you in it."

He did not respond.

"I was never unfaithful to you. I had a lapse of temporary insanity I cannot explain, but I guarantee you that it will not happen again."

"It has nothing to do with him or any outside person, Persi. Our marriage has to do with us. You and me—pure and simple. If we're solid—"

"You are right. Absolutely, unequivocally." He'd cut to the core and she looked clearly into his eyes. "I know what I see in you . . . home." Fresh tears sprang and fell from her eyes.

Nick cut his eyes so he couldn't see the woman he loved more than himself. He wiped his thumb across his mouth.

"I see my soft place to fall in this crazy world," she continued. "I see the father of my children. My partner for life. I see a man of integrity, principal, and loyalty that even when his wife does something uncharacteristic, he still has a commitment to the institution of marriage, to his wedding vows. A man who will keep us always turning *toward* one another, not *on* or *away* from each other. I see a man who believes *we* can handle anything that comes our way . . . together."

Nick looked at Persi. She thought she saw his hurt melting behind his eyes. Or was it indifference? Or was she just hoping she had another chance?

"If this is the kind of marriage you want, Nick, then I am the woman for you. Nothing has changed for me."

"Did you ever *really* love me, Persi?"

It was her turn to close her eyes against the hurtful question. She couldn't speak. She breathed and stepped toward him and said, "Nick, I am ready to surrender all I have to you. No holding back. From this moment on. If you just believe in me, like I believe in you."

And there it is, Nick thought. *A proclamation. She is ready to love me without reservation.*

"If you cannot forgive me for this one and only Pavlovian, knee-jerk reaction to a stupid stimulus from the past, then . . . I understand."

She gritted her teeth, fighting the urge to start crying again.

Nick exhaled like weight from his psyche had been removed. The admission and relief, a hurdle cleared, made him smile imperceptively.

Was he smiling? Persi eyed him hopefully.

"Like Emerson said, 'What lies behind us and what lies before us,'" Nick said softly, "'are tiny matters compared to what lies *within* us.'" He smiled fully and gathered Persi in his arms. "If all you say is true—"

"It is Nick, I love you, I love you, I love you." Tears of joy eased from her eyes. "It scares me that I love you so much."

"How do we work our way back?"

"One kiss at a time," Persi suggested. She tiptoed to reach his lips. Perfect but unresponding. She kissed him again. This time she felt an involuntary twitch on the left side. She pecked him again and she felt a slight pucker in response. Then she kissed him fully on his perfect pair, and he kissed her back. Forehead to forehead. Nose to nose, they smiled into each other.

"Then let's see where this thing goes," he said.

"Excuse you!" Persi protested and looked into her husband's playful eyes.

He laughed and she joined in—full, sexy, and plump as the notes from his sax.

Their laughter lilted through the window across the street to where an old man in a black beret walking his dog glanced over and saw the couple so in love . . . so happy to be together. The man did not recognize the Drifters "Save the Last Dance," but he smiled as the man and woman, who never saw him, danced in the second-floor flat.

"*Amour*," the man whispered, smiled and followed his dog down the street.

Notes

Notes